A FATE UNKNOWN

A PARANORMAL RH NOVEL

SINCLAIR KELLY

DEDICATION

To my husband, for all your love and support. I promise to add 'throbbing-cock' into the next book just for you, babe. Yes, I'll even add that incorrect hyphen, grammar be damned.

CONTENTS

Prologue

What. In. The. Ever-loving. Fuck.

I must've had one helluva time last night if the pounding in my head is any indication. My entire body aches like I went one too many rounds with a boxer - and lost. Taking stock of every ache and pain, I'm startled to realize everything feels...heightened. More intense some-how. It's like all of my senses are misfiring, making every breath, every throb and sting, every small movement send tiny pulses of electricity zinging across my body. That can't be good, can it?

I try to swallow, but it's a struggle. My mouth is dry and gritty and tastes like ass. Sweaty, dirty ass. Not that I've ever licked dirty ass. Though I wouldn't be opposed to licking a curvy, *clean* ass. The image of an alluring heart-shaped mole on a nicely sculpted ass cheek pops into my head.

Wait, what? That's it. I'm never drinking again. Ever.

Bringing my arm up, I run my hand down my face, and even my skin feels hypersensitive. Brushing my fingers over my eyelid, it's like I can feel every ridge and groove and detail of my fingertip. I can suddenly distinguish each indi-vidual blade of grass as it tickles the back of my neck. A wetness pools around my feet, along with the distinct grittiness of sand and the coolness of damp pebbles.

Where in the hell did I pass out?

My hands drop to tangle in the long grass beside me, and I use that simple touch to ground myself before opening my eyes, concerned about what sort of shit I might have gotten into.

As everything slowly begins to come into focus, my gaze locks on the stars twinkling in the clear night sky. Each one seems brighter than it should, closer and clearer. I look to my left, and the lights on the bridge above me are almost blinding in their intensity. Quickly shutting my eyes again, I take a deep breath to calm myself. It could be worse, right? I could be staring at a set of gleaming silver gates nestled in soft, fluffy whiteness, just beyond which are isles of clouds with a river of light flowing between them. Or a land full of screams, where every surface is made from black rock and the only light is from the lava that oozes upwards with a reddish glow from the ground to the ceiling high above.

Ok, that is oddly specific. What in the actual hell?

Opening my eyes again, I scan my surroundings. The roaring rapids I hear are actually just a wide, slowly flowing creek, its water gently trickling over the rocks at the shore...and my feet, apparently. There's an owl hooting and car horns blaring somewhere off in the distance, but they all sound like they're right next to me.

I release another breath and instantly regret it. My mouth *smells* like ass too. Other scents begin to filter in. The smell of earth - dirt and grass and flowers. Bluebonnets, maybe? How the hell I know that, I have no idea, but it's so strong I hold my breath to avoid the overwhelming assault of odors.

Deciding I need to figure this shit out, I sit up. My head

pounds, and I reluctantly take a few more deep breaths to get the world to stop tilting on its axis. At least I'm wearing clothes - a blue, button-down shirt that's shockingly unrumpled despite my apparent fun last night, a pair of black trousers with the hems slightly damp from the water at my feet, and tan suspenders.

Where are my shoes and socks?

Nothing around me looks familiar, but I feel like I've been here before. Each side of the creek is heavily lined with trees. The grass slowly giving way to rocky banks edging the water. Sitting next to a large pedestrian bridge, I'm flooded with this feeling of peace and love. Which doesn't make one damn bit of sense.

"Where the fuck am I?" I ask the night, my voice hoarse like it hasn't been used in years. Unsurprisingly, I get no response.

Then I'm struck with another thought. *Who* the hell am I?

My heart starts to pound, panic rising.

"Knox. That's my name. I'm Knox..." I trail off, coming up blank. I don't know my last name.

As I attempt to keep the ensuing dread at bay, I sift through my memories only to realize I have none. Nothing. I don't know how old I am, where I came from, or what happened to me.

Bringing my hand up, I slowly rub the center of my chest. There's a pounding there that I thought was my heart's erratic beating thanks to the panic attack I'm somehow managing to stave off, but it's more than that. I flatten my hand, feeling the thump thump of my heartbeat, but somewhere deeper there's a tug, this invisible pull telling me I need to get up. I need to go...somewhere.

I should probably be worried about finding food, and

maybe some shoes, but the tug is growing in intensity the longer I sit here. Those heightened senses I was experiencing seem to be lessening somewhat, the power pooling somewhere inside me instead. Gathering strength and morphing into a powerful draw that is insisting I follow it. But where? And why?

Standing up slowly, the world spins for only a second before I'm steady enough to turn around. I stumble up the embankment, through the trees, over rocks and roots, until I'm stepping out onto a sidewalk next to an empty street. I glance left and see nothing but more trees and a dark road leading to God only knows where. To my right, I see a well-lit area a few blocks down along with more traffic, both people and cars, and I'm suddenly overwhelmed with feelings. Happiness, excitement, jealousy, sadness. So many emotions slam into me it's almost crippling. I stagger slightly and look down to find my palm resting on my chest again, the tug there starting to physically ache. I should head toward the people, someone who could help me, but the tether linking me to some mysterious pull is adamant that I go left, into the uncertainty that lies down that desolate road.

I glance right again, my belly rumbling and feet throbbing after walking through rough rocks and sticks. A thought strikes, and I quickly check my pockets but find no wallet or identification. I have no idea who I am or where I'll go, and I've got no money to get me there.

Deciding to listen to my stomach rather than some weird *feeling* I don't know if I can trust, I head toward the sounds of life. As I approach the busy street up ahead, I slow my pace and pause in the shadow of the nearest tree, suddenly realizing something is seriously wrong here. There's a large crowd on the corner and music filtering out the door which is open to allow the long line of people inside.

Women dressed in short dresses and thigh-high, heeled boots laugh and talk while waiting outside. The men are in pants that flare out widely at the bottom and tight button-down shirts which are unbuttoned down to their chests. Their hair is as long as the women's, and they run their fingers through it while they stand by, smoking cigarettes and scanning the growing line. But why is everyone surrounded by this hazy fog? Everyone is encased in colors, muted pinks and purples and yellows, shades of blue, and hints of red. It's like someone placed a rainbow over the crowd, and they're all swimming in it, causing the colors to swirl and mix.

Those feelings I've been experiencing have only grown stronger with every step I take toward the group in front of me. Throw in some frustration and anger, desire and despair, and it's too much for my fragile mind right now. I can feel it all, and no matter what I do, I can't seem to shut it off. I grab my head with both hands, trying to get it all to stop, but it simply grows stronger with each person that walks up to get in line.

Risking another look at the crowd of people then down at my own outfit that seems drastically out of place, I know with a curious certainty that I don't belong here. I belong...somewhere else. Some*when* else.

I glance behind me again, down the quiet darkness of the road, and my feet slowly turn me around, directing me back the way I had come. An almost involuntary action that I don't fight. Because at this point, I have nothing left to lose. I can only hope that whatever I find is worth the struggles I sense are waiting for me.

"Here goes nothing," I mutter to myself as my feet start

moving. What I'll find down this road is unclear. I only know I'm heading toward some mysterious unknown...fate.

Chapter 1

Fate

Ghost Girl Fact #1: All the eye candy is good. Exorcism is bad. The fact that I'm more focused on the former might not be a good thing.

My life, or lack-thereof, is a total shit-show at the moment. I am neither here nor there. Stuck somewhere in between life and death. I ramble around this monstrosity of a house with its beautiful wood floors, winding staircase, antique fixtures, and covered furnishings with no real reason for being. Nothing about this place seems familiar, yet here I am. I can't leave the property. Trust me, I've tried. I wander day in and day out because – let's face it – ghost girls don't exactly sleep, hold jobs, or have active social lives. I'm assuming I'm a ghost because...what else could I possibly be?

Walk through walls? Check. Slam random doors? Check. Make lights and other electronics go bat-shit crazy, scaring the crap out of unsuspecting people? Check and check.

I guess I'm just your average, everyday poltergeist. I can manipulate my environment but little else. No one can see me or hear me. I can't touch anyone either, much to my very real disappointment. It gets lonely being a ghost girl.

My penchant for putting on a show - aka my boredom - has made this place a revolving door for the paranormal community. The Most Haunted Home in the Midwest. Yup. That's right. I turned this otherwise normal home in the middle of Nowhereville, Illinois, into a regular circus sideshow. It's been on the market since the day I appeared, and my performances have scared off every potential buyer or renter that has stepped through those double front doors, with their gorgeous, antique iron scrollwork and frosted glass.

What can I say? I'm a badass. Albeit one that doesn't seem to know much about who she is, where she came from, or what she did that could have resulted in her current predicament.

So what *do* I know? I know that my name is Fate. Ironic, right? How I know that, I can't be sure. Just like I can't be sure how I know that there are three things I miss more than life itself. Yes, I mean that quite literally.

First – coffee. Just the sight of it alone practically sends me into an immediate orgasm these days - if ghost girls could have orgasms, that is. Every time a real estate agent sets up for an open house with a pot of the steaming, yummy goodness, my mouth waters, figuratively, of course, because ghost girls do *not* drool.

Second – wine. Something tells me that wine and I used to have an ongoing love-hate relationship. I bet it was my kryptonite. Cheap, expensive, dry, sweet. I don't even care. If I concentrate hard enough, I swear I can taste the bountiful flavor rolling around on my tongue. Again, immediate almost-orgasm.

Which leads me to the third – sex. I know, obvious,

right? I'll admit that there have been a few times throughout the years where thrill-seeking couples have broken in and gotten down and dirty right in the front living room or shagged it up in one of the upstairs bedrooms that still has a dusty ass bed...and...I may have stayed to watch with unabashed longing, wishing I could at least touch myself to take care of the ache that seems to be perpetually present.

What? There's nothing wrong with a little voyeurism when your life is no longer yours to live. Instead, you live vicariously through those around you. If there's anything I've learned in my time here, it's that I must have been a very sexual being in my past life as every fiber of my phantom body aches for the touch of another.

Life – or rather death – just isn't fair, dammit!

Pouting over all of the things I'll never get to experience again is pointless, but what else do I have to do? Dramatically draping my wrist across my forehead, I sip from an imaginary wine glass with the other. Anything to give some depth to my little self-indulgent pity party. Just when I'm really getting into my spectral sobfest, the sound of approaching cars hits my ears. I roll my eyes, cross my arms over my chest like a stubborn toddler, and refuse to give in to my curiosity. Considering the randy locals prefer the dark when they want to sneak in and defile the property, it's either a real estate agent bringing yet another client that will inevitably piss themselves when they get a taste of my renowned paranormal experience, or another group of those pesky ghost hunters that think they can get rid of me. I simply do not like to share what I perceive as my own personal space. I may be lonely, but I'm not stupid. The living do not like to co-exist with the dead, and ain't nobody got time to deal with cleansings or exorcisms to rid the home of my presence. This place is mine, and it's going to stay that way.

The slamming of car doors is my signal that it's time to get off my ass and evaluate my next move. With a huff of annoyance, I lift my head from the covered arm of the chair I'm sprawled across and fling my legs to the ground. How my transparent self doesn't sink right through the furniture or floors is a mystery, but one simply does not look a gift horse in the mouth. As I amble over to the nearest window, I try to remember the last time I felt a plush cushion sinking beneath my weight or the velvety softness of it beneath my fingertips, and I come up empty. Always empty.

Spotting the black convertible Mustang of my nemesis – the current agent who handles the listing for the property – I fake a gag with one finger down my throat. Immature? Maybe. Let's blame it on my rusty social skills considering it's been just me, myself, and I for way too damn long.

She steps out, her long blonde hair pulled back into a sleek ponytail. Black stiletto heels add another four inches to her already tall figure. Her red dress is excessively tight over her slender body, while her fake boobs are almost popping out of the low-cut neckline.

Oh, I'm not judging. Just stating facts. Trust me when I say she's not at all shy about the work she's had done. I can't even begin to count the number of phone conversations I've had to listen to where she gushed about how awesome they looked post-recovery and how she likes to fondle them herself.

Ugh. TMI, am I right?

She and her whole outfit are just a little too inappropriate to be considered professional, but that doesn't matter to Agent Barbie. No, that is not her real name, and no, I've never really cared enough to figure out what it is. Why would I when she'll be just another in a long line of fools that have attempted to sell this property - and failed.

I scan the driveway, trying to seek out the poor souls unlucky enough to stumble into my lair – *insert evil villain laugh here* - but my eyes snag on the logo-covered doors of the two black SUVs parked in the circular drive. The company name stands out in large, white lettering outlined with silver.

V.I.P.S. Valley Investigations & Paranormal Society.

"Oh my ghost! Really?" I groan aloud while also giving in to another eye roll because - ego, much?

These groups always fall into one of two categories. First, the fame whores who want to make a name for themselves at the Most Haunted Home in the Midwest, hoping to earn their own TV show. Like there aren't already a million other YouTube and TikTok users out there looking for their fifteen minutes in the spotlight.

Then there's the second group. The genuine researchers who are trying to discover answers to the unexplainable - whether that means proving the existence of the paranormal or debunking all the reported activity by chalking it up to swamp gas or drafty windows.

My guess is this group is of the former variety. I mean, V.I.P.S.? Really?

I could ignore them and let them think the rumors of paranormal activity are just that - rumors and highly exaggerated, leaving them disappointed and dejected. Or, I could give them the experience of a lifetime. It's been a while since I've put on a good show, and this may be just the distraction I need to avoid tumbling even further into the depths of my despair.

Just add melodramatic to my long list of ghostly sins.

Movement below grabs my attention, and I watch as a

man glances toward the window where I'm standing. My breath catches, and a sudden tingle tickles my belly with a strange sense of familiarity. It doesn't make any sense, and unease begins to slither through me. He's tall – well over six feet. His sandy blond hair brushes the collar of his shirt, with a stray piece falling in front of his face. A large, masculine hand comes up to run through the offending strands, pushing them out of the way, then drops to run over his scruffy blond facial hair. His bicep flexes under his tight black t-shirt bearing the company logo, and his low-slung jeans hug his long, lean legs. He has a sort of Thor thing going on, and my sex-deprived self just wants to get a peek at his - ahem - hammer.

His brows narrow slightly as he stares my way before his attention is dragged to the man walking up to him.

My gaze slides to the new guy, and the tingles I was feeling before turn into a full-blown riot of sensation in my nether region. Pretty sure I'd be soaking my panties if ghost girls could do that sort of thing. Then something else slithers along with the arousal coursing through me. Something that is gut-wrenching and makes me want to wrap my arms around myself in comfort.

Alpha - as I decide to call the new guy - is just as tall as his friend, but where Thor is lean, athletic grace, Alpha is six-feet-plus of utter badass. Broad shoulders nearly stretch his black logo t-shirt to its limit, and tattoos cover muscular arms that flex as they carry two steel gray cases. His jet black hair is cut into a faux hawk that totally suits the whole bad boy vibe he has going on. Aviator sunglasses cover his eyes from view, but the tightness in his mouth is unmistakable even from a distance. My thumb itches to run along his lips soothing the tension there, offering a reassurance only I can give.

Oh my ghost! Where the hell did that thought come from?

The two have a quick conversation I can't make out, which is cut off by the approach of Agent Barbie. She sashays up to the duo, and I fully expect them to ogle her and her fake tatas. What is it about a pair of boobs that reduces most guys to simpering puddles of mush? Men...*so* predictable.

Much to my surprise, her attempt fails, and after a few brief words from Alpha, Agent Barbie turns and heads toward the front doors. She purposely sways her hips to catch their attention, and I wait for their eyes to snag on her ass. It's an unspoken test. Will they pass, ignoring Agent Barbie's second attempt at seduction, or will they fail like so many others before them? I'm shocked when their gazes turn in sync to the window where I stand, and for a brief moment, I'm frozen. Unable to move or think or even breathe – if my lungs could actually do that sort of thing. Then they turn and head toward the house without another glance, and the moment is over.

The sound of the front door opening barely registers as I'm lost inside my own mind, taking a step back as I try to figure out what the hell just happened. Throughout the years I've been stuck in this afterlife limbo, this is the closest I've come to feeling alive. Dormant emotions are beginning to resurface along with a strange sense of awareness. I swear my fingertips are tingling with power, and long dead nerve endings are sparking to life. I don't know what's going on, but I'm definitely going to have to figure it out. Being caught unaware is annoying.

A deep and husky voice coming from below pulls me from my introspection.

"Guys. I'm picking up a strong feeling of irritation."

Eyes widening as confusion wars with curiosity, I

quickly make my way down the hall to the top of the staircase that descends into the middle of the foyer. My translucent hand grips the beautiful mahogany banister, and I stop myself from taking another step as I stare down at my new visitors.

Agent Barbie has planted herself at the base of the stairs with Alpha and Thor standing off to one side. Three other guys are standing just inside the front doors, their feet surrounded by silver cases. As my gaze scans over the crew, I'm momentarily stunned by all of the eye candy currently taking up space in the foyer. Until this moment, I thought the hot, paranormal researcher was mostly a myth like Big Foot or aliens. Although Zak and Aaron from the GAC could come research me up any time they'd like.

Suddenly, Thor looks up at the spot where I'm standing.

"What is it, Knox?" asks Alpha in a low, rich voice that sends shivers down my spine.

"I don't know. Now I'm feeling curiosity, or maybe confusion." Thor seems to ponder this for a moment, falling silent in a brief pause. "It's hard to tell."

"What do you mean 'it's hard to tell'? What color is the aura?" demands Alpha.

"That's just it. I can't see an aura. It's like I'm experiencing the feelings myself. I've never felt anything like this," muses Thor. "I could swear it's coming from the top of the stairs."

The group turns as one toward the staircase, each of them looking around as though they can find the source of his unexplainable feelings. It's silent as they listen for any sound that could point them in the right direction.

I stand as still as a statue. Afraid that if I move, I'll shatter whatever the hell this bond is with Thor, or Knox, or whoever the hell he is, and I'll go back to being utterly alone. For the first time in too many years, I feel a connection with another being. I can't fuck this up. His eyes, that I can now discern are a beautiful hazel, seem to stare right into mine.

"Are you picking up any other vibes? Male or female? Young or old?" one of the newcomers asks.

He's slightly shorter than Alpha and Thor but still taller than average. Same black logo shirt that's hiding what has to be an impressive chest if the muscular arms are any indication. His dark brown hair is messy like he just rolled out of bed. It's long enough that my fingers itch to run through the silky strands. His black square glasses are super sexy on him, pushing buttons I wasn't even aware I had.

Thor looks around and shrugs, his brows furrowed in thought. The guy who I decide to name Sexy Nerd pulls out a gadget from one of the silver cases and attempts to turn it on.

A sense of excitement fills the air as the others all wait expectantly. Well, except for Barbie. She's checking her phone and twirling her hair around one of her fingers, looking slightly bored by it all.

Sexy Nerd smiles, revealing an adorable pair of dimples, and says, "Maybe this will help. I've got the digital EMF Meter set up. Let's see if it wants to play."

It? Oh, hell no! I am definitely *not* an it, dammit! I'm five feet, nine inches of curvy, ghostly woman. That's what the hell I am. Of course, they can't see me, but that's beside the point.

"I'm experiencing irritation again. A lot of it. Definitely coming from the direction of the stairs. I'm guessing female if the mood swings are any indication," mutters Thor.

Well, that's just demeaning. Though I'm also honest

enough with myself that I can acknowledge the validity of that statement, letting it go with a shrug.

Sexy Nerd starts moving around the room with the EMF meter. It's the tool of choice for most ghost hunters these days. It measures the level of electromagnetic energy in an area, spiking when it gets close to things that give off an electric current. Ghost hunters believe it can prove or disprove the presence of paranormal activity. Assuming the person knows what they're doing. If the user is standing in the middle of a room, far away from anything electrical, and receives a spike, it could indicate ghostly phenomena as ghosts are supposedly known for emitting their own current. Yeah, this isn't my first paranormal rodeo.

It stays silent until he gets closer to the bottom of the staircase.

"We've got a spike right here – almost five milligauss. Looks like a temperature dip here too. Almost five degrees cooler in seconds."

His excitement is obvious and has me smiling a bit. Just as he prepares to head up the stairs, Agent Barbie lays a hand on his arm. The smile falls, and I experience a stab of emotions that pass so quickly I can't even recognize them all. Just as I'm reeling from whatever the hell that was, the EMF meter starts beeping frantically, and Sexy Nerd's eyebrows furrow deeply. I want nothing more than to kiss him there to smooth out those lines.

What the fuck?

Apparently my libido and I need to have a little sit-me-down. I'm all for sexy times, but this feels like so much more than simple desire. There's a level of intimacy here I can't even begin to fathom.

"Come on, guys. Y'all can't really believe there are like... ghosts living here, right?" she asks with a nervous little laugh at the end. She grabs a chunk of her blonde ponytail and twirls it around the fingers of her left hand, the other still clinging to Sexy Nerd's arm. The contact is making me feel a little slap happy.

Dammit! What I wouldn't give for a set of solid hands right about now.

He seems to suddenly realize that she's touching him and quickly drops his arm before looking to the top of the stairs once again. Obviously reluctant to stop researching the cause of the activity, he turns to Alpha who gives him a simple nod. He shuts off the EMF meter which is still beeping wildly.

"Come on. Let's get these lease contracts signed, and then I can give y'all the keys to the place...and a personal tour if you'd like," Agent Barbie offers with a little wink.

She walks over to her bag sitting on the table in the middle of the foyer and pulls out a stack of papers and a pen. With a little come-hither gesture, she motions for Alpha to meet her at the table. He steps up to her right, with Thor moving up to her left. They begin going over the terms, and only then do her words register.

Lease contracts? They're moving in? Well, fuck me sideways!

Chapter 2

Fate

Ghost Girl Fact #2: Don't piss us off. We make shit explode.

My hands land on my hips, and my head falls back with a dramatic sigh that no one can appreciate because no one can hear it. This can't happen. These guys, no matter how drool-worthy, absolutely *cannot* take up residence in my house. I'll be facing months of spirit box sessions, and video cameras always recording, and digital recorders placed in random locations, and...yeah, okay...loads of inevitable sexual frustration.

Dammit!

How did I find myself here? I've spent years in relative peace. Now, in a matter of minutes, I'm witnessing my solitude go up in flames. And not just a cozy little fire that warms you up while you roast marshmallows and sing camp songs. This is a full-on inferno engulfing every last scrap of my sanity. Kumba-fucking-ya!

New voices draw my attention back to the present and the maddening situation I have found myself in.

"Ouch! What the hell was that for?" says a blond giant

near the door, rubbing his shoulder and scowling at the man next to him.

"Come on, dipshit! Let's grab the rest of the gear," replies an identical blond giant standing next to him.

These two guys are mirror images of each other. Taller than the other three by at least a couple inches, their shoulders probably struggle to fit through a door frame. I'm honestly astounded by the elasticity of those black logo tees. *Someone should definitely leave the manufacturer some five-star reviews on Amazon.*

They're both in black jeans that encase their long legs, black boots, and matching aviator sunglasses. Their long hair hangs in luxurious waves past their shoulders, and I feel a twinge of hair envy. Even their full beards match. *Does their underwear match too?* Boxers? Maybe boxer briefs? It seems imperative that I find out.

"Fine. Let's go, wankstain," mutters Dipshit.

They turn and head out the door. From the back, the only noticeable distinction between the two would be the tattoos covering opposite arms and hands. Their asses are most certainly identical. I had to double check that little detail - all in the name of research, of course.

As if my overactive imagination needed anymore stimuli, now my mind is swirling with all sorts of naughty thoughts about being the female meat to their twin sandwich. Yup. I'm headed straight down the one way road to Frustration Central. *Ugh! #GhostGirlProblems.*

I plop down on the top step, my elbows finding my knees, and look down on the chaos that was once my peaceful foyer.

"Ok, Fate," I say out loud, which helps me think. "They're intrigued now. This damn connection with Thor and that little fiasco with the EMF meter have given them ammunition for their research. They won't leave." I let my mind skim over all of my potential plans. "Maybe I'll just ignore them. Let them think it was all just a fluke. If I can manage to stay far away from Thor, he'll have to assume it was a fluke or something, right? They'll get bored and high-tail it out of here. It might be a half-assed plan at best, but at this point it's all I've got."

No one responds, of course, because no one can hear my ramblings.

But is that really what I want? For them to abandon this place and leave me alone. I may appreciate having the space to myself, but the loneliness has grown to become an insistent, gnawing despondency. For the first time in my recent existence, there's a flicker of hope that I might be able to find some answers to my situation. These guys are key. I can feel it every time one of those damn hints of familiarity brushes against that empty space inside my soul. It would suck them in and keep them if it could, but they bounce right off, leaving me feeling emptier than ever. If I can somehow figure this out, maybe I'll finally get some resolution.

What that means, I'm not sure. Head off into the light? Yes, please. Get sucked down into the fiery depths below? An image suddenly pops into my mind of embers and screams and bleakness, all in terrifyingly vivid detail. My eyes widen, and I swear I can smell wisps of sulfur. Then it's all gone, and I'm left trying to figure out, once again, what the hell just happened.

A girlish giggle draws my focus back to the chaos of my unlife, and I look down to find Barbie packing up her paper-work while stealing glances at Alpha. The other guys have finished unloading the equipment and are surrounded by so many cases there's barely enough floor space to walk.

"Well, you boys are all set. I could give you that tour now if you'd like? Maybe I can come back another night and make you all a welcome home dinner?" she simpers, turning to look at Alpha and not so subtly pushing her chest out.

Something starts to slither through my body as I stand, my hands clenching into fists from the power coming to life inside me. I look down at them, momentarily confused at my body's sudden involuntary responses, but my focus is drawn back to the group below when I hear his voice.

"I don't think that will be necessary, but thank you for getting everything set up here for us," Alpha says, taking a step back.

She smirks. "Oh, it was nothing."

Obviously not put off by his easy dismissal, she steps toward him and lifts her right hand to his chest. She lets it drag down slowly until it stops on the waistband of his jeans. "I'd be happy to give you a...private tour...if you'd prefer?"

Before he can respond, a sudden blinding rage sweeps over me. A red haze covers my vision, and my entire body begins to tremble in response to the overwhelming level of power, the likes of which I've never experienced. I try to calm myself down but have no control over the tide of emotions assaulting me - one of which feels a lot like jealousy.

"Guys. I'm not sure what's happening, but I'm feeling some serious anger building," Thor states with a worried look on his face just as all the lights start to flicker wildly. "I can actually feel the fury growing stronger by the second."

Alpha looks his way, only to swing his gaze back to the blonde leech who has suddenly attached herself to him with both hands on his chest, taking fistfuls of his shirt.

She looks afraid, and that only brings a sinister grin to my face.

Placing my foot on the first step, I start to make my way down the stairs.

"Shit! I can feel it getting closer. Everybody move away from the stairs." Thor slowly backs up, attempting to avoid the clutter on the floor around him.

Again with this 'it' business. Another rush of frustration and anger floods me.

I take one more ridiculously slow step, wanting to draw it out. For the first time in years, I feel powerful, as though I'm in control of something other than a shitty pity party. I'm in control of my surroundings. Of my own fate. The fear permeating the air makes something inside me come to life. It wants to revel in the chaos I'm creating. Wants to rejoice over the growing panic in the room. I lift my hands, glancing down at the pretty pink sparks of electricity pulsing off my fingertips. That's new. So is the desperate need for release from this riot of feelings consuming me, which is as intoxicating as it is alarming. I know I should be terrified of what it all means, and a part of me definitely is, but not enough to give a damn at the moment.

As I descend another step, the power leaking from my hands suddenly shoots out. A pair of light bulbs burst inside the light fixtures in the foyer, directly below where I stand. All six people in the foyer drop down, covering their heads at the sudden explosion of noise and glass.

Well, that was...unexpected.

I must have powered up in the poltergeist world because this shit has never happened so effortlessly. I've always had to work my ass off to demonstrate my paranormal proclivities. A ghost girl could get used to this.

Alpha jumps up, grabbing Agent Barbie's arm and

tugging her away from the stairs. The action sends another wave of rage crashing over me, and any curiosity I had about my newfound abilities is washed away. In its wake, I feel nothing but the intense desire to make her pay for touching what's mine. The thought has me pausing momentarily, but the emotions roaring through my body insist that I keep moving - my sudden possessiveness all but forgotten.

The others follow Alpha and rush back toward the door.

The stairs beneath my feet pass one by one, the progression of bursting bulbs following me as I descend. The sound of feminine whimpering brings a manic smile to my face.

I keep moving. Bulbs keep exploding in my wake.

Alpha pushes the now crying agent behind him. "Knox, what do you feel?"

"Still feeling this extreme rage. Maybe some jealousy and satisfaction mixed in. Something set her off, and we need to figure out a way to get her to calm down!"

"*Her*? You're sure about that now?"

"Definitely a female. She feels threatened. And pissed. Really, really pissed!"

"Macklin. Any ideas?"

I see the thoughtful look on Sexy Nerd's face just as I reach the bottom of the stairs. A table and a shit load of equipment are all that stand between me and the group of people that have royally destroyed my peace. A wicked smirk still tilts my lips as I tip my head and wait to see what he comes up with before I make another move, my curiosity temporarily getting the upper hand on the plethora of emotions rolling through me.

"I have a theory," Sexy Nerd, or Macklin, mumbles. Clearly lost in his own musings. "Cole, put your arm around Mandy."

Alpha's eyebrows go up questioningly.

"Just...bear with me and let's see what happens."

My eyes narrow as I watch Alpha, or Cole, grab Agent Barbie's hand and pull her alongside him. His left arm wraps protectively around her shoulder, and she buries her tearstained face into his side. His other arm comes up reflexively, wrapping her in an embrace.

I'd like to say that I saw the act for what it was. A way to goad a response. That I am a mature, adult ghost and could ignore the emotions creating a tsunami inside me. I'd like to. Really, I would. But I can't. Nope. This ghost girl can apparently be just as immature and irrational as any other living, breathing, warm-blooded female on the planet that's had a run in with the green-eyed monster, otherwise known as jealousy.

A low growl startles me for a second until I realize it's coming from me.

Huh. That's interesting.

"What the hell, Macklin?" mutters Knox. "Not a good idea, guys," he warns, shaking his head.

Smart guy, that one. They really should listen to him. Especially considering the sheer level of energy coursing through the room. Maybe it's time to throw in something special from my ghostly repertoire.

Doors slam shut throughout the house, and the clatter has everyone looking around, waiting for what will happen next.

"That theory, Macklin. Now," Alpha shouts.

"It's just as I thought. The few times we've been able to get a reaction from the entity were always when Mandy was touching one of us. If I had to guess, this entity really does not take kindly to that."

Oh, just peachy. First, I was an *it*. Now, I'm an *entity*. What's a ghost girl gotta do to get a little respect up in here?

Aretha really had the right idea.

My mind zings back to Macklin's words. Why *don't* I like Agent Barbie touching these guys? I don't know them. I certainly shouldn't feel so possessive of them.

Fuck!

What the hell is happening to me? The panic I've been keeping at bay begins to creep back in. The power, though diminished, is still buzzing at my fingertips.

Just as I'm about to turn around and find a place where I can calm down and work through all of the craziness, I hear Cole hushing Agent Barbie – because no way in hell am I calling her by her real name – and whispering to her just low enough I can't make out the words. Her head tilts up, and she stares into his eyes, his shirt once again clutched between her perfectly manicured fingers. For a split second, I think they're going to kiss and am hit with the strongest sense of déjà vu, like I've seen this play out before.

The fire in my veins is instantly reignited, all rational thought disappears, and the growl has returned. All of a sudden, the built-in sound system throughout the house starts blaring a popular pop song.

Barbie screams while the guys all cover their ears. I stand there, with a death glare aimed at the blonde interloper. If looks could kill, she'd be nothing but ash right now. Lucky for her, I don't even have a solid body let alone super-death-powers. But I do have enough energy zipping through me to add a little extra oomph to my usual bag of tricks.

I concentrate on my power. Holding my hands out in front of me, I wave my right hand to the side, and a portion of the silver cases on the floor start to slide toward the far wall. Doing the opposite with my left hand, the remaining cases slide to the other wall. With each step I take toward the door, I spread the sea of cases.

"Shit!" Cole exclaims over the loud music.

His gaze follows the cases that are seemingly moving by themselves across the beautiful hardwood floor. "Thad. Levi. Get Mandy outside. Now! We'll follow in a minute."

Dipshit or Wankstain – not sure which is which – tries to pry Barbie's fingers from the front of Cole's shirt. When she's finally detached, she struggles to stay with Cole and ends up over one of the twin's shoulders, crying hysterically. I don't even have time to react to the contact before they rush her outside, shutting the door behind them.

The effect is immediate. The angry haze that has been consuming my vision clears, and the addicting power running through my body slowly diminishes. I'm left standing in the middle of the foyer, shattered glass around my feet, with the music still belting out a last warning that everyone will get what's coming to them - before suddenly cutting out.

Talk about perfect timing on my part. *Yes! #Ghost-GirlFTW*

And...silence.

No one makes a move or says a word, too stunned to come up with anything coherent. Or at least that's my excuse. Not sure what the guys are thinking.

It's Macklin that breaks the standoff.

"Holy shit! That was epic!"

Cole turns to scowl at him and then faces Knox.

"Knox?"

"Nothing. It's like all the intense anger and irritation just disappeared. I sense a little bit of confusion, maybe, but that's it. She's still really close. Not sure where exactly, but definitely close."

"Any ideas what the hell that was all about, Mack?" Cole asks.

"For whatever reason, it..." Macklin starts.

Back to *it* now, am I? My fingers spark in response.

"Whoa! She doesn't like that at all," Knox states with a light chuckle.

Why is he amused? I'm sure as hell not.

"Um. Ok. Sorry! Uh. For whatever reason, *she*..." he pauses, looking at Knox who surveys the room for a second, gauging my reaction.

Satisfied, I give them two thumbs up. Like they can see it. Which they definitely can't so I just look ridiculous. *Ugh. #GhostGirlProblems*

Knox nods to Macklin, giving him the all clear. This whole thing is just too weird for words.

"Right. So she definitely has an issue with us being touched. Why that is, I can't say. Maybe it has something to do with why she's stuck here? Some sort of incident from her past that's stirring up all of these feelings. We'll have to dig deeper for answers," Macklin finishes.

"Okay," Cole starts, "let's work on getting everything set up as soon as we can. We need to start documenting our experiences and digging into the history of the house. Mack, walk Mandy's bag out to her and make sure she's ok to drive home. If not, drive her car and I'll have one of the boys follow you."

My temper flares at that, but before it can escalate, Knox cuts in.

"Yeah. She doesn't like that either. Apparently it's more than just the touching she has an issue with. How about we get Mandy a taxi if she's still shaken up?" Then he proceeds to look around as if he's waiting for my approval.

A warmth spreads through me at his words. For the first time in too long, I can communicate with someone else, even if it's indirectly. His thoughtfulness causes a pang in the region where my heart would be, if ghost girls had beating hearts that is, and a small smile finds my lips.

"Uh. Yeah. Okay. I think she likes that idea," he says, then clears his throat.

No doubt he's feeling all of these mushy feelings coursing through me and doesn't have any idea what they're about. I suppose that's for the best. Because right now, I don't have any idea either.

Chapter 3

KNOX

EMPATH FACT #1: HARD ONS SHOULD NOT BE A PROBLEM IN THIS LINE OF WORK. EVER.

To say tonight was a clusterfuck is an understatement. I'm exhausted, both mentally and physically. After the chaos of earlier, there is nothing I need more than the drink in my hand and the surprisingly comfortable leather seat under my ass. We're all trying to settle down now that the house is somewhat in order – the broken glass cleaned up, furniture uncovered, and the bedrooms situated enough for one night.

Macklin was able to get a fire started in the large, ornate fireplace in the study, and its crackling warmth is enough to calm even the most restless soul. The room is massive, with bookshelves on the far wall, a woven rug that covers a majority of the dark wooden floor, and leather sofas that are arranged in a U-shape in the center of the room facing the large window seat overlooking the front lawn and circular drive. Most of our equipment is still sitting just outside the study door. Untouched after being moved by an unseen hand.

Once the glass stopped exploding, slamming doors quieted, and the music went silent, it was as if she just vanished. The onslaught of emotions diminished with the distance, and I was left feeling oddly...hollow. It may have been mere moments out of this long life I've lived, but the connection was more powerful than any I had encountered before. It was as if I experienced every nuance of what she felt, when she felt it.

Most don't understand my unique abilities. They don't believe that I can see the aura of those around me, both the living and the dead still on this plane. They can't fathom that I hold the power to see the essence of who a person or spirit is on the inside. Whether that's because they're naturally skeptical or they don't want to accept the fact that I may be able to see the real person beneath all the lies, I can't be sure.

A person's aura is like a misty haze that surrounds their body, changing with their emotions, but also with a core of stable color based mostly on their inner self. A yellow haze, for instance, usually represents happiness or a friendly nature. Red can signify anger or strength. Green is health or jealousy. Every color has its own meaning, and I use that to my advantage when meeting new people.

She didn't have an aura, unlike every other entity I've encountered. The spirit that seems to reside in this house just exists, and I can feel her in the very center of my soul.

I take another drink of the dark amber liquid, the ice cubes clanking against the glass. The warmth flows through me and smooths out the concern that wants to rise again.

Who is she? Why is she here? What is she doing to me?

Cole walks in with a tower of pizzas that he unceremoniously drops onto the coffee table. Thad follows with a stack of paper plates and napkins, and his twin, Levi, with the bottle of Jack I helped myself to earlier.

"Dig in," Cole says. "Then we can work through the plan for setting up our gear and where we want to begin."

"Is no one going to ask the obvious question here?" Levi mumbles around a mouthful of pizza. "What the fuck was all that earlier?"

Most people have trouble telling the twins apart even though they tattooed opposite sides of their bodies. I don't have that issue, of course. Their auras are enough for me to differentiate between the two.

"The entity..." Macklin pauses as if he's waiting for her to smite him where he sits. "Uh...sorry...the *female spirit*... seems to be more powerful than anything we have previously come up against. Shattering light bulbs and slamming doors are one thing. Moving multiple cases and turning on a sound system with a totally relevant song is another. It should be interesting to see if she can manifest in other ways," Macklin responds excitedly.

Leave it to our resident nerd to get excited about shattered glass and Taylor Swift.

"Mack," Cole starts, and I already know what he's going to ask before the words leave his mouth. "Do you think she could be the reason we were drawn here?"

The five of us are...different. Unusual in ways the world would deem impossible. We have no history. We were never born. We have no families. Don't know our last names, if we even have any. We've lived for fifty years but don't age.

Waking up one day under a bridge in Austin, TX with no idea who I was or what had happened to me, I had this overwhelming sense that I needed to find something. I journeyed across the country, following an unseen tether that constantly tugged at my soul.

In a crowded diner outside of Chattanooga, TN, I found Macklin. He had woken up in New York City and, like me, couldn't resist the pull to hunt for something unknown. The second he pushed open the glass door of the diner, two missing pieces in the puzzle of our lives clicked into place. His aura was a bright blue, with a haze of yellow around it - telling me he was loyal, friendly, and held an intelligence that went beyond what was normal. This deep sense of brotherhood formed, and we spent hours talking about our journeys.

But the tug didn't disappear. It was still there, insistent that we keep searching, but for what, neither of us knew.

We used his innate knowledge of anything and everything, a gift that is as useful as it is annoying, to our advantage. We scouted out routes and potential locations as we set off to follow our instincts.

Together, we found the twins in Chicago a couple months later. They hadn't wandered like we had. Instead, they'd ignored the pull, following their guts, and stayed put, which is probably a good thing where they're concerned. Their tendency to wreak havoc has caused us a number of close encounters with law enforcement throughout the years.

Where Thad's aura was a deep red, tinged with a blackness in the middle, telling me he was strong and passionate with a hint of darkness somehow mixed in, Levi's was a surprising indigo, slightly white at the center, an indication he was intuitive and benevolent, with a level of purity mixed in. Which all made sense once we got to understand them and their powers.

Not long after they came into consciousness, they had a run in with an aggressive spirit. When one of them attempted to bitch slap the thing, something only Thad or

Levi would think was a good idea, they discovered they could force the spirit to cross over into whichever realm they were destined for. Seeing an opportunity, they quickly began offering their ghost exterminating services to those wanting or needing to get rid of undesirable guests. Their ingenuity and enterprising spirit, which we've come to understand is their default way of thinking, was much appreciated as they were able to fund our continued search while we criss-crossed the country. That was the start of our paranormal team and our cover for our supernatural abilities that would later become known as Valley Investigations & Paranormal Society.

Our rag tag group scoured locations for close to six months before we found Cole outside a poorly lit bar in Phoenix, Arizona. He was drunk, his clothes a tattered, bloody mess. His knuckles were shredded and bruised, obvious signs he had been in a fight. The twins managed to get him back to our hotel, where we forced him to sleep off the alcohol. When he came to, he was confused and angry with a cloud of unexplainable depression drowning him in his own misery. It all matched his aura which was a dark gray, with swirls of angry red. Determined to keep the urge to hunt buried under liquor and fighting, it had taken us several weeks to convince him to sober up and join us.

Even though we were no longer being pulled toward the unknown – the puzzle pieces all in their rightful places - there was still this sense of something missing. Something that would keep the puzzle from breaking apart ever again. Forty years went by until one day, the tug was back. The pull was diluted, different from the others, but persistent nonetheless.

After years of searching, we may have just found our glue.

"She *could* be the reason we were drawn here," Macklin

muses, his thoughts mirroring mine and drawing me back to the present. "I'll start researching the estate as well as the surrounding areas tomorrow and see what I can come up with."

"Make sure you tell the twins where you'd like to see the video and infrared cameras set up," Cole states. "I want answers, so let's make sure we document and log anything that could help us solve this mystery."

I take another large swig from my glass. It's coming. I can feel it. The question I don't have any answers to. Uncertainty has my stomach in a vise grip, and I'm wondering if another glass of Jack will help or hinder the situation.

"Knox," he says, eyeing me like he knows where my mind has gone. He probably does. He always seems to. "Tell us about what you experienced earlier. You said there was no aura. Explain."

Jackass. He knew if he asked me, I'd skirt around the question with half answers and small truths. Instead, he simply demanded I explain. An innate part of me is unable to deny the command. Sometimes his power sucks ass.

"It started outside," I begin, remembering the unnerving sensation that inundated me as I stood in the driveway. "All of a sudden, I was hit with this intense flood of emotions. It was live action, as if I was experiencing them as they were happening. And not just a general sense of the emotion. It was the real deal. Like they were my own."

"And this has never happened before, right?" he asks, already knowing the answer but wanting me to acknowledge it.

"Never. Emotions are like rain. Normally, I have a figurative umbrella which shelters me from getting drenched. The rain could be pouring down, but it flows right off that layer of protection. I know the rain is there. I can see it. Hear it.

Feel the pressure of it somewhat, but I remain mostly unaffected. With her, it's like stepping straight out into the downpour without an umbrella. The rain drenches me in seconds. Invades every sense, leaving me vulnerable. And even when it's dried and gone, I can still feel the aftermath throughout my body."

"Damn. That's deep, bro," Thad snarks from his seat on the sofa next to his twin.

"Shut the fuck up, Thad."

"Alright. That's enough," Cole commands. "We need to figure out what's happening here and what this all means."

"This is definitely an intelligent haunting, not a residual one," Macklin states as he grabs his own slice of pizza. "She's responding to our actions directly, not just reenacting her last moments over and over again. Her level of power is astounding."

"Bro, you sound way too excited about that," Levi mutters as he tips back his glass and downs his Jack, which he immediately refills.

"Of course he does. Dude practically creams his pants when he's got a new mystery to solve," Thad chuckles.

"For fuck's sake, you two. Knock that shit off," Cole orders. He's the only one the twins will listen to, with or without his power. He has this domineering quality to his personality and naturally gravitated toward the leadership position once he pulled himself out from the bottom of the bottle. "We've got a lot of work to get done, and something tells me this could be it. This could be where we finally get some answers. Knox, can you still feel her?"

I finish off my glass and hold it out for Levi to refill while I expand my sense of the room and beyond. Instantly, I feel her. This warm presence that's surprisingly stronger than it was before. Her emotions swarm my own, and it feels like coming home, a thought that alarms me on a primitive level. It takes me a second to gather myself enough to describe what I'm experiencing.

"She's just as confused as we are, and that seems to irritate her. But she's excited too. She can sense that I'm linked to her," I murmur, lost in my own thoughts and wondering why this all feels so damn familiar.

Her nearness puts me suddenly on alert, as if our conversation has summoned her. Curiosity, annoyance, and something else I can't quite pin down swirl through me - each battling to be the victor of some emotional war.

How the hell do women handle this shit? Emotional roller coaster, my ass. It's more like an emotional tsunami.

"Knox, what is it?" Cole demands.

"She's here," I reply quietly, "and she's close."

"Mack," Cole snaps, "get an EMF meter in here now, along with a digital recorder."

Macklin jumps off the sofa and rushes into the foyer, the opening and closing of cases accompanied by mumbled curses as he's trying to find what he's looking for. The rest of us remain silent - not wanting to scare her off.

Her amusement catches me off guard. As does her level of satisfaction – which I'm sure stems from the fact that she can get a rise out of us simply by being in the room. I put a stop to the smile that's tempting my lips as her emotions mingle with my own. It's becoming harder to distinguish the two.

Then I feel it. That unnamed emotion from earlier.

Attraction.

She knows I'm tuned into her, and she likes it. Suddenly, it feels like she's right in front of me. Like if I reached out, I could touch her. A wave of longing that is not my own assaults me. Not just lust or desire, but this deep need to connect to another person. To touch and be touched. I'm practically frozen in place, my knees spread wide as I lounge on the sofa. My arm is slung over the side with the glass of Jack in my right hand. I tilt my chin up slightly, as if I can look her right in the eyes.

"Knox? What's happening?" Cole asks from the sofa across from me, but I don't look his way.

"She's right here," is all I manage to say.

There's suddenly rustling around the room. People moving and shuffling about, but I don't see any of them. My focus is on the space in front of me – on the woman who has captured my complete attention when I can't even see her. A hint of vanilla and cinnamon settles low in my belly, stirring an arousal I wasn't expecting.

A tingling starts on my left cheek, trailing down my chin and over the front of my throat. I swallow reflexively. It continues across my collar bone and over my left shoulder before flowing down my arm and pausing slightly on my inner elbow, swirling around in a small circle - which I find both playful and sexy as hell. It moves down my left forearm to my hand that is resting on my left thigh.

My gaze follows the movement as I let her explore, because that's what this is. An exploration. Her reaching out to someone on the most physical level she's capable of and I'll be damned if I don't like it and want more. My jaw clenches as I struggle to get a handle on my desire. Thank fuck for my jeans which are hiding the evidence of just how excited she's got me.

"Dude. What's going on over there? You look like you're a little tense," Levi questions.

"Bro, from the looks of things, bet those jeans are becoming damn uncomfortable," Thad jokes.

So much for hiding anything.

The touch that had paused on my hand at Levi's words starts up again. Whispering over my knuckles and down to my fingertips where she stops. My hand is pretty damn close to my cock, and I'm slightly ashamed to admit that I want nothing more than for her to explore that area a little further.

I look up and stare into the nothingness in front of me, and whatever she sees when she looks at me must give her the answer she needs. I release the breath I wasn't even aware I'd been holding as the tingles move up my inner thigh and right over my erection, lingering there. Even over my jeans it feels as though small bursts of current are being sent straight to my dick, and I'm dangerously close to embarrassing myself right in front of my brothers.

"Fuck!" I moan out, dropping my head onto the back of the sofa. Her touch ghosts up and down over my shaft, and it takes all of my self-control to not buck my hips up into the invisible hand that I can all but see.

This is definitely a first for me. A fully clothed hand job given by an invisible woman. The guys will never let me live this down.

Right as I sense her amusement that is heavily laced with a desire of her own, a blast of those damn tingles courses through my dick, down and around my balls, and doesn't let up. My hips jerk, my body taking over, while my left hand grabs hold of the cushion to give me leverage. I curse and groan loudly as I come – unable to stop myself.

The tingles slowly begin to fade away as my body recovers from one of the hottest – and fastest - damn orgasms of my life. I'm left breathing like I just ran a marathon, staring up at the ceiling wondering what in the actual hell just happened.

"I feel like I need a cigarette after watching that little show," muses Levi.

Raising my head, I glance around the room, seeing all of my brothers standing in a loose semi-circle around the coffee table in front of me.

"Can she do me next?" Thad snickers.

Only a few seconds pass before his whole body suddenly jolts, followed by a bellowed, "Fucking hell, woman! You do *not* zap a man's junk like that. I want the good shit Knox got."

The rest of the guys chuckle as he rubs his hand over his scorched crotch.

"She's highly amused right now," I manage through my own laughter. I can practically feel her grinning in satisfaction.

"A woman with a dark sense of humor. I like it," Levi proclaims.

Followed by Thad's barely contained, "That's so fucking hot!"

Bringing the glass of Jack up to my lips, I notice my hand shaking ever so slightly. Quickly, I finish off the drink, needing the alcohol to calm my rioting system. I'm relaxed yet wound tight at the same time. I'm not sure what to make of our ghostly woman or the fact that it seems I'm becoming as possessive of her as she is of us.

Our ghostly woman, Knox? Really?

"You care to explain what the hell just happened?" Cole asks, his raised eyebrow the only indication he's not only interested but also amused, which is a rarity for him.

"Thought that was already evident?" I smirk lazily, knowing my non-answer is going to bug the shit out of him until he demands that I give him the details.

It's then I notice the guys all have a piece of equipment

aimed my way. So that's what all the commotion was. Macklin has the EMF meter. Cole with the digital voice recorder. Levi has a thermal imaging camera, and Thad has a video camera.

Just fucking fantastic. This moment will be replayed and re-lived just to torment me for years to come.

"I've got to say," Mack starts, "that was one hell of a show of power. She drained every single one of our batteries. And she's got control too."

"I would agree with that statement. Her control was phenomenal," I respond, sending the twins into simultaneous groans of envy.

"Knox, what did you feel?" Cole asks, a hint of his power in the question.

I release a long sigh.

"She's lonely. Almost desperately so. She knew I could see her, figuratively, of course, and took advantage of the unique connection we seem to have. It was like..." I trail off, trying to come up with the words to describe the feeling of her ghostly hand on me in words that won't make me sound as desperate for a repeat as I am. "Like all of her desire and need coalesced into this electrifying sensation, but there was no pain. Just really, really intense pleasure. I couldn't stop my body from reacting. It's like it recognized the feeling and welcomed it."

That last part is what worries me the most.

"Now I need to get cleaned up."

I feel her presence slowly fade away, satisfaction and a hint of sadness both trailing in her wake.

"She's gone," I murmur.

Her departure leaves me with an emptiness that doesn't make sense. A lingering hint of vanilla and cinnamon remains, reminding me of my favorite snickerdoodle cookies, stirring up a longing somewhere deep inside me. I just want to eat her up. Which is beyond weird since she's a fucking ghost.

"We should probably all head to bed and get some rest. Something tells me we'll need to stay sharp around here," Macklin suggests.

"Agreed," Cole mutters. "Head to bed. That's an order. We'll figure out the rest in the morning after a good night's sleep."

The chill in the night air has me slowly coming awake, and for a second, I can't remember where I am. After years of traveling and not having a home base, places start to blur together.

I'm in a fairly comfortable bed. Sheets and comforter must have been kicked off at some point as they're tangled around my feet. I manage to open my eyes, though my body protests. Lying on my right side, I'm facing the only window in the room - which I confirm is closed - and can just make out the leaves from the ivy plant growing around the outside window.

That's right. Illinois. Haunted house. Coming in my pants. A ghost who is quickly taking over most of my thoughts. Good times.

It's 3:15 in the morning, and the illumination from the alarm app on my phone is the only light in the room. *What in the hell woke me up?* I close my eyes, roll over, and get comfortable, fully intending to go back to sleep.

The faintest shift of air in front of my face has my eyes flying open this time. For a moment, I'm frozen - my body refusing to move. I force my heart rate to slow down and my breathing to calm, even as panic grips me.

Because a few inches from my face, she sleeps. A slender nose, turned up just slightly at the tip. Her almond-shaped eyes are closed with long lashes brushing her transparent cheeks. Her lips are large and full, completely kissable, though they're relaxed in sleep. With one arm bent under her head, the other is stretched out and halfway through my body.

I've found my wake up call.

Trying not to make a sound, I take in the rest of our little ghost, as there's no doubt that this is she. I can sense her somewhere deep inside of me. Something urging me to close the gap between us.

Her long hair is in messy waves, flowing over her shoulder and spread out on the pillow behind her, the exact color lost in shades of darkness. She's wearing a t-shirt with short shorts, but the simplicity of that does nothing to cool my rush of desire. This time I can't even blame it on her. I feel nothing from her but a sense of peace as she sleeps, unaware of my inspection.

I slowly lift my right hand, wanting to know if I can touch her. Feel her. Is she responsible for the sudden drop in temperature, as ghosts have been known to be? Is she made up of mist or just shadow and light?

Just before my fingers brush over her arm, her eyes open. I can't discern the color, as transparency doesn't allow that, but they're strangely beautiful in a haunting sort of way. She starts to pull her arm back, her gaze catching on my hand frozen in midair. Her eyes fly to mine, and I watch as they widen in surprise. Her lips part, and I should be ashamed of all of the ways my brain tells me I could put those pouty lips to use...but I'm not. Not one fucking bit. Because she wants it too.

She quickly shoots up to her knees, and I rush to follow, freezing when we both find ourselves kneeling on the bed, facing each other. I tower over her by at least a few inches. The fact that I can see the outline of the door through her hazy form is a little disconcerting, but now I've got a clear view of her spectacular ghostly body. My eyes roam. From the hair that lays in sexy waves down to the middle of her back, to the short shorts that stop at the bottom of her ass cheeks. Her t-shirt is tight, hugging ethereal curves that are starting to make morning wood become a reality, definitely something I never thought would be an issue in this line of work.

She's younger than I would have expected. Maybe mid-twenties. The slogan across her shirt reads *#GhostGirlProblems*, and I can't stop the tilt of my lips at her apparent sense of humor. Who is this delicious anomaly?

A small pang of sadness hits me when I realize that whoever she once was, those days have passed. She won't get to leave this place unless it's to find peace on the other side and will never get to experience the life she could have had.

She tilts her head as though she senses the sudden shift of my thoughts. She's nervous and unsure, but I can also sense her surprise and a heavy dose of anticipation.

"I'm Knox," I whisper, not wanting to startle her.

Her lips move, but I hear nothing.

"Wait. I can't hear you. Say it again, slower."

I watch those luscious lips intently as they form what must be her name.

"One more time."

I receive a quick flash of frustration, but she tries again.

"Fay?"

She shakes her head and rolls her eyes. The irritation level in the room isn't the only thing skyrocketing; my dick is rising with every movement of her perfect fucking mouth.

I watch as she tries one more time, putting so much emphasis on the last part that my face is hit with a blast of cold air.

"Did you just ghost spit on me?" I ask with obvious amusement.

Her eyes widen, and she throws her head back in soundless laughter. I desperately wish I could hear every noise this gorgeous creature makes.

Once her laughter stops, she starts to do something with her hands. Is she... signing?

I bring my hand up to run through my bed tousled hair because...shit! I don't know what the hell she's trying to tell me. I could yell for Macklin, but a part of me doesn't want to have to share her with someone else - even one of my brothers - when I've just found her.

"I don't know sign language."

Her hands drop to her sides, and she just glares at me like this is all my fault. With another roll of her eyes, she uses both hands, maneuvering them until they're in the shape of a letter.

"F. Got it!"

Her hands come back up in an awkwardly shaped A. Then a T. Then with one hand in the shape of some sort of squared-shaped C, she holds up one finger from the other hand in the middle forming an E.

"Fate?" I ask, thinking that there's no way her name is a coincidence.

She nods enthusiastically, a beautiful smile appearing on her face.

"What are you doing here, Fate?"

She simply shrugs, shaking her head. The smile disappears, and wisps of sadness filter through our connection. So she doesn't know much about her own situation either. Interesting.

"Is anyone here with you?"

Another shake of her head, along with a wave of total sorrow that damn near has me grimacing from its intensity.

"Maybe there's something my brothers and I could do to help you. Would you like that?"

Again, more enthusiastic nodding.

"Let's go see if the guys..." But I'm cut off by the bedroom door slamming open.

Suddenly, she disappears, leaving nothing but a trace of her scent behind.

"Dammit, Cole!" I growl. "She was right here in front of me."

"What the fuck do you mean, she was right in front of you?" he snaps back.

"I could see her. She was so fucking close. What the fuck, man?"

"Well, shit! The EMF meter outside your door started lighting up and beeping wildly, so Macklin thought we should check on you."

It's only then I notice Macklin behind him, shouldering his way into my room.

"Did she do anything to you? What did she look like? Did you talk to her? Why is she here?" His barrage of questions comes faster than I can even keep up with, and I run my hand through my hair, tamping down on my irritation born of disappointment from her disappearance.

"She didn't do anything. She was...stunning. Much younger than I expected. But when I asked her name, she had no voice. She literally signed the letters of her name. Which is Fate – honest to God. And if that's not intriguing enough, get this. She has no idea why she's here."

"That can't be a coincidence," Macklin remarks.

"No. I'm pretty sure it's not. I was just getting ready to lead her to all of you since she said she'd like our help, but then asshole over there had to scare her off."

Cole looks slightly chagrined at his rookie mistake, but rather than apologize, he immediately orders, "Let's go get some of our equipment and scout the room. See if we can find anything unusual. Do you still sense her?"

I take a moment and reach my senses out to her. I'm still on my knees in the middle of the bed, surrounded by her scent and the memory of her smile. She's no longer close by, but I'm slightly relieved when I feel that she's just as disappointed as I am. When I lift my hand to push hair out of my face, I notice something on the inside of my left wrist. It's a solid line broken only by two small dots in the center. A tattoo that I most certainly didn't have just moments ago.

"What the fuck?" I ask no one in particular, staring at the offending appendage like it can give me an explanation.

"What is it?" Macklin strides over, grabbing my left hand and pulling it toward him. "When did you get a new tattoo?"

"I didn't. This wasn't here before."

"She marked you?" Cole exclaims.

"I'm not sure what this is or who did it, but there's only one person who might be able to give us some answers," I respond thoughtfully. "Now we just have to convince her to show herself again."

"We'll need to find a way to communicate with her since she won't be able to just answer the questions outright. Maybe we keep it simple for this first attempt. A yes or no interrogation," Macklin rambles, already creating a list of questions in his head for the lovely little ghost.

"What, Mack, no Ouija board?"

"Hardy har har. Aren't you hilarious," he mutters, rolling his eyes. Then he yawns. "I'm a tech genius, Knox. Not a teenage girl. I'll figure something out."

"Okay. We all need some sleep if we're going to draw her out again. I want everyone ready and alert at all times," Cole demands.

"You got it, boss." What I don't say is that my soul is already restless, wanting to reestablish the connection with her. The tug I felt earlier has nothing on the deep-seated need to see her again that courses through my veins like an unrelenting wildfire. Hot and dangerous. Ready to consume me if I'm not careful.

What the fuck has she done to me?

Chapter 4

Fate

Ghost Girl Fact #3: GTDs (Ghostly Transmitted Diseases) really are a thing.

igures. You sleep with a guy one time, and he gets all possessive and shit, marking his territory. Want to know the real kicker? We didn't even have sex! No orgasms for this ghost girl. What the hell? Come on, universe...can't a ghost girl get some action? I've got to say, I feel a little cheated. I mean, he got an orgasm thanks to my generosity. It's only fair that he share the love, right? Sharing is caring after all.

The dark line broken by two small dots in the center is staring at me from my left bicep. This strange voodoo stuff has me all sorts of weirded out. My fingers trace over the line again and again as if it can tell me how it got there. Who knew ghost girls could get tattoos? I sure as hell didn't, and something tells me this one isn't your average ink. *More mysteries to solve. Fantastic.*

With my finger still trailing over the heavy black line, I'm suddenly hit with a sensation I barely recognize. Skin on skin contact. Touching my other hand, I hope for a miracle but sadly feel nothing. Yet when I touch the tattoo again, I *feel* it. It's a warmth where there was only coldness for so long. It's the most amazing feeling ever. Maybe this tattoo isn't so bad after all. I may not know what's happening to me, but it's about time I get some perks.

When I cozied up next to Knox, I hadn't intended on falling asleep. Honestly, I didn't even know I could. I just wanted to be close to him, this man who's the first to sense more than my mere haunted existence, the first to sense *me* in over ten years. *Huh, ten years. How do I suddenly know that when time has always been an abstract concept for me?* We have a connection, him and me. He gets me, which I know, I know, sounds like some cheesy rom-com cliché, but this is the real deal. He knows what I'm feeling almost before I do. And on some strange level, I get him too. A soul-deep familiarity touches the very core of my being every time he's near.

As I lounge on the covered, antique Chesterfield settee in my little attic hideaway, I wonder for the umpteenth time what it is about these guys that calls to me. Hundreds of people have passed through this house, and I haven't spared them so much as a second glance. These guys though. There's just something about them. As if they're my first drink of water after being stranded in the desert...and no way am I going to share.

Then why the hell are you sitting up here when you should be down there? a little voice in my head asks. Honestly, I'm not sure how to answer that. Being near them soothes my soul, but it also freaks me the fuck out. These dueling emotions of want and wariness are driving me a little crazy, to be honest.

Just as I'm really getting introspective, the tattoo on my arm starts to burn, then itch. What the fuck? Did he give me some weird STD? Though I guess it couldn't be an STD because again - no sex. Maybe GTD – ghostly transmitted disease? Ew!

My body goes hazy, or at least, hazier than usual, and I feel like I'm being sucked into a vortex. The next thing I know, I'm standing in the middle of the coffee table in the study, staring right into Knox's beautiful hazel eyes. He doesn't seem to see me at the moment, which I'm slightly grateful for considering he isn't alone. The other four are with him, and that's just a tad bit intimidating.

He's rubbing his wrist like crazy, and I notice a dark line that looks suspiciously like mine. Oh! Matching couple's tattoos. Isn't that sweet? I mean, a little premature considering we just met, but hey...ghost girls can't be picky, right?

Then I remember my tattoo burning like someone was trying to scrub it off with sandpaper. Coincidence? I think not.

Wait a damn minute! Is this some sort of ghostly summoning device? Can he force me to appear with a quick touch of his tattoo? Is that what his hand was doing when I woke up next to him? Here I was thinking he was trying to cop a feel, which I totally would've been okay with, but *this*? Oh hell no! I definitely didn't agree to this shit, and he's going to need to reverse it. *Now*.

I take a step out of the coffee table, because that's just weird, throw my hands on my hips, and take in the room around me. The study has always been one of my favorite places in the house, with its window seat where I could watch the living world go by. Now, it's even more homey. The covers are off the furniture, and a small fire is lighting up the room, plus the amount of eye candy doesn't hurt either.

The clock on the wall shows that it's barely past five in the morning. I do a quick scan over the guys, noting early mornings don't look bad on any of them. Each is holding a mug, and I'm hella pissed that they get to enjoy coffee when I'm stuck here in the ether with nothing but some weird ghostly voodoo on my arm.

"Here we go again, guys," I hear Knox murmur.

Oh yeah. He knows I'm pissed off. See? He gets me.

"Let me guess, the temperamental little ghost is gracing us with her presence?" questions the one with black hair and ice blue eyes - Cole, if I remember correctly.

He's dressed all in black again, but damn does he make monochrome look good.

"Can you see if you can get her to appear for all of us? It's time we get some answers."

What is his problem, anyway? If he's not making demands, he's asking questions. Demands, questions, more demands. Is he conversationally illiterate or something? Are those the only two forms of speech he's capable of?

When I stop staring at those pretty blues, because at least those eyes make up for his serious personality flaws, I realize everyone is quiet and looking around the room.

"All right, guys. I know you can't hear a damn thing I'm saying, but we need to get a few things straight here." I pause and take a deep breath, ready to go into a rant that will ultimately lead nowhere since, you know, invisibility is kind of my thing.

"Can anyone feel anything?" Macklin interrupts. "The EMF meter is showing some significant spikes and a temperature drop, but are there any physical manifestations?"

I can tell from the look on his face that this guy gets super excited about his research. His hair is still tousled, and his button-down baby blue dress shirt is misbuttoned, with the sleeves rolled up to his elbows. He's an adorably hunky mess - from his glasses down to his bare feet. I didn't know forearms could entice, but watching his muscles flex as he messes with his gadgets is seriously doing something for me.

"Come on! Seriously?" Knox asks the room, his arms thrown in the air like he's exasperated with me. "Your sex drive is higher than the twins', and that's damn near impossible."

Thank fuck they can't see me because my blush has probably got me as red as a tomato. One word. Horny. I just can't seem to help myself around these guys.

"Our ghost woman is a little dirty, is she?" quips one of the twins.

"I can make her a little dirtier," offers the other.

Oh yeah. These two are trouble with their matching white tees and jeans that fit just a little too well. The three of us together...

"For fuck's sake. We're never going to get anything accomplished here. Fate's as easily distracted as they are," mutters Knox.

I turn to glare in his direction. It's not nearly as effective as I'd like considering he can't see me, which pisses me off more.

"Fine. You want to get something accomplished? Then hell, let's get something accomplished," I sneer, really starting to get into this. I'm pacing in front of the window seat now, and I swear, if I could crack my knuckles, I sure as hell would. Arms start flailing around, hands gesturing wildly, let the rant begin.

"I'm here, living my best ghost girl life until the five of you come along and totally destroy my peace and quiet. Then you," I point directly at Knox, "form some sort of connection with me - *without* my permission, I might add. Make me feel like I'm not alone for the first time in way too long. And when I come down later to find you, you're lounging on the sofa looking all delectable and shit. How the hell am I supposed to pass that up? So what do I do? I give you an orgasm knowing damn well I won't get one in return, but I'm generous like that. It was basically torture. You get the happy ending, and I get zilch. But do you give that a second thought? No. Then I accidentally fall asleep in your bed because I can't help but be near you, and when I wake up, you can actually see me..." My voice trails off, though that's lost on everyone but me.

Pausing just long enough to relive that moment, I continue on, softer now. "You can't even begin to imagine what that felt like. To be seen. For the first time in years, I felt like I was alive again."

I stop for a second, turning to stare out the window, trying to get a handle on my emotions. If I could cry, tears would be streaming down my cheeks. But I can't, so I stand there and let the emotions roll through me. The room is silent, but they're probably just waiting for Knox to give them the play-by-play. I take a deep breath and exhale. Then I do it again. I glance down and notice the tattoo, and suddenly I remember what pissed me off in the first place.

I spin around, pointing right at the dark line on my arm.

"And then I see *this*. What the fuck? You put some sort of goddamn summoning device on me? What am I? Some sort of suped up science experiment to you? Think you can play around with me and make me appear at your beck and call? Well, I've got news for you. I don't jump for anyone. I'm my own damn woman, and you *will* reverse whatever the hell this is right the fuck now! Do you hear me?"

By this point my chest is heaving with anger, and I've managed to reappear right in front of Knox. I'm staring at him with my finger damn near poking through his chest, our noses just an inch apart.

And he's staring right back with wide eyes.

I risk a glance around the room, suddenly realizing I'm the center of attention.

They. Can. All. See. Me.

Fuck!

My own eyes widen, and my mouth opens, but I close it quickly, not knowing what to do or say. My hand drops to my side, and I do a quick scan to make sure I'm not standing here naked. What can I say? Attire or lack thereof isn't always a huge priority when one is invisible. Luckily, I'm in a pair of skinny jeans and another white slogan t-shirt. This one says *Ghost Girls Don't Get Mad. They Get Even.*

One of the few perks of my current situation. I can manifest whatever clothing I want. It's pretty cool, actually, but even that lost its excitement years ago.

They're all still staring at me, so I take a small step back and do something completely embarrassing.

"Um...hi!" I say and give an awkward little wave. Like I'm a damn beauty queen in some sort of fucking pageant. I grimace slightly.

Quite the first impression, Fate.

And cue eye roll because I'm just hopeless. Socially inept. Eh, solitude does strange things to people.

Knox is the first to break the silence. He shoves his hands into the back pockets of his blue jeans, the move stretching his black long-sleeved shirt tight across his chest. And what a nice chest it is too. I kind of want to run my hands down it to feel up the eight pack I know is also hiding there after last night.

"Focus, little ghost," he murmurs, a smirk tilting those full lips of his.

This time, all the guys chuckle because...they can see me, and they just watched me eye fuck Knox. Fabulous. All of them except Cole, that is. What's his malfunction anyways? Do I even care?

"Brothers, this is Fate. Fate, my brothers," Knox says as he begins to point to each one. "This fucker to my right is Cole. Self-proclaimed leader of our merry band of misfits."

Cole nods his head, and I do another awkward hand wave because what else can I do?

"This hot mess to my left is Macklin, resident genius."

"Hello! We have so many questions for you. Like how long have you..."

"Dude, we're not going there yet. Hold your damn horses," Knox mutters.

"Sorry," Macklin apologizes, an adorable blush staining his cheeks.

"Nice to meet you," I sound out slowly, hoping he can read my lips and understand what I'm saying. I'm graced with a small smile in return.

"And finally those two numbnuts next to Mack. Thing One and Thing Two - otherwise known as Thad and Levi. Since they're almost impossible to tell apart, just look for the tats. Right arm, Thad. Left arm, Levi."

"Damn, woman! You're smokin' hot. You and I could have some fun together for su—" He's cut off by a smack to the back of the head. "What the hell? I didn't do shit that time!"

"Nice to meet you, Fate! I apologize for my uncouth brother. We really do have manners. He just forgets his most of the time," Levi says.

I laugh, because the twins are like my spirit animals. Lots of fun to be had there, I'm sure.

In the quiet that follows, Macklin looks at Cole, who

gives him a small nod. The man really is in charge. Wonder if that applies in all circumstances...like the bedroom. Before I can let my mind wander down that rabbit hole, Macklin starts the inquiry.

"Fate, I've got to be honest and admit that we've never done this before - communicate with a spirit in real time, I mean. You're a first for us. Most of the time, spirits can't manifest enough to make talking a possibility. And of course, the twins have a tendency to act first and ask questions later."

"Hey now, we always give them a chance to do things the easy way," Thad grumbles.

"Most of the time," Levi quips.

"Some of the time," Thad retorts.

"None of the time, if it were up to you," Levi chuckles.

"Seriously, what is wrong with you two? Ignore them. We're going to do our best to help you. Since we can't hear you, we're going to stick to yes and no questions to make it easy, though I have a digital voice recorder on. It could pick up anything you try to say that falls outside our normal hearing range. Is that ok?"

I nod.

"Ok, good. I guess the first thing we'd like to know is if you know why you're here?"

I shake my head since I have no idea.

"Ok. Do you know how long you've been here?"

I nod, holding up all ten fingers.

"Ten...months?" he asks.

Another shake of the head.

"Years?"

A nod.

"Wow. You've been here a long time." He shares a quick

look with Knox that I can't decipher, before turning back to me. "Your level of awareness is extraordinary."

Extraordinary is not the word I would use to describe my time here. Though I guess it's pretty accurate when you consider the fact that I didn't know it had been ten years until these guys showed up and my powers kicked up a notch.

I walk back through the coffee table, admittedly a little weird now that I have a whole room watching me, and plop my ass down on the window seat. My expression must give my thoughts away because he quickly back tracks.

"I'm sure it's been hard for you. All that time alone. Hasn't there been anyone else that's come along? Other spirits, even?"

A quick shake of my head is all I can manage. The sadness inside me wells up, close to overflowing. My head drops, and I study the pattern of the cushion beneath me through my transparent legs. Anything to distract myself from the reality of being utterly alone.

"Easy, Mack," Knox says softly. "This is hard for her. Her anguish is damn near drowning me."

"I'm so sorry, Fate. I can't imagine what you've been going through. Is this place familiar?"

I shake my head.

"You just appeared here, ten years ago."

I simply nod. He's not asking. More like confirming the information he's already piecing together.

One glance at my arm and my determination pushes aside my sorrow. I raise my hand, like I'm in school or something, needing answers to some questions myself.

"You have a question?" he asks, seemingly surprised.

Slowly, I say, "What. The. Fuck. Is. This?" I punctuate each word with a jab at my damn bicep.

"Bro, the way those lips say fuck is damn hot. Can I keep her?" Thad begs.

"Shut up, dipshit!" replies Levi, with a punch to Thad's arm.

"So you have a mark as well," ponders Macklin, apparently not noticing my rising temper.

"It's his fault!" I growl, jumping to my feet and pointing at Knox angrily. Walking closer, I continue, "And he needs to fix it, right now!"

"Little ghost, we can't hear you, so aim that righteous anger somewhere else. *You* did this to *me*," Knox asserts, pointing first at me, then himself.

Staring up at those hazel eyes, I order myself not to be distracted and pulled into their depths, and quickly look to Macklin, willing him to understand.

I point to Knox. Point to the tattoo on my arm. Rub my wrist in an imitation of Knox's gesture. Then fling both hands down toward the floor where I stand.

"Wait. So you didn't put that mark on him," Macklin states rather than asks, like he's starting to see where this is going.

I furiously shake my head side to side and once again point an angry finger in Knox's direction, really hammering this point in.

"Hmm," Macklin murmurs. "He didn't do this. Something must have happened when the two of you saw each other. Did either of you feel anything?"

Both of us shake our heads this time.

"Interesting. We need to figure out what this means. But wait, you motioned to your wrist," he says as if he's having an epiphany. Looking at Knox, he continues, "You were rubbing your wrist as if you could wipe the mark off." He looks back at me. "Then suddenly you were here?"

I nod with a purse of my lips, throwing my hands to my hips in what I hope illustrates my level of indignation. There is no way this was all just an accident.

"Is she trying to say that Knox called her here by rubbing on his mark? The one she swears she didn't have anything to do with?" Cole asks doubtfully, aiming a glare in my direction.

I've opened my mouth, ready to show him just where he can shove that doubt he's throwing my way, when Knox cuts me off.

"Whoa. Calm down, little ghost. This is all just a little confusing. He didn't mean anything by it. Plus, he's naturally a prick, so you might as well get used to it."

"Hmph!" I release the pent up breath I had been holding in and cross my arms over my chest. I hate when a well-deserved tantrum is interrupted.

"Let's give it a try," Macklin invites eagerly. "Fate, you go...wherever it is you go when you're not here with us. Let's see if Knox can call you back."

I look at him for a moment, trying to discern his angle here. Is he really trying to help, or is this all some sort of game? Can I trust him? Can I trust them? That little wary voice in my head says I need to be careful, that I could get hurt, but my heart wants me to throw myself at them and never let go. When did I become so damn fickle?

Macklin is watching me patiently, waiting for me to make a decision. He isn't pushy or demanding. He looks a little curious, almost hopeful, and a lot excited.

I'm starting to think maybe they know as little as I do. Decision made, I nod before poofing myself back into my little attic space. Poofing isn't the technical term for it, but cut a ghost girl some slack. It's been quite an eventful morning already.

I'm not waiting long before I feel the burn, followed by a sort of itch. As I begin to go hazy again, I try to fight it, try to stay locked in place, but it doesn't work. Before I know it, I'm once again standing in front of Knox. Like I'm a damn genie or something.

I glare up at him, not at all happy that he has this power over me.

"Well, obviously that worked," Macklin exclaims, way more excited about this than I am.

Knox leans down near my face and whispers loudly, "Don't worry, little ghost. I won't make you do anything you don't want to do." Then he winks.

His nearness, along with that easy charm of his, sets all my nerves a buzz. I can't even respond as I'm held captive by his hazel eyes.

"What the hell does all of this mean, Macklin?" Cole snaps.

Macklin glances my way. He takes me in, his brown eyes considering all of the details we've just learned and formulating a hypothesis. I wish he was using his uber smarts to somehow formulate a plan to make me real again because damn, these guys have me worked up something fierce. *What? This ghost girl can dream.*

"We've seen firsthand her level of power and heard about the history of the house, the stories of people experiencing all sorts of phenomena. It's what brought us here in the first place." He pauses for a moment. When he continues, though his response is aimed at Cole, his eyes never leave mine. "I honestly believe we were drawn here for *her*, not the house or the area."

Then he speaks directly to me. "Don't worry, Fate. We're here now. You're not alone anymore."

And I melt, the rightness of those words settling somewhere deep inside me. They're here...for *me*. My soul wants to weep at the thought.

My eyes are holding his like they're my lifeline. There's a softness there but also a hidden strength he doesn't let many see. He doesn't pity me. He simply understands and wants to help.

I mouth a simple, "Thank you."

He whispers back, "You're welcome."

Chapter 5

Macklin

Techie Fact #1: Nerds need love too.

The laptop screen is starting to blur. I rub the heels of my hands over my weary eyes, exhausted after analyzing the data we've collected over the last few days. The voice recorder was a bust, and that is highly disappointing. I expected to capture at least a few solid EVP - electronic voice phenomena - considering her level of power and the fact that she tends to rant and ramble to herself a lot. That much we've all noticed. Honestly, though, I really just want to *hear* her. Talk, laugh, something. A part of me is desperate for that connection to her, and that thought is a little disconcerting. Lack of evidence usually doesn't cause a pit of sadness in my chest. I make a mental note to think more on that later. I'm not usually one for avoidance, but this seems as good as time as any to start.

I've been sifting through the video evidence for so long now that I feel like my body has melded with the chair I've been sitting on. And still no sign of our beautiful spectral resident. Sure, she's been manifesting in front of the group fairly often over the last few days, almost like she knows when we're talking about her and refuses to be left out of the discussion, but I was hoping to catch a glimpse of her unaware. Learn more of what makes her tick when she's not putting on a face for our benefit.

She still doesn't trust us, not that I blame her. I'm sure spending ten years isolated and alone has really affected her ability to open herself up to anyone new - people and spirits alike. I have to remember this is all uncharted territory for her as well.

"Any luck with the video?" Cole asks from the doorway to our command center.

It's really just a storage room that I claimed early on as a place to set up the numerous computers, charging stations, and other spare equipment we'll use during our time here. As one of the only empty rooms on the main level, it gives us plenty of space to work with. No windows means no light or sounds from the outside to distract or interrupt us when we're reviewing all the material we've recorded. It's also an ideal place to watch the live video feed from the cameras we have set up around the house.

I pick up my glasses and put them on before turning to Cole. "Nothing on the voice recorder. Video is coming up empty so far as well."

"Any luck with the research on the property?"

"I'm expecting a call from the local library any time now. They were hunting down some old news articles for me that were only available on microfiche. They expected it to take a few days to get it all together."

"Has she dropped in on you at all? I know she's been showing up to all of our group meetings, and she's spending a lot of alone time with Knox. I swear, if he's giving her confidential information, I'm going to throat punch him."

"I haven't seen her outside of the group meetings."

"Okay. Keep me posted if she starts coming around.

There's something about her that makes me uneasy. If you find anything about the property that's worth discussing, send a text to the group so we know we'll need to meet up. I'm going to do a more thorough search of the attic and see if I find anything there. Thad and Levi have the basement. I'll check back in later."

With that, Cole walks out. No goodbye or see you later. His mind is already on his next task, leaving little room for small talk. He's visibly irritated, or maybe distracted is a better word, and I'm not sure what to make of that. He's normally so self-assured and confident that seeing him off his game is a little disconcerting. But hasn't she done that to all of us? Thrown us off and forced us into circumstances we aren't exactly used to or comfortable with?

I'd meant it when I told her that we're here for her now. Her predicament is enough to send my mind into a million different directions, all of them wanting to solve the mystery of her existence. But there's also something about *her* that draws me in just as much, if not more. For the first time, I don't need a puzzle to piece together or a riddle to decode to capture my interest. She's done that all on her own without even trying. The fact that she's a ghost rather than a living, breathing woman simply makes it less intimidating and takes the pressure off. I don't have to try to be someone I'm not.

The other guys have never suffered from lack of female companionship. Women have come and gone throughout the years, none of them sticking around for more than a night or two. When you move around as much as we do, long-term relationships just aren't in the cards.

As the resident and self-admitted nerd of the group, I've always been too busy to bother with dalliances. Honestly, I'm much more comfortable in the background, working out our next steps once Cole has decided on a path and making sure we'll have what we need to get us there. My ability, this endless well of information that I can pull from at any given moment, has gotten us to where we are today but isn't really a highly sought after trait with women.

Need a map of the area? I can help with that, no Google Maps required. Need to know what the average temperature of Nebraska is in the middle of June? Roughly seventy-two degrees - in case anyone was wondering. If it's factual information you seek, I'm your guy. Our team definitely utilizes that fount of knowledge on a daily basis. There are plenty of other things, though, that I can't answer. Things about an individual's life or circumstances, for instance. I could have saved us years of useless searching otherwise. Though I suppose all of our seemingly meaningless wandering has brought us here, to her.

Until now, women have never really held my attention long enough to pull me away from my instinctive quest for answers.

Until her.

It might be the sense of familiarity we've all admitted we feel when we're around her. It might be the way her eyes light up when she's worked up into a fury. It could be the sheer mass of power she somehow contains within that lithe ghostly body of hers. Or it could just be the simple yet stunning smiles she's graced me with that have made me a bundle of nervous mush where she's concerned.

And I know it's not just me.

Knox is borderline obsessed, seeming to seek her out on an hourly basis. Something about their linked emotions has formed a strong and immediate connection between the two. He may use his looks and skills to get what we need when we're out hunting down information for our research, or on the rare occasions we go out for entertainment, but I know it's really all for show. Down deep, he's as desperate for a real connection as I am.

Meanwhile, the twins are jealous of the attention she gives Knox. They're doing their damndest to tempt her away, and I'm sure they'll succeed eventually. Apparently, the whole twin thing is a big draw, and girls just swoon over the chance to be with two guys at once. I mean, they share everything else, why not women too? Personally, I don't get it, not that I have much experience, but to each their own.

Cole, on the other hand, is openly hostile toward her, practically snarling in her direction any time she's close by. His attitude is something I can't explain. He's never been the social butterfly of the group, hell, he's almost more closed off than I am, but his obvious contempt seems unwarranted and is starting to grate on everyone's nerves - including my own.

The Mario theme song starts playing somewhere in the room, startling me.

Dun dun dun - dun dun da dun.

I search the tops of both desks and under the table on the far wall before I find my cell. Unfortunately, I've missed the call, but I recognize the number as the library. Looks like it's time to get some answers.

"What the hell am I doing here, mate?" asks Knox, for what seems like the millionth time. I'm seriously questioning my logic in bringing him along on my library adventure at this point.

"Mate? Really? Have you been watching the Crocodile Hunter again?"

"What? I'm trying out something new. I mean, it's your fault for telling me that mate actually derives from the German word gemate which means to share a meal at the same table. That makes us mates. It's kinda catchy."

"Remind me to never share knowledge with you again. It gives you crazy ideas."

He just rolls his eyes.

"Anyway, you're here to help me sift through this mountain of information. The others are busy scouring the house for clues."

"Who are we? The gang from Mystery, Inc?"

I just cut a glare in his direction.

"Fine," he sighs, "and what are we looking for exactly?"

"Anything unusual that might give us a lead on Fate's background. I've requested all records from the last hundred years or so."

"Dude, that's a lot of data. You'll never get through it all."

"Hence the reason you're here with me. You can sort out the irrelevant information, so I can focus on the important details. This should help me later. Since I've been exposed to it, I'll be able to recall all of the facts and can piece together a theory a lot faster."

"Lucky me," Knox mumbles as he bites into an apple.

"You know there's no food allowed in here, right?"

"Does it look like I give a damn? You want me here, this is what you get. Do you want me hangry, or do you want me helping?"

"Helping. Definitely helping. I've seen you hangry, and it's worse than a mogwai fed after midnight."

"Then you're safe from the gremlin. For now. So, where do I start?"

Debate settled, we finally get down to business. Sitting at a table deep within the library where they have their microfiche machines, I get him set up. The librarian provided everything she could find. News articles for the surrounding area dating back a hundred years. Title transfers and tax documentation on the house from the time it was built back in 1865. Any and all photographs taken at or near the property.

There is a real possibility we'll be here all night.

"What do you think happened to her?"

Before answering, I take a moment to contemplate his question while flipping through the first article.

"We know so little about her and her situation, but I know it can't be a coincidence that her story so closely resembles ours. The only difference is that we aren't spirits. Hopefully we find something here that will help us unravel both mysteries."

"Do you think..." he trails off, and I notice him running his fingers over her mark on his wrist.

"Do I think...?"

He hesitates, obviously reluctant to say what's on his mind.

"Do you think she's really a ghost?"

"I think the activity we've witnessed so far leads to her being a spirit stuck in the mortal realm as the most likely explanation. She must have something left unresolved, or the circumstances surrounding her death were so violent that she can't find her way to the other side."

"You don't think her abilities - the fact that they far exceed the average poltergeist - or her incredible self-awareness might indicate she's something...*more*?"

"I suppose anything is possible. Look at us, after all. The evidence, however, doesn't necessarily fit with that theory."

"I just..." He pauses, running his hand through his hair, his tell. He's unsure, and that frustrates him. He angrily chucks the apple core into the garbage can at the end of the table. "She *feels* so much more than any spirit we've ever encountered. The emotions I get from her are more like what I get from you guys or other living beings. The fact that hers seem so intimately tied to mine...I don't fucking know."

I study him for a moment. Knox has always been more sensitive than the rest of us. Which is only logical considering he's bombarded by emotions twenty-four hours a day seven days a week. His line of questioning, though, has me wondering if this obsession is far more serious than I even anticipated. The answer is obvious.

"You've developed feelings for her."

"What? No. Of course not," he denies quickly, absently rubbing his wrist.

"Knox, I've known you for fifty years, and I've never seen you like this. Constantly wanting to be near a woman. Worried about her. Caring about her. I get it. You formed a deep bond with her rather quickly. It would make sense if you feel deeply for her, but I have to suggest proceeding with caution. At the end of the day, she's still an apparition. She's not alive. Her future ended the day she died, and a relationship can't go anywhere."

Somewhere, deep in the recesses of my mind, I repeat that mantra to myself. More than once.

"Obviously I know that. I just can't help feeling like she's meant to be here. Not just with me. With all of us. I can't explain it, but it feels like it's always just been this way." He pauses for a moment, then releases a deep sigh. "But you're right. Maybe I need to back off for a while. Give myself some space. Maybe it's just the fast connection and close confines of the house that are making this connection seem like more than it is."

"I think that's a smart idea. Take some time. Clear your head."

He nods and turns back to the machine. I can tell he isn't happy with my suggestion, but I know Knox will do what needs to be done. Though I'm sure it won't be easy given that Fate isn't held by the same earthly confines we are. Locked doors are no match for her.

It feels like we've been sitting at these machines for hours when Knox's sudden exclamation has me almost knocking my coffee right off the side of the table.

"Crikey, mate! I think I've got something! Look at this."

I narrow my tired eyes at him.

"Sorry. I couldn't resist. Seriously though, I found something." He points to an old photograph showing the back portion of the property.

"Ok. What am I looking at?"

"It's what you're *not* looking at."

I scan the photo again, noting the large yard with lots of green grass and a bit of the stone patio in the corner. As the resident know-it-all, I'm a little ashamed to admit that whatever he's seeing, I haven't found it yet.

"Look to the left. What's missing?" he helpfully suggests.

I look again, and then I see it. Well, actually, I *don't* see it. That's his point.

"There's no willow tree. When was the photo taken?"

"October 5, 1920. Right before a big party celebrating some dude whose name they mentioned at the beginning of the article, but I can't remember now. Figured it wasn't important."

"Ok, but what does this tell us?"

"Now look at this photo. It was taken two years later."

I look at the new photo and realize what he's getting at. A willow tree can reach full growth in roughly fifteen years.

At only two years old, this willow tree looks as though it's fully grown already. This is an anomaly worth looking into.

I quickly do a mental scan of anything else I know about the willow on the property and come up remarkably short. I know it sits toward the far back corner and has an old swing that sways in the breeze. Not very technical, but it is what it is.

"That's not normal, right? I'm no tree expert, but even I know a tree takes a while to grow. What do you think it means?" he asks. Again, I notice him touching the tattoo, as if being away from her for this long is starting to get to him.

His obsessive need for her is concerning. I make a mental note to ensure he's putting some real space between the two of them starting as soon as possible. Maybe I'll have a talk with Fate, though that brings about some dangers of its own - mostly to my diminishing self-control.

"I'm not sure. It's definitely suspicious since there's a huge gap in the timeline. We didn't appear until 1970, forty-eight years after this last photo. Forty years after that, so 2010, Fate appeared but spent another ten years on her own here. Not to mention, willow trees typically only live an average of fifty to seventy-five years if given the right conditions. That tree is roughly a hundred years old. How does this all tie together?"

"Mate, that's on you. I'm just the manual labor. You're the architect behind this little operation."

"Hmmm...that's starting to grow on me. So, what does that make Cole?"

"He's the foreman - keeping all the working parts in order."

"And the twins?"

"They're the green guys. The newbies. They get the shit work - like fetching us water and cleaning the tools."

I chuckle at that. Pretty sure neither Thad or Levi would approve of his analogy.

"Let's see if we can get this evidence in a to-go package so we can get back."

We quickly print off the photos and any other supporting documentation we can find and pack it up to head home. Odd that I would refer to the old house as home when we've lived there less than a week. Makes me wonder if it's not so much the house but the occupant that has prompted that noun to be replaced for the first time in our existence. She's effecting change within our group, and she has absolutely no idea. That thought is as troubling as it is exciting.

Chapter 6

Macklin

Techie Fact #2: Talk nerdy to us. It doesn't take much more than that.

The moment she enters the command center, the aroma of freshly baked cookies fills the room and my senses are on high alert. She's never sought me out before. Then again, maybe she's looking for one of my brothers. Knox, most likely. I throw the hint of disappointment that sneaks through my shield right back where it belongs - in the box labeled *Don't Go There*.

I turn away from the evidence I've been organizing to see her hazy form wandering around, her fingers drifting over the numerous pieces of equipment stacked on the tables. She's not looking my way, and I use the opportunity to catalog every detail.

She's only a few inches shorter than my own six feet, putting her roughly around five-eight, give or take an inch. She's slender, but with delectable curves my eyes can't help but trace over. Her hair is a mass of dark waves tumbling down her back, and I wonder what it would look like spread across my pillow.

The way she holds one arm behind her, while her other

hand whispers over each piece like it's a priceless treasure, alludes to simple sophistication. She's a walking contradiction. Her inherent grace is something I haven't seen in someone as young as she appears to be, yet her style is that of someone that could blend in with today's twenty-somethings with no problem.

The dark-colored shirt she's wearing reads #GhostGirl-Goals in white letters. Her sense of humor I can appreciate, as it resonates with the nerd in me. Simple jeans and light-colored Converse complete her look. The blend of the modern elegance she wields so effortlessly and the street style she pulls off with ease somehow makes her that much more interesting.

When my eyes come back up, I realize she's been watching me, watching her. I blush a little, feeling like a fourteen-year-old boy caught ogling his crush.

"Hi," I say awkwardly then grimace slightly. Now I sound like a teenage girl. Great.

I watch as she waves, a small grin on her gorgeous face. She knows she unnerves me, and she likes that. And I like that she likes that. *What is wrong with me?*

"Are you looking for Knox?"

She shakes her head then points one beautifully manicured fingertip at me. Do ghosts get manicures? I mentally add that to my growing list of questions to ask her.

My pulse is racing. I adjust my glasses, though they were already as straight as can be, but it helps me feel in control. What can I say? I'm living up to the quintessential nerd stereotype - minus the suspenders.

"You're here...for me?"

She nods, a hint of her tongue peeking out before biting her bottom lip.

That small action awakens a need in me that's so strong I

have to clench my hands into fists to stop myself from reaching for her.

"Oh. Well...sure." I clear my throat before mumbling, "Um...what can I help you with?"

With one finger, she points to me, then taps her lips.

For a brief moment, I think she wants me to kiss her, and my eyes widen and meet hers. They're beautiful in an ethereal sort of way.

She simply smiles, her lips quirking up on one side. I'm amusing her. Usually, the embarrassment I'm feeling would be enough to have me hightailing it in the opposite direction, but with her, it feels like this is something that's completely normal for us. Second nature. Me being awkward and her loving my awkwardness.

Whoa! Love? Slow down, buddy.

She points to me again, then brings her finger up to her eye, then down to tap her lips again.

"Oh! You want to talk?"

Right. Lip reading because we can't hear her. Get your shit together, Mack!

She nods again.

A mixture of relief and disappointment whirl through me before I can tamp it down.

"That I can do. I'm ready when you are."

I watch her lips form the first word.

"Do."

A quick nod before she's moving on to the next word.

"You."

Nod.

"Have."

Nod.

She signs the letter A.

"A."

The next word is a little trickier. The distraction of her pouty lips getting the better of me.

"Goat?"

She laughs silently while shaking her head. Watching her lips forming the word again is the sweetest kind of torture - my jeans suddenly a little tight. My imagination, which I didn't even know still functioned, is suddenly running wild with all the other things those lips could be doing.

I must have been staring a little too intently, as she starts waving her hand in front of my face to get my attention.

She tries the word again.

"Ghost?"

She nods, then she holds up her hands in the shape of a square and mouths the next word.

"Box? Do I have a Ghost Box?" Surprised, I ask, "You know what that is?"

She nods, excited now, and moves a little closer.

"I do. Just let me find it."

Her sexiness just increased ten-fold. Beautiful *and* smart? *Yes, please!*

I head over to the far wall and begin to hunt through the cases we have yet to open, quickly finding what she's asking for. I have a system. Everything is put into groups by use - sound, video, tools, accessories - and then placed alphabetically by name. The guys say I'm OCD, but I think it's called organization. A Ghost Box Ovilus III is a small handheld device that has a built-in database of over two thousand words. In theory, a spirit can manipulate the environment, selecting the words needed to answer questions which are displayed on a small, simple screen. Sort of a high-tech ouija board, minus all the demon summoning. It could be a tremendous help in communicating with her, and I should have thought of this before. I'm blaming the sweet little ghost for my inability to think straight. That's the only possible explanation.

"Found it. Just let me get it fired up."

Walking over to the table with the chargers and spare batteries, I feel her come up next to me, watching me intently. I spare a sideways glance and note that she's focused on each step, each part of the process, taking it all in. The academic in me appreciates that, and the man in me appreciates the way her chest gets pushed out when she moves her arms behind her back so she can lean in. Her hair falls forward, and if she weren't an apparition, it would be brushing my arm right now. Would it feel like silk against my skin?

"Uh...it's ready. Want to give it a try?"

She gives me a thumbs up.

"Okay, let's see..." I pause and try to think of innocuous questions I could ask, but my mind keeps circling back to her.

Are your lips as soft as I've imagined they are?

What would your body feel like against mine?

What sounds do you make when you...

Jesus, Mack! Get your head out of the gutter!

"So...uh..." I clear my throat again, my face probably beet red. "Let's start with, where are we right now?"

I watch as she looks at the Ghost Box intently, and then a word crosses the screen.

Room.

She claps excitedly and motions for more.

"What color is your hair?"

She grabs a hold of the long locks and then looks at the box.

Dark crosses the screen, followed closely by *Brown*.

"Do you know what day it is?"

She appears to think for a second.

June.

Sixth.

"Wow! That's impressive. For a spirit, you're very aware of your surroundings. Hmm...how about this one. Where do you go when you're not here with us?"

Attic.

"What do you do all day?"

Her head tilts to the side, and her eyes wander around the room. Her pouty lips are pursed in thought, and I've never wanted to kiss someone so badly in my life.

Wander. She shrugs. Then a mischievous grin lights up her face.

Spy.

"Spy? On us?"

She holds her thumb and index finger just a bit apart, scrunches up her adorable nose, and shrugs again.

"A little?" I laugh. She is the most intriguing woman I've ever come across, and I find myself wanting to learn everything about her. Her likes and dislikes. Her fears. Her desires. What she wants for her future.

Then I remember that she doesn't have one. Her time for hopes and dreams has ended. She's not meant to be on this plane, and there can never be anything more between us. The laughter slowly dies off, leaving us caught in each other's gaze.

I'm the first to break the silent stand off.

"I'm sorry you've been alone for so long," I practically whisper.

The light leaves her beautiful eyes, and she looks at the floor as if the hideous gold and burgundy pattern of the carpet is of significant interest.

"But you have us now, and I promise we'll help you. I know that's probably not enough…" I trail off. What does a man say to a stunning, ghostly female standing right in front of him looking so damn sad that his own heart is just seconds away from breaking?

"So sorry we can't give you your life back?"

Or maybe, *"At least you'll be in a better place."*

There's always, *"Hopefully you'll end up in Heaven, not Hell!"*

Dammit, pull it together man.

Then an idea strikes. Wanting to do something that will take that sad expression off her beautiful face, I'm opening my mouth before I can think it through.

"I know you want answers, but there *is* another option. Thad and Levi have these…abilities. They could help you cross over, and you wouldn't have to be stuck here anymore."

The minute the words leave my mouth, I regret them and want to take them back. I don't want her to choose that option; I want her to stay with us for as long as she can. The guys will hand me my ass when they hear what I've offered. Except Cole. He might actually approve.

She looks up at me then, her heart in her eyes. She takes a step closer, so we're almost chest to chest. The lights in the room begin to flicker a little, and my heart starts to pound. I briefly wonder if Knox is going to come flying through the door but remember he ran out to grab dinner. She lifts her right hand and places it over my chest, right on top of my heart. It sort of hovers there, not exactly touching, but it's as close as she's able to get without putting her hand right through me. I feel a tingle at the connection. Like that feeling you get when you shake someone's hand, and there's a jolt from the static electricity, except this is all pleasure and no pain and doesn't disappear. The longer her hand rests there, the more the sensation starts to slowly expand across my chest. It feels *amazing*, and I totally understand Knox's obsession now.

She starts to talk, but she's going too fast for me to make out what she's saying. I'm watching her lips move until sound abruptly breaks the silence like someone just unmuted a TV.

"...a good man. I've been alone for so long that I've forgotten how nice it is to be noticed. To be seen. Thank you for giving that to me again and for offering to help me, but I can't leave without knowing why I'm here in the first place. I need answers."

I'm still staring into her eyes, but the sudden sound has rendered me incapable of speech. Her voice. It's...like the sweetest honey or the richest whiskey. Smoky, mysterious, alluring, and the hottest damn thing I've ever heard. Before I can find my own voice again, she's stepping away, wandering back through the room while she continues on.

"You guys were so unexpected. I had accepted this solitary life I've been forced to live, and then you guys came barreling in and shattered it all to hell. I was confused. On one hand, I was excited that this might be my one opportunity to figure everything out. But on the other hand, I wasn't exactly thrilled that I'd have to share my space with a group of hot guys. I'm not gonna lie, ghost girls have needs too, ya know. Imagine watching the hottest porn and not being able to jack off to relieve the pressure. Yeah, one word. Torture. Right?"

She spares a glance in my direction before continuing on, not waiting for my reply. Completely unknowing.

"This thing with Knox. Matching tattoos? Seems a little much if you ask me. I mean, I just met the guy. Then he rubs his damn wrist and *BAM*, I'm sucked through some vortex and placed right in front of him. What the hell is up with that, anyways? Then you have to go and be all sweet and stuff. Offering me help and telling me I'm not alone. You have this whole sexy nerd thing going for you. That was my nickname for you that first day, by the way. The twins...well, Jesus. They're just as dirty as I am. Or, at least that I assume I am, because let me tell you, my mind is a scary place to be. And Cole, what is that dude's problem?"

I watch as she paces in front of the table full of cameras and REM-pods. Her heartfelt words quickly turning into a ghostly rant that is, admittedly, as adorable as it is amusing. This isn't the first rant I've witnessed, but it *is* the first one I've had the pleasure of watching up close and personal, so I lean back against the table behind me and cross my arms over my chest. Just taking in all of her ghostly glory. She doesn't realize I can hear every word out of that gorgeous mouth now, and I'm not about to tell her yet.

"Oh. And what the hell was that while you were at the library? I kept feeling the tug of Knox summoning me, which, by the way, I absolutely abhor, but since he wasn't here, I would get sucked into the vortex and spit out in random locations throughout the house. Face first against a wall. On my back, out on the front lawn staring up at the sky. Once, I even appeared right in front of Levi on the toilet. Can you say *awkward*? Was Knox doing that on purpose? Did he forget I'm confined to this damn place?"

She releases a heavy sigh like she just can't deal with it before turning and facing me head on, placing her small, elegant hands on her hips.

"One more thing. What is this about abilities? Do you all have one? That's not normal, right? I mean, I've seen a lot of people come through this house, but none of them could do what you guys apparently can. So, let me guess. Knox feels or senses emotions; *that* one is obvious. You said the twins have some sort of power that could send me to the afterlife. What about you? You seem to be the techie of the group. Is there more to that? And what's Cole's super power? Being an asshole?"

She chuckles at that, and the sound is like nothing else.

"Fate..."

She throws her hands up and her head back in obvious frustration.

"Ugh! I know. You can't hear a damn word I'm saying. What the fuck does a ghost girl gotta do to be heard around here?"

I let the silence linger, wanting to draw out the moment for just a second longer.

"So...sexy nerd, huh?"

Her head snaps back down, and her eyes go wide.

"You heard me?" she whispers.

"Almost every word."

"You can really hear me?" she asks, a little more enthusiastic now.

"I can," I reply around a grin of my own.

The flickering lights flare brightly. Before I can stop her, she's launching herself in my direction and, since she's not solid, flies right through me. I feel a blast of cold air and a rush of tingles. When I turn around, she's sitting on the ground, legs spread out in front of her, her head partially through the table and computer along the wall.

"You forgot, eh?"

"Yup. Totally forgot about the whole spectral body thing there for a second."

"I'd offer you a hand up, but..."

"Well, aren't you just a gentleman!"

"Most of the time."

At that, she turns and looks at me. Her eyes do a quick scan of my body before meeting mine.

"Is that right? And the rest of the time?"

"Guess you'll have to find out."

"I knew I liked you, Sexy Nerd," she says as she manages to get to her feet. She's still standing in the middle of the table, but that doesn't seem to bother her.

"Come on, let's go tell the others that you got your voice back. I have some other interesting news that turned up during our library search today to discuss with everyone as well."

"Ready when you are. Plus, I say we have some fun with the guys before we let them in on our secret. Bring the Ghost Box."

I follow her out of the room, or at least I do once I open the door that she just glided through. I'm not sure what she has in mind, but I'd bet money the guys aren't ready for whatever she has planned. And to be honest, I'm not sure I am either.

Chapter 7

Fate

Ghost Girl Fact #4: Ghost girls are temperamental and somewhat irrational thanks to their insubstantial existence. Yeah. Let's go with that.

Poor Macklin. He has no idea what he's in for.

I strut into the room like I own the place. I mean, in my own way of thinking, I do. It's mine. I don't particularly care if I've never made a single payment, or if I have no proof of how the house came into my possession. Isn't common law home ownership a thing? If not, it really should be.

Most of the guys are waiting in the study, drinks in hand, discussing their apparently fruitless searches. I could've told them it would be pointless, but until a few moments ago, I was as silent as the women in Cole's bed. There's no way his grumpy ass can get any sane woman to the point of screaming his name.

I know. Bitter doesn't look very attractive on me, right? Guy's always a jerk to me though, so he can bite me. Hmm...that doesn't sound like a bad thing at all actually.

Thad is the first to see me as he sits sprawled out on the sofa facing the door.

"Get that fine ghostly ass over here, woman! I've missed you."

I playfully sashay my way over, walking through the sofa, facing him. It just so happens to also be right where Cole is sitting. Slowing down, I accidentally on purpose pause slightly when my ghostly form is aligned with his fully alive body, then continue on. Risking a glance over my shoulder, I see him fighting to contain a shiver in reaction.

"Fucking temperamental ghost," he mutters under his breath as he takes a drink of the amber liquid in his glass.

I smile and wink at Thad who has a front row seat to my childish but highly satisfying behavior. What can I say? Cole and his cranky ass bring out the worst in me. I take a seat between Thad and Levi like I have every right to be there. Like I've always been involved in these meetings.

Fake it 'til you make it, right?

Thad leans in and whispers in my ear, "Oh, you and I are going to have some fun together, aren't we, woman? Why don't we skip this little get together and go make some plans of our own?"

I smirk in his direction and waggle my eyebrows at him.

"Bro, what about me?" asks Levi, leaning in on my other side. "You're not going to let him leave me out, are you, sweets?"

"Knock it off," Macklin barks from across the room. "Fate's got enough on her plate without having to deal with the two of you. Where's Knox?"

"Right here, fucker! Dinner is served," Knox says as he enters the room carrying two large white bags full of take-out. He sets them down on the coffee table and starts to pull out the foam containers.

"Who ordered the Kung Pao Chicken, extra spicy?"

"That's mine." Thad raises his hand. "I like it spicy - just how I like my women," he finishes with a wink in my direction.

This guy is like a male version of me. If that isn't a frightening thought, I don't know what is.

As they continue to divvy out the food and begin to eat, I find myself wishing that I had a sense of smell and could take in the aromas around me. That I could enjoy the simple act of eating a meal. That I could savor every bite and actually feel full. Who knew one could miss something as basic as chewing? Hell, even the bloating that will most likely follow the fried rice and egg rolls seems appealing when you've felt nothing but emptiness for far too long.

I shake myself out of my sullen mood and observe their interactions just as I have over the last few days. They're comfortable with each other in a way that only siblings can be. They may call each other brothers, but I highly doubt there's any blood relation happening here, aside from the twins obviously. They joke and laugh, rib each other over stupid shit, and support each other when it's needed. I envy that closeness and their camaraderie.

Looking up, I notice Macklin watching me intently. He's sitting on the sofa opposite us looking as disheveled and adorable as usual. He pushes his glasses up the bridge of his nose, and the muscles in his forearm flex with the movement. Damn, he doesn't even know what that does to me. His gray button-down is rolled at the sleeves, untucked, with his undershirt hanging out. His jeans fit nicely over his toned legs, and his practical work boots are like new. Pretty sure he spends more of his time behind a computer screen than he does out in the field. His brown eyes remind me of the most scrumptious chocolate, and I would love nothing more than to devour him whole.

Knox must pick up on my ever increasing desire because a loud throat clearing comes from his direction.

"Are you two done eye-fucking each other yet?" Knox taunts.

I've never seen a grown man blush as much as Macklin does. It's totes adorbs. No, I don't care if that phrase went out of style years ago. I'm a ghost, dammit - basically timeless - which gives me the right to say whatever hellishly ridiculous slang I want.

"What? She's eye-fucking Mack?" Thad cries. "The fuck? When did that happen? What about me, woman?"

"I wasn't even sure he liked women," ponders Levi.

"Fucking right? Never seen him with one. Yet here he is, making moves on my woman before I can get more than a little zap to my dick!" exclaims Thad.

Knox smirks. "As if either of you have a chance."

"Shut the fuck up, pretty boy," Thad retorts. "She likes us more than you. She just feels guilty because you have to deal with her crazy ass emotions."

Crazy ass emotions? Who? Me? Yeah, okay. I'll give him that one, but it's totally their fault.

I try to get Mack's attention as he watches the play-by-play with amusement. Sensing my ghostly stare, he looks over at me, and I motion to the Ghost Box sitting on the floor next to his feet. Somehow, some way, he knows what I'm thinking and gets this mischievous look in his eye. He picks up the device just as Cole interjects himself into the conversation.

"What the fuck is wrong with all of you? She's a goddamn ghost, for Christ's sake. None of you can have her."

"I think I may have a way to solve this problem," Macklin declares, maintaining eye contact with me. I mash my lips together to avoid letting out an excited squeal and giving myself away. "Why don't we let Fate choose which one of us is the best?"

In this moment, I fall head over heels for my adorably nerdy gentleman. He's willingly offering himself up as my accomplice in a prank against his brothers, and that is better than pretty flowers or a box of chocolates any day. Not that a ghost girl can enjoy or appreciate either of those things.

"Let her choose? Mack, have you lost your damn mind right along with these other fools?" Cole snaps.

Macklin ignores Cole and continues, "Fate came to me earlier today and gave me the idea to use the Ghost Box to communicate. It will allow her to answer our questions within the limited scope of words that are available in its database. So, Fate. Who is it? Which one of us is the best?"

All five sets of eyes find me. I slowly stand up and eye Levi. Trailing a finger across his shoulder, I hear Macklin read the word from the screen in his hands.

"Big."

"I'm big all over, sweets," Levi croons.

I consider him and all of his significant bulk, wondering just how big he's talking. My mind is pulled out of the gutter I find it lodged in on the regular with these guys around when Thad tries to touch my ass, his hand passing through it instead. I run my fingers through his hair, using a trickle of my power to brush the strands back.

Macklin chuckles. "Dirty. Boy."

"Hell yes, I am, woman," Thad proclaims, trying to reach for me but swiping his arm through my waist instead. "Dammit!"

I walk over to Knox and lean in like I'm going to kiss him

but trail my finger along his scruffy jaw instead. Then I hear Macklin.

"Saw." He pauses. "First."

I shift my head to look at Cole without moving my body an inch. He just glowers at me.

"Ass. Hole," Mack chokes out. The other guys chuckle, and the muscles in Cole's jaw clench. He obviously doesn't find it as amusing as the rest of us.

I slowly straighten and look at Macklin as I walk through the coffee table. *What is it with me and this damn table?* Then stop when I'm mere inches away from him, pushing my body as close as it can get with the device between us. I look up and his eyes meet mine.

"Sexy. Nerd." He grins.

I place my hand on top of the one holding the Ghost Box and let it rest there for a moment, speaking without saying words, and totally ignore the fact that all of his brothers are looking on.

"But really, why choose?" I suddenly say out loud, turning around to look at all of their stunned faces. A moment later, chaos ensues, the brothers all talking at once.

"What the fuck?"

"Wait, we can hear her!"

"Why the hell didn't you tell us we could hear her?"

"Fuck! Her voice is like angels singing!"

"Okay, okay," Macklin shouts over the noise. "It happened just before we walked in, and we knew we had to let you all know."

"Then why all the theatrics?" Knox retorts.

"Um...because it's hella funny?" I scoff with a roll of my eyes.

"Who the fuck uses the word *hella* anymore?" he quips back.

"This ghost girl. That's who."

"Do you always refer to yourself as *ghost girl*?" He snickers.

"Hmmm." I tap my bottom lip with my finger, thinking. "Actually, I do. Weird, right? But it seems familiar like everything else lately." I shrug.

"So you feel it too?" Mack asks. "The familiarity?"

"Totally. Since that first day. You guys too?" I look around the room and see them all nod - except Cole. Macklin raises his hand to push his glasses up, and my eyes snag on his wrist.

"Holy shit!" I point at the offending mark. "You have one too!"

He pulls his hand back, and right there on the underside of his wrist is a solid black line broken only by three small dots in the middle.

"Wait. Yours has three dots," Knox says, eyeing Macklin's hand. Then he looks at me. "What about you? Got anything?"

Damn. Didn't even think about that. I turn my head to look at my left bicep and sure enough, just above Knox's line, is a replica of Mack's.

"Dude! What the fuck?" I whine.

I mean, I like these guys, but permanently marking my body is not something I would agree to at this point in our relationships.

Relationships. Heavy emphasis on the S. *Huh. Plural. Ghost girl's got game.* I mentally high-five myself.

"What is so damn amusing over there?" Knox complains.

"Oh. Nothing."

"Do you think yours works the same way mine does?" Knox asks Macklin.

There's a joke in there somewhere, I just know it, but Mack interrupts before I can work it out.

"We should test it!" Mack beams.

"Whoa! Wait a minute there, Sexy Nerd. I didn't sign up for another round of *Let's summon the ghost girl*."

"If you're all done ogling the new marks she's going to deny having any involvement with, can we start to discuss what Mack and Knox found at the library today?" Cole snaps.

"Oh right." Suddenly all business, Macklin walks over to the desk by the bookshelves and pulls a file from his bag. As he walks back to the group, he eyes the twins. "So, here's the summary since I know you guys have short attention spans."

"Thank Christ!" Thad mutters under his breath.

I walk over and perch my ghostly ass on the arm of the sofa next to Cole. He may be a douche canoe, but the guy is super pretty to look at, and I'd be lying if I said I didn't find myself drawn to him more often than not. Like two magnets, constantly being pulled together but fighting it.

"Knox found an old photo that dates back one hundred years, and he noticed the willow tree was missing."

"Knox actually helped?" Levi asks, looking at the man in question. Then he chuckles, "Bout damn time, bro!"

"Shut the hell up," Knox grumbles from his seat.

"The next photo, taken only two years later, shows a fully grown tree. That's unheard of. There is no such thing as coincidence. We all know that. One hundred years ago, there was no tree there. Fifty years ago, we came to be. Forty years after that, Fate appeared in this house where that exact tree was planted. I'd hazard a guess it was the same day we all felt that tug spark up again, which sent us *searching* for something while she spent another ten years *waiting* for something." Mack looks my way before continuing. "You were waiting on *us*. Our stories are almost identical. Coming from nothing. Remembering nothing. The fact that the second we arrived, we all felt *something*. I don't think we can deny it anymore. Our histories are intertwined. Now we just need to find out how and why."

The room is stunned into silence, myself included. Considering I now have a voice for the first time in ten years, that's an impressive feat.

"So, let me get this straight. You all are fifty years old?"

That earns me a glare from Cole.

"What? I mean, you all look phenomenal for fifty. Just throwing that out there. Haven't aged a bit."

Cole rolls his eyes at me, then his face relaxes into the serious expression that's usually plastered on his gorgeous face. He clears his throat before hesitantly saying, "I think I may have at least a small part of the answer to that."

The entire room turns to Cole. Something about the way he's sitting, leaning forward, his muscles tense and ready for flight, tells me I'm not going to like what he's about to say. No one says a word as he takes a moment to speak. Whatever this is, the fact that his brothers don't know about it does not bode well for this conversation.

"You guys all know about my nightmares..." He pauses while the guys nod their understanding.

"What nightmares?" I blurt out.

The glare he shoots my way is, yet again, familiar.

For a moment, I don't think he's going to respond, but finally he starts again. "I have nightmares quite often, and the sequence of events is always the same. At the end, I shout out 'Don't go!' before I immediately wake up. But there are details I've never told you. Things you need to hear."

He studies his boots intently, his hands clasped together

with his elbows on his knees. Before he continues, he takes a deep breath.

"They used to happen once every couple of weeks. Then the moment we started planning our trip here, they started coming every few nights. After that first day in the house, they've been happening nightly. Sometimes multiple times a night. If I fall back asleep, it starts all over again."

"You've had the same nightmare for over fifty years?" I ask incredulously.

"No..." He hesitates, looking at me for the first time without a hint of his trademark glare.

Those ice blue eyes pierce my soul, and that gut-wrenching feeling I had the first time I saw him hits again, full force. I wrap my arms around my middle like it will make the hurt go away.

His eyes haven't released mine when he begins to speak again, a softness to his voice that I've never heard before. "They started ten years ago." I'm once again rendered speechless, but the same cannot be said for the other guys.

"What the fuck do you mean, they started ten years ago?" Levi shouts.

Thad, always ready to back up his twin, fumes, "So it's okay for you to keep secrets, but the rest of us practically get court martialed if we forget to tell you we took a dump? What kind of bullshit is that?"

"You didn't think to tell us this a few days ago when we learned how long Fate has been here?" Knox growls. He gets up and storms over to the window seat. With his left arm straight out, he rests his hand on the wall while he stares outside.

The sky is a beautiful mix of pinks and purples and oranges. Normally, I'd bask in the glorious sight before me. Maybe admire the way the colors blend, the way they shift as the sun moves across the sky. But that beauty is lost on me right now. I almost welcome the night and the way the darkness that follows will be hiding the world beyond. It seems fitting, somehow, like a metaphor for my life. All the color and life being taken over by a void of darkness.

The twins have gone quiet, but I can sense their growing tempers. With their arms crossed over their chests and the scowls on their faces, you don't have to be Knox to figure that out. Macklin seems as intrigued as ever. That brain of his is processing things faster than any of us can comprehend.

"There's more," Cole says quietly.

"Christ. Here we go. What else have you been keeping from us?" Knox demands angrily.

"The details of the dream have become increasingly clear over the last few days. I'm remembering more than just the last few seconds. I'm in some sort of cavern with a large natural pool built right into the ground. It has the clearest water I've ever seen. I'm desperate to make someone understand something. It's as if..." He trails off for a moment, his eyes tracking some unseen memory in his mind. "It's as if my life depends on it. But I'm also confused. Whatever has happened, my brain can't seem to figure it out."

He shakes his head, frustrated that he's only getting bits and pieces. He's still staring off into space, lost in his nightmare and a memory of something he can't fully remember.

"She's looking right at me, the girl from my dreams. Tears are streaming from her beautiful gray eyes, down her cheeks. The look on her face is utter devastation, and my heart feels like it's being ripped from my chest. She finally turns and starts to run away from me, back through the cavern entrance. I try to grab her hand to stop her, but she slips out of my hold. I chase after her, but she's suddenly vanishing in front of my eyes. Like smoke that slowly starts to dissipate. That's usually when I shout, 'Don't go!'...but it was slightly different this last time."

"This girl? Who is she? Can you describe her?" Macklin asks.

I'm watching Cole intently. A sick feeling starting to roll through my body as a memory, long since locked away, finally breaks free. I already know the words he's going to say. I can hear them in my head, in his voice, loud and clear.

"You shouted, 'Fate, don't go!'" I whisper. "Didn't you, Cole?"

His eyes are full of despair when they reach mine.

"Yes. It was you. It's *always* been you. That first time we saw you, I knew you were the girl that haunted my dreams, but I don't know what I did. Or what you did. Or what the hell is happening at that moment. That's why I can't trust you. Something happened, and whatever that something is, there's a damn good chance it's the reason we're all here. No memories of who we are or where we came from. No idea who we are to each other." He stops then and stands, his fists clenched at his sides. "Now we're all back together again. And here you are, tempting each of my brothers. Batting those eyes of yours at all of them. Maybe this is your revenge. Your way of getting back at me for all of that pain I caused you. Or maybe this is your way of apologizing for whatever bullshit *you* pulled that day. Hell, for all we know, this has something to do with one of them. I don't know, and I don't really fucking care. All I know is that until we figure this shit out, I. Don't. Trust. You."

By this point, he's in my face, towering over me. My power starts to rise along with my anger. It starts in that empty space inside me and slithers out in all directions, lighting up nerve endings along the way until it reaches my fingertips. The lights start to flicker. The fireplace roars to life.

It's not a surprise there's no love lost between us. I've let his constant hostility flow through me like water through a sieve since the day he got here. But now this ghost girl's switch has been flipped, and I refuse to stand here any longer and take the brunt of his anger that I've done nothing to provoke. Time to remind this asshole just who he's dealing with.

The sound system once again starts blaring a rather appropriate tune if I do say so myself. *Yeah, fuck you very much, Ass-Cole.*

We're toe to toe, Cole and me. Both breathing heavily, our eyes locked on each other. If I didn't know any better, I'd say this sounds like the start of a very sexy, drool-worthy scene that culminates with his and her pleasure. Unfortunately, as an active participant in the current situation, I can assure you that it is not in the least bit mouthwatering, and there will be no happy endings.

That alone is enough to have me lashing out at him.

"Just who in the hell do you think you are? *You* came to find *me*. Not the other way around. If there is anyone here who should be suspicious right now, it's me!" I shout over the song.

Realizing how ludicrous it is to yell over the music, I use my power to turn the volume down to a reasonable level while keeping the song on repeat because I know it will piss him off.

"What in the hell do you have to be suspicious of? You're dead. A ghost. No one can do shit to hurt you. My brothers and I, on the other hand, have everything to lose, and I'm not trusting our lives to a hot-headed nymphomaniac!"

"Nymphomaniac?" I sputter.

I'm slightly outraged. Slightly in agreement. I mean, it has been god knows how long since I got laid, and I tend to have a one track mind where these guys are concerned. Though that's totally beside the point right now. He thinks that I don't have feelings just because I'm no longer alive? That I can't be hurt? Well, he's wrong. Because right now, that empty space in my soul that's been begging for even the tiniest scrap of their attention, any teensy hint of connection, is shrinking in on itself. Closing itself off when it had only just begun to open itself up again. *Fuck him!*

"Maybe we should all calm down," Macklin says, trying to stem the rising tide of anger and revulsion in the room. Of course, we ignore him.

"You're wrong. I may be powerful, but I'm not invincible. There is one particular weakness you guys can exploit. Mack said the twins can send me to the afterlife. One little touch and boom! Bye bye, Fate."

The room is suddenly in an uproar, the guys all talking over each other.

"What the fuck, Mack?" Knox shouts.

"You told her we'd send her to the afterlife?" Thad demands.

"You told her about our abilities?" Levi asks.

"That was *not* your decision to make!" Cole growls.

"I only offered to help. I didn't want her to be alone anymore," Mack snaps, squaring his shoulders, which would be totally sexy if I had time to really appreciate it. Sadly, I don't. I have to make an asshole remember his place.

I tune them out and focus on Cole.

"Maybe that's what's really going on here. You came to eliminate the threat. I mean, you said it yourself. I've been haunting your dreams for *years*. Were you tracking me down so you could finally put an end to the nightmares? Or maybe you wanted to rid yourself of whatever guilt you feel every time you look at me? It's starting to look like I'm the one that shouldn't trust any of you."

I punctuate that last statement by stabbing his chest with my pointer finger. Unfortunately, it's highly ineffective as it just sails right through his body rather than meeting the resistance it so desperately desired.

"Fate, we're not here to harm you. We want answers, just like you do," Knox tries to interject on his brother's behalf, and I don't pay any attention, but I do note the sense of strain in his voice. Poor guy is probably inundated with all these hostile feelings being slung around the room. I make a mental note to make it up to him later.

There's a silent stand off as Cole and I glare at one another. The routine has become familiar in the days since the guys showed up, but this time there's more than just seething anger in those beautiful blues. If I didn't know any better, I'd think I'd hurt him somehow.

"You know what? I can't deal with this right now. Why don't you go give away orgasms like Oprah gives away cars and leave me the hell alone," Cole snarls as he stomps out of the study, silence following in his wake. A few moments later, the back door opens then slams shut.

I'm staring at the doorway he just walked through, wondering why he gets under my skin so damn bad...and how in the hell he knows so much about Oprah. The man is an enigma I may never get the chance to figure out.

In that hint of a memory I have, the anguish in his voice is undeniable. I never would have expected him to aim that particular emotion at me or tell me not to go, for that matter. Our current, unspoken *stay the fuck away from me pact* must not have existed then.

He's right about some of what he said, at least. We don't

remember who we are to each other, and we don't know what that means for the rest of us.

"Give him time to cool off. One of us will go get him and bring him back in. We'll need to discuss everything we just learned," Macklin soothes as he walks up behind me.

I can't bring myself to turn around and face him, but I have to ask what I know we're all thinking.

"What does this all mean, Mack?"

"I'm not sure, Fate, but we'll figure it out. Together."

"Together..." Drawing out the word, I take a second to gather my spiraling thoughts before I continue. "Funny how only moments ago that word would've had me swooning at your feet."

I look over my shoulder and find him focused on me.

"Is that all it takes to get you on your knees, woman?" Thad asks, earning a smack to the back of the head from his brother.

"Ouch! What the fuck, man?"

Not even the twins' naughty sense of humor can ease the pain that is slowly encompassing my heart like a slow-moving poison through my blood.

"But now," I say slowly, turning to fully face Macklin, "now, I'm not sure together is such a good thing to be."

The hurt I see flash across his face causes a twinge in my heart, and I quickly scan the faces of the others, finding the same. I don't want to be the cause of those looks. Ever.

Hope. It's a dangerous emotion I had always managed to avoid. Until now. Until them. Now look where that's gotten me. Alone in a room full of people. Been there, done that, have the t-shirt.

"I'm going to go. I'll find you later." With that, I poof myself into one of the upstairs bathrooms and throw myself into my second favorite place in the house, the large empty tub where someone, at some point in time, left an empty wine bottle sitting in the corner. That person is someone I would probably get along with. I mean, I'd totally bring a whole bottle of wine to a tub soak...*yes, please*! Getting comfortable, I give in to a much-deserved pity party of one, imagining a full bottle of wine and a tub filled with luxurious bubbles. A ghost girl can dream, right?

Chapter 8

LEVI

TWIN FACT #1: WE DON'T EXPERIENCE EACH OTHER'S EMOTIONS (THANK FUCK, BECAUSE MY TWIN IS A DIPSHIT).

*L*ying on this somewhat comfortable twin bed, I think back to the clusterfuck that was this evening. The look on Fate's gorgeous face as Cole broke her spirit down is stuck in my damn head. She was finally starting to trust all of us, to ingratiate herself into our group, filling a spot that seemed to be custom-made just for her. The more time she spends around us, the more I notice the ever-present sadness in those haunted eyes slowly being replaced with a confidence and power that stirs something inside my soul.

Which is a first - for my soul, that is. Normally, it's there in the background of my consciousness, with about as much feeling as a doormat. After meeting Fate, it's as if it's waking up from a long slumber. This intense possessiveness and a growing sense that we need to protect her at all costs, along with a healthy dose of fond affection, are screwing with my mind, and the sexy as fuck ghost is responsible.

Fond affection? She's turning me into another Macklin. Fuck my life.

Except, after tonight, we're back to square one. A loud sigh escapes my lips before I can stop it.

"What the fuck are you pouting about over there?" Thad asks from the twin bed beside me. It's like we're kids again. Except we don't remember ever being kids, which is fucking strange. Even so, given our unique bond, we'd still prefer two small ass beds that barely fit half our bodies over being in separate rooms. When we're apart for too long, we get antsy and irritable, the sense that something is missing making us agitated and more aggressive. We've been lucky we've never had to see what would happen if we were separated indefinitely. Something tells me it wouldn't be good.

"You think she's okay?"

His eyes shutter, and whatever joke he was going to crack is gone like the wind.

We sit there for a moment, our eyes locked onto each other. Sometimes serious talks like this are just easier when you don't have to speak the thoughts out loud. Thank fuck for our twin connection making this one big silent conversation in our heads.

You know she's not okay, bro.

How can we make this right?

His eyes leave mine for a moment to stare at the ceiling, his large hands moving up and under his head. When his head finally tilts toward mine again, the serious look on his face tells me just how much this is bothering him too.

We can't. If we tried, we could end up doing more harm than good.

What do you mean?

Think about it, bro. One small mistake and we could accidentally send her off to the afterlife. We get too close to her, get a little too excited, let one spark fly from our fingers, and she's no more. You want to risk that?

It's my turn to look away. He's right, which is not something I often say. Of the two of us, he's the loose cannon. The one more likely to fuck things up and then smile at you in apology. Then I sweep in to smooth things over. But right now, he's one hundred percent right.

The fact that he's the rational one in this scenario is surprising and actually kind of fucking annoying. That's my usual gig, and I'm not sure how I feel about this role reversal. Is my whole world turning on its axis?

Despite the fact that everything in my being is begging me to go to her, to assure her that we would never hurt her, I can't because that's not a promise I can make. And that thought tears a new hole in my already tattered soul.

"Dammit!"

"We'll figure things out tomorrow. Let everyone cool off tonight," Thad says quietly, like it's the last thing he wants to do.

As my brain circles back to Fate, the one thing that's become increasingly obvious is that somehow, in a short amount of time, she's managed to carve out a place in my heart - a place that's hers and hers alone. With every frantic beat in my chest, I know that neither my heart nor my soul is happy that we're so fucking helpless. That there's nothing we can do to change the fact that our girl is hurting. I can only pray that the next time we see her, we'll be able to tell her just how important she's becoming to us. How much we're here for her and despite what my dipshit brothers do or say, she can always count on us to be in her corner.

"Right. Tomorrow," I say quietly, already knowing that sleep is going to be elusive, and I'm in for a long ass night.

Chapter 9

COLE

ASSHOLE FACT #1: WE DON'T ALWAYS WANT TO BE ASSHOLES. IT'S JUST PART OF THE JOB DESCRIPTION.

The dreams have been coming more frequently over the years. With the chaos of the last few days, I fully expected them to get even worse. God, I hate it when I'm right. After seeing Knox and his sudden, almost obsessive connection with this spirit, I have begun to dread the night. I'm not one to believe in coincidences and have finally conceded they have everything to do with the girl. Ghost. Whatever the fuck she is. There's no denying it now anyway - not after seeing her.

Until today, my brothers hadn't known all the details. Guys don't ask a lot of questions. They don't want to discuss feelings - well, except maybe Knox. In true male fashion, most men wait until you're ready to talk about it. I had never reached that point. Until Mack pointed out that our histories are somehow tied together, and I was forced to.

Fuck! I should've told my brothers. Our bond has survived the years because we're open and honest with each other.

It's the very foundation we've built the last fifty years of our brotherhood on. The fact that I'm the one to put the first crack in it adds another bruise to my battered soul.

Sitting in bed, drenched in a cold sweat, I take deep breaths to calm my racing heart. This one was more realistic than any I've had before. The look of despair on her face shattered my heart, and the tears coursing down her cheeks were so real that I swear if I wiped them away, I'd wake up with the dampness still lingering on my fingers.

The sense of impending doom that always follows the nightmare - because, hell, I always call it like it is - leaves me irritable and moody. This time is no different. I take that back; with everything that went down tonight, it's worse than usual.

I throw the covers off and get out of bed. Padding to the en-suite bathroom, I head for the sink, turn on the chrome tap, and splash water on my face. Gripping the edges of the granite countertop so fiercely it's a wonder it doesn't crack beneath my hands, I lift my head and stare at myself in the mirror. I take a good, long look at the features I've seen every day for the last fifty years. The ice blue eyes are the same. Nose is still straight despite numerous attempts to change that. There are no new wrinkles, scars, or marks lining my skin. My hair is styled differently now but is still as black as night. I'm the same man that woke up in Phoenix all those years ago, but how long will that last? Something tells me that my past is catching up to me. With no idea what that means, I'm scared shitless for the first time in this life.

Avoiding the pain and anger and confusion that were building inside me was easy when I could pick fights or drink myself into a stupor every night. I could ignore the itch just under my skin caused by the unease that threatened to devour me whole at the first sign of weakness. Then my brothers saved me. Pulled me out from that pit I had fallen into before I could let the fear consume me, because underneath it all, that's what it was. *Fear*. Channeling my power into keeping them safe helped me stave off this sense of impending doom that follows me around like my own personal rain cloud.

My power, the ability to command those closest to me without question and outsiders by a simple touch, comes with a hefty price tag. I'm always cognizant of each choice that needs to be made, not wanting my brothers to ever feel like I'm making them do something they truly don't want to do, but when push comes to shove, I'm the one that has to make the tough calls. Our survival has always been my burden to bear. I may be an asshole and naturally take charge, but the weight of responsibility is a load too heavy even for me sometimes.

When we got word of a house that had been haunted by a spirit intent on scaring buyers away, that this spirit was powerful and not to be messed with, my gut tried to warn me. I chose to ignore it. I mean, what were the chances this was in any way related?

Now, after seeing my nightmare manifest right before my very eyes, that fear is slowly clawing its way to the surface again, and neither my power nor my brothers will be enough to stop it. The only thing that can, the only *one* that can, is someone I refuse to get close to.

The moment she appeared in the study, I knew there was no denying it any longer. While the hazy form made it impossible to discern the color of her hair or the exact shade of her eyes, I knew. Her hair was a deep brown, like the dark chocolate I enjoy so much. Those eyes were gray and could pierce you with a single look. The large, pink lips were tilted into something other than an expression of utter sorrow, a rarity that *almost* brought a smile to my face.

That's usually all I ever remember when I wake up. Her beautiful, devastated face. Aside from that, I can recall nothing. No prior memories of her. No prior memories of us. No prior memories of my brothers. Nothing.

It's for that reason I don't trust her. *Can't* trust her. My brothers' lives are on the line, and an unknown such as our ghost girl, with as much power as she's packing, is a dangerous thing. There are just too many questions. Why am I always screaming for her not to go? Is that look of sorrow from my dream for herself or for all of us? Maybe just one of us? Is it a premonition of things to come or something from our past? Is it caused by guilt or devastation? I'm not the one with the ability to sense emotions, but even I know that I'm missing something important. We need to find answers, fast.

Frustrated, I leave the bathroom and head for the kitchen. It's the middle of the night, and the house is dark and quiet. The stairs under my feet are silent as I follow them down and around, through the foyer, to the back of the house.

The two sets of French doors on the back wall are the first things I see. The moon is high tonight, giving me just enough light to see the spectacular view. A stone patio sits just outside the door. Though it's empty right now after being abandoned for so long, it's big enough for a large patio table and a few lounge chairs. Maybe even a fire pit, though I doubt we'll be here long enough to get to enjoy that. A massive yard with green grass that seems endless lies just beyond the stone pavers. The old weeping willow, the tree that is somehow linked to *her*, is off in the distance, the branches nearly sweeping the ground beneath. An old swing still hangs, ready to be put to use. I wonder how many kids have been pushed on that thing? How many families have called this place home?

I stand at the door, looking out into the tranquility of a cloudless night sky. It's calm. Peaceful. I'm not sure I've ever felt that particular emotion. I'm positive I won't any time soon, and that's fine with me. I'll give anything, do anything, to ensure my brothers get to experience it, and that's enough for me. Though something tells me our little spitfire is about to turn our whole world upside down, and there's nothing I can do to stop it.

Chapter 10

Fate

Ghost Girl Fact #5: We do not lose our tempers. Only when provoked, or faced with assholes, or so damn turned on we can't think straight. See also Fact #4.

Crying is highly underestimated in my opinion. The release is so utterly invaluable, but no one realizes that until the tears can no longer flow. I wonder how many people out there are physically incapable of crying. Chances are probably less than one percent, kind of like the chances of a smile on Cole's kissable lips. Guess that leaves little old me. The ghost girl whose tension slowly builds up like water inside a water balloon without the ability to cry it out. How much can it hold before it simply bursts? When that pain can't break free through tears, how else does it escape?

I was once a relatively happy ghost girl. I had my own space. My own sense of self. My own unlife - pathetic, though it may have been. Now, for the first time since I appeared here, I'm lost. This connection to the guys is taking a turn in a direction I hadn't anticipated. I wanted answers, but I only got more questions.

Are they really the reason I'm stuck in this afterlife limbo?

What does this mean for me moving forward?

Who am I, or maybe more accurately, who *was* I?

If Cole's nightmares are actually memories, then I wasn't exactly human, right? Humans don't disappear in clouds of smoke. I already know the guys are something *more*, though they haven't had time to explain to me what that entails.

Maybe it's time I demand some answers from the one person who will give it to me straight regardless of whether the truth hurts like a bitch.

I sit up and harden my resolve. They aren't the only ones whose past is coming back to haunt them, and I deserve answers just as much as they do. If they didn't want to share, they shouldn't have sought me out, right?

Damn straight!

I repeat a new mantra in my head.

I will not lose my temper. I will not lose my temper.

Oh...who am I kidding? I'm totally going to lose my temper. He and I go together like gasoline and fire.

I poof myself to the kitchen and look out the doors at the blackness of the night. The grounds are beautiful in the daytime, but I stopped enjoying them years ago when I realized the sun no longer warmed me, and the yard was more like a set of iron bars than a relaxing haven.

I spot a shadowy figure that can only be Cole out by the willow.

Before I can change my mind, I'm standing next to him. He's staring the tree down like its very existence pisses him off, and it probably does. Everything does. So I stare down the damn willow like it's personally aggrieved me too.

"What did this tree ever do to you?" I blurt out, and Cole startles slightly. That makes me smile, feeling a tad bit triumphant. The man is normally as unshakeable as a damn stone statue. I mean, I would've loved to see him jump and scream like a girl, but I'll take what I can get.

"What the fuck do you want?"

"Straight to business. I like it."

"Didn't I tell you to leave me the hell alone?"

"Did you actually expect me to listen to you?"

He turns to face me then, anger and frustration and something else flashing in those pretty blues. For a second, I just stare at him. I know this man. Maybe not the man standing before me, but the man he used to be. I can feel it in my soul; a little spark of a connection flares brightly every time he's around. It feels like passion and pain, love and sorrow. It so badly wants to break free from the confines it's been placed in.

I ignore the damn thing.

We're obviously not the same people we once were. Hell, even if we did remember each other, I'm not so sure new me would like new him. Letting that teensy connection grow once again could be our final demise.

I let my gaze drift back to the tree, refusing to let those eyes draw me in.

"It's frightening, isn't it?" I murmur.

"What is?" he practically growls.

"Not knowing who you are or where you came from."

There's a brief pause while he takes me in and releases a long sigh, turning back to the tree. Out of the corner of my eye, I see him put his hands in his back pockets.

The silence drags out until I can barely stand it. He drops his head back for a second and mutters something just low enough that I can't make it out. Then he's staring at the tree once more with a determined look on his face.

"I never actually had a problem with that until the

nightmares started," he finally responds. The reluctance to converse with me is evident in his tone. Still, he continues. "I knew they were more than just dreams after the third or fourth time, which meant nothing good could have happened. Why else would I be forced to relive that moment over and over? Makes it hard to keep going when you're not sure what you did so wrong to get you to where you are."

He takes a deep breath. His shoulders straighten ever so slightly, and his biceps tense up with his agitation.

"There's a lot you don't know, Fate. About us. About what we've seen and experienced over the last fifty years. About what we're capable of. If you did, I'm not sure you'd be as eager for answers as you think you are."

The Cole I had grown to know would rather stick hot pokers in his eyes than give me even a tiny hint of vulnerability, so to say his response surprises me is an understatement. I want to keep him talking. Need him to give me the answers he seems to think I shouldn't want.

"So why don't you tell me? Help me understand."

"I can't. My responsibility is to my brothers. To keep them safe. Alive. Until we know more about who you are and what happened, I can't risk it. I won't."

While I understand and respect his loyalty to his brothers, my frustration begins to grow. Once more, I'm an outsider looking in. Except this time, I'm not just watching frivolous activities and playing games with unsuspecting people. This is my very existence on the line, and I'll be damned if he just brushes me off.

With impatience clawing at me, I repeat my *I will not lose my temper* mantra until I'm reasonably sure I won't bite his head off - figuratively, of course, because this ghost girl isn't a fan of blood.

Once I'm fairly confident I have myself under control, I ask, "What do *you* think happened to us, Cole?"

He's silent for a moment, and I'm totally fine with that. It gives me a chance to appreciate the darkness although I'm almost sad I missed the sunset casting gorgeous colors across the sky. The creatures of the night are starting to quiet down in preparation for the day ahead. How long has it been since I've purposefully stepped a foot outside the house? I may be a ghost, and I may be stuck here indefinitely, but there are still experiences to be had in this afterlife, right?

Breaking me out of my reverie, his voice is soft again when he replies, "We hurt each other somehow. Badly. Now we're here, like this, because of that."

Even though I knew that already, I consider his words and take a moment to search inside myself. There are memories there that are just beyond my reach. That pain I experience that I can't quite name might give me some answers, but it's buried so deep that I can't get a good grasp on it no matter how hard I try.

"Don't you think it would be better if we worked together to try to figure it out?" I plead.

He turns to look at me again, his gaze searching for something when our eyes meet in the shadows.

"No. I don't."

A little shocked despite myself, I'm sure my brows have hit my hairline, and my frustration surges to dangerous levels.

"Why do you hate me so much? I'm here with a damn olive branch, and you just slapped me in the face with it." My voice wavers slightly, mostly from the anger building within me, but also from the hurt I'm trying desperately to ignore.

"I don't hate you. I hate how you make me feel."

I take in that seemingly innocent statement and let it roll around in my brain. There's a challenge in his eyes I haven't seen before. Like he's begging me to prove him wrong. I want to - desperately. If I only knew why he seems to think he's so right.

"How do I make you feel, Cole? Other than pissed off, that is."

His eyes are still locked on mine, a myriad of emotions in their depths.

When his gaze moves to the ground, I think our conversation is over. Then his low, rich voice is rushing out into the night, the words spat out gruffly like his mouth took control before his brain could figure out what was happening.

"Like I'm on fire every time you're near me. Like my skin is too tight. Like there's something inside me just begging to be free so I can consume you whole. Like my very soul recognizes its other half."

I'm speechless. These weren't flowery compliments or tender declarations of love. Just a few harshly spoken sentences, yet he has melted my ice. Broken down my walls. Drained the poison right from my veins, leaving me open and exposed and so damned shocked I can't think straight.

I should've known it wasn't that simple though.

"But you also make me feel like my heart is being broken in two every time my eyes catch yours. Like the very soul that belongs to you is being shredded into pieces and laid at your feet. Like I will burst into flames the second I get too close. I trust my gut, and that's why this," his finger moves between the two of us, "whatever *this* is...can't happen. Won't happen. Maybe Macklin was right. Maybe the twins should give you a personal demonstration of their powers. The temptation you offer on an open platter is likely to get us all killed, and I'd rather see you gone than to see my brothers suffer any more than they already have."

A slap across the face would've been less harsh than those words. He lured me in. Hooked me. Then dragged me out into the open, gutted me, and threw me on the fire.

If this is what my existence is to consist of, if I only have two options in this ridiculous afterlife, perpetual loneliness or emotional battery, then I think I'm ready to wave the white flag and surrender. I realize I'm tired, a soul-deep sense of exhaustion stemming from the fact that I live day in and day out but don't really live at all. I simply exist, barely. There will never be more for me than this, and a ghost girl can only take so much before she simply gives up.

"You win," I say simply, and his stunned look holds no satisfaction for me.

"What do you mean, I win?"

"You win. I give up. I surrender. Call the twins and have them do their thing."

"Fate..."

"No. You don't get to backtrack now. You've thrown it all out there, and I've listened. Come to terms with the fact that this is all there will ever be for me. I choose my own fate." I take a deep breath and release a self-deprecating chuckle. "Ironic, right? But I won't let anyone else decide what happens to me. So, call them. Let's get this thing done."

"Come on. You don't actually mean that."

"Oh, but I do. I'm one hundred percent dead-fucking serious right now. Call. Them."

"I'm not going to..."

"Since when did you grow a pussy? A few seconds ago, your balls were so big they wouldn't fit through a door. You got what you wanted. Take it. Call them. End me. You. Fucking. Win!"

By the end I'm shouting at him.

The look on his face would be comical if I wasn't practically vibrating with anger. My power, which had been fairly dormant until now, is blazing inside of me. Rolling just under my skin, looking for an escape. My fingertips tingle and my toes curl as my body attempts to keep the beast inside of me contained.

"Well? Go on. Do it!" I snarl.

"Just calm down and let's…"

Calm down? He wants me to calm down after he just swung a damn sledgehammer through what was left of my non-existent heart? As if.

Another surge of power has my knees almost buckling, but I keep my balance. Aware that he's now the one in imminent danger if I can't release some of this power that's inside of me, I stumble back a few steps. I frantically look around, seeking something to aim all of this anger and frustration and energy at.

My eyes land on the willow tree, and something inside of me snaps free. Whether it's a snippet of a memory or a figment of my imagination caused by the stress I'm currently under, I can't be sure. But suddenly I know this willow tree and I really do have a history. We have a connection, the two of us. One forged in death.

Before I can even think about what I'm doing, I'm stalking up to the tree. Something is calling to me, like to like. Power to power. A connection that is awakening from a long slumber.

"Fate? What are you doing?"

I ignore Cole and keep walking through the hanging branches and over the uneven ground with sections of roots sticking out until I can lay my palm against the rough bark. The second contact is made, I feel it. The power. So much like my own that the two forces surge forward, needing to reunite.

"Fate? What the fuck is going on?"

So he sees it too. The glow that has started to spread out from where my hand is joined to the trunk. I move to pull away but can't. My hand is locked into place, my fingertips digging into the bark until it's almost painful. *Wait a minute. I can* feel *pain. What the hell is happening?* Panic starts seeping through the anger without lessening the power inside me.

"I don't know. I can't move my hand."

"Here. Let me help..."

"No! Don't get too close. My power is growing. I won't be able to keep it contained much longer. Just go."

"I'm not leaving you here like this."

"You have to. You've got your brothers. Keep them safe. Tell them..." I pause, coming to terms with the fact that this is probably where my existence ends. I take a shuddering breath. "Tell them I said thank you for making sure my last days weren't spent alone."

"Fate..."

"I'm sorry, Cole, for whatever happened in the past. And just in case sorry isn't what's needed, I forgive you. Hopefully one of those is enough to stop the nightmares and help you move forward."

The glow is now a large, ghostly flame, illuminating the entire space under the willow's hanging branches. There's no heat, just an intense light that's growing by the second. The ground begins to shake, causing the branches to sway which throws a beautiful light pattern out into the yard beyond. It would be a stunning sight to take in if it wasn't so damn terrifying.

"Don't do this."

"I don't have a choice. Now hurry."

Just as I say that, bolts of lightning start shooting out from between my hand and the tree. The power in my body has recognized the power within the tree, and nothing is going to stop the two from having a happy little reunion.

"Now, Cole! Run!"

I watch as his hands fist and his jaw clenches when the realization hits that there's nothing he can do. The emotion in his eyes is one I am intimately familiar with. Regret.

"It's okay. Go. Please," I whisper desperately.

With one last look and a simple nod, he runs off into the night.

I hold on with all my might for as long as I can. Praying he's a safe distance away, I let my head drop forward and take a deep breath. On the exhale, I release the tight hold I have on my power, setting it free.

There's a blast of bright light and a sudden surge of power like I've never felt, then the world goes black.

Chapter 11

Somewhere in the Gateway...
Present Day

Personal Assistant Fact #1: Do your job even when there's no one around to appreciate your hard work. But seriously...where the fuck is everyone?

If I have to dust another damn piece of furniture, I'm going to lose my shit. Dusting has never been in my job description. I am 'Assistant to the Queen.' This sort of menial labor is beneath me. Or at least it *was* until all hell broke loose.

One second, we're all going about our daily duties, and then wham! The queen goes AWOL, ghosts start to panic and flood the chambers, and then...double wham! Her crew appears - laid out on the floor - unconscious. Before I can so much as blink, a highly unexpected shockwave blasts through the room. The riff raff disappears in wisps of smoke, and I'm left standing in the center of it all, staring in stunned disbelief.

I'm a little embarrassed to say that it took me a few moments to get my shit together. I've always been unshakeable; that's why the queen chose me. Well, that and she needed some estrogen and serious sarcasm appreciation around here - kindred spirits, she and I - but this was something I'd never experienced in all my years on this plane.

So, I did the only thing I could do. I made sure my friends were kept as comfortable as possible. She would've expected nothing less. For years, I watched over their prone forms, making sure no one and nothing got to them. Not that there was a lot of activity here. For the first time in centuries, the place was as silent as a tomb. Which is pretty ironic considering we deal with death on the daily around here. Or at least we did.

It's simple, really. This is the Gateway. The plane the deceased must pass through before judgment. Think of it like a very busy processing center. Hundreds of thousands of spirits walk through here, all awaiting their turn to be sent off to their final destination. That's our queen's job, to oversee it all with her handpicked crew by her side.

Except now, they're all gone, and I'm left here to wonder what that means for the surface world. Without this place in operation, those spirits we saw day in and day out are trapped. Stuck somewhere between planes, unable to cross over. That means the surface world is probably all sorts of crazy right now. Like a clogged drain, the backup has to go somewhere.

Just when I thought things couldn't possibly get any worse, one day, many decades ago now, the crew simply disappeared. And when I say disappeared, I mean *vanished*. Poof. Gone. Right in front of my very eyes.

My link went silent and has stayed that way, and that is highly disconcerting.

I know they'll all be back one day. She wouldn't let anything keep her away from this place or from them. Which leaves me here, cleaning, to make sure that when they show up, it's as immaculate as the day they all left. I'm such a good little assistant. See, that's some high-quality sarcasm right there.

The rag floats through the air, clearing the dust that has gathered on the queen's chair. She hates the word throne, and to be honest, she hates the fact that I call her queen. In her eyes, she is merely a woman with an extraordinary and highly satisfying day job.

Highly satisfying - hell, I'd be satisfied too with all that eye candy surrounding me. I think they like to see who can get the biggest shock out of me with their damn near pornographic public displays of affection. Horny bastards. And though my preferences don't run along the same lines, a girl can still appreciate an attractive man when she sees one. Of course, I can't enjoy that particular pleasure either way. Assistant to the queen I might be, that doesn't change the fact that I'm still as dead as a doorknob.

With another swipe of the rag and a very dramatic sigh, I move around the chamber. It's a large room; the raised dais sits at the back with a deep red runner that flows from her throne - I mean, her *chair* - down the steps, across the sparkly white-tiled floor, all the way to the doorway. All of the doors throughout the entire compound have remained closed and locked down tight since the shockwave slammed them shut. Doesn't stop me, of course, but any unspelled spirits out there can't get in.

The once stylish, white and black damask walls have taken on a gray hue - actually, the whole damn place has. It's like the Gateway senses its queen's absence and demonstrates its grief by bathing the entire plane in tones of gray. It would be utterly depressing if not for the hundreds of portraits that cover nearly every available inch of wall space. Some in black and white. Some in muted color. All memories from centuries gone by. I make sure each is gleaming, just like the day they were hung with love and care. They are the only reminder that this place was once lively and bright, or at least as lively as a place that temporarily houses death's occupants can be. The colors here were once more vibrant and richer than the surface world.

I pass by the door off to the left of the dais that leads to her office. I cleaned in there yesterday. Or maybe it was last week? Time works differently here. Her desk is exactly as she left it, papers and writing utensils neatly placed on the dark wood's surface. The comfy, burgundy sofa and chairs that sit in the center provide a cozy seating area; they're ready for more of the conversations and laughter that used to fill this room. The fireplace is cold but stocked with everything needed to fill this place with warmth once again.

For now, I continue to clean and straighten things that aren't really untidy in the main room, but it keeps my mind from going completely batshit crazy. A hundred years will do that to even the strongest of spirits.

Suddenly, a zap of current sparks through the room, lighting the sconces along the wall and sending fresh air throughout the chamber. Didn't realize how musty the place had gotten. Not that I can smell it or anything. It's more the feel of the air as it moves through me. It isn't as dense. If that makes any sense. Which it probably doesn't, but such is life. Or death. Whatever.

My link that has been dormant for longer than I care to contemplate unexpectedly goes live again, and I'm flooded with an overflow of information coming so fast that I can't keep up with it all. My head spins, figuratively, of course, because hello, I've seen the *Exorcist,* and I'd never do something so uncouth as to let my head rotate 360 degrees. Off-balance, I fall right through the wall and into the hallway outside the main chamber, stumbling a bit before dropping to my knees.

Reeling from the re-established link, I grab my head in my hands and try to work out what it's trying to tell me.

It's hard to explain this link, this tether between us, when I don't fully understand it myself. It's more than a simple means of communicating. Not alive, per se, but somewhat sentient. It's like the telephone, GPS, and an alarm system had a magical baby, and each one of the queen's crew cares for and responds to the baby in our own ways.

What? Weird explanation? Sometimes my mind works in mysterious ways. Another reason the queen chose me. Kindred spirits, remember?

Right now, the link is flooded with stuttered voices and garbled shouts. It sounds like one hell of a bad cell phone connection, and that's never a good sign. When it's over-whelmed, the link can be a bastard to understand. I wait it out, knowing that once it calms down, I should be able to get a location on the queen or at least one of the others. That's all I should need to find them and figure out what the hell is going on.

I've got a century worth of bitching and moaning just bottled up and waiting to rant on about. And they have some explaining to do.

Chapter 12

COLE

ASSHOLE FACT #2: WITH GREAT POWER COMES...A LOT OF FUCKING HEARTACHE.

My head is pounding like I've had one too many whiskeys, except I'm pretty damn sure I haven't had so much as a sip in years. I slowly open my eyes and take stock of my surroundings.

The moon is still high in the sky, the yard shrouded in darkness, but I can make out the house, which is somehow tilted on its side, up ahead. The grass beneath my face starts to tickle my nose, and I realize I'm actually the one who's sideways, sprawled out on the back lawn, just shy of the patio.

Taking a quick inventory of the rest of my body - fingers and toes, hands and feet all move with no pain - I tentatively push myself up off the ground, getting to my feet. I'm covered in dirt and grass but otherwise seem unharmed, all things considered.

Running my hands over my face, the fingers on my right hand sink into something wet and sticky. Gently, I prod around above my cheekbone and, with an embarrassing wince, discover a ragged cut at my temple. It's small but bleeding like a son of a bitch.

Guess this could've been a helluva lot worse if I had made it a few more steps onto the stone patio. At least the grass acted as a cushion. I have it to thank for keeping my skull mostly intact.

Bright light is suddenly flooding the area from the numerous backyard lights, and I shield my eyes from the glare. The back door flies open, and I look over to see all four of my brothers rush out. When they get a good look at me, they come to such an abrupt stop I imagine their feet squealing and smoking like tires, all four of them doing a pretty awesome impression of that cliched cartoon moment. It would be comical if it weren't for the bass drum thumping out a rhythm inside my skull. Maybe I hit my head a little harder than I thought.

"What the fuck happened to you?" Levi asks. His total lack of concern has me rolling my eyes, which my head does not appreciate.

Macklin is the first to recover from his shock and makes his way over to inspect me. "Looks like it's just a scratch. I don't think you need stitches."

Knox interrupts Macklin's check up. "What in the hell happened out here? The whole house started shaking." His voice is full of impatience and something else I can't quite name as he scans the yard and beyond. "Then we heard a loud blast, almost like a grenade or bomb had gone off. Woke us all up."

"I just woke up face first in the dirt. Haven't had time to figure out exactly what happened yet."

"Tell us what you remember," Macklin says gently.

"I woke up after another nightmare, and I came out here to calm down. I was standing at the willow tree, looking for anything unusual, and berating headstrong, beautiful ghosts when Fate…" I trail off as the last few moments hit me with all the force of a mack truck.

Us arguing. The tree. The light. The look in her eyes. Her apology. Her saving my life.

Without saying a word, I turn and sprint in the direction of the willow, the last place I saw Fate. As I approach the spot, it takes a moment for the sight in front of me to register.

I can hear my brothers close on my heels, someone shouting my name, and I stop just shy of where the tree once stood, my brothers' voices cutting off as soon as they've reached me. All of us are in a line, staring at what was once a large, ancient willow tree. Now, it's nothing more than scrap wood spread out in all directions. Leaves and some larger tree limbs that somehow managed to avoid being decimated are scattered about. Clumps of dirt and grass are tossed amongst it all, leaving divots in the ground from where they were violently ripped up. The swing is upside down, its ropes mangled and twisted.

It does, indeed, look like a bomb has gone off with the tree at the epicenter. But it wasn't a bomb or a grenade. It was the ghost girl. *Our* ghost girl.

"Seriously, what the fuck happened?" Levi snaps again.

I can't answer him. My heart, which could rival the Grinch's in size, is now shriveling to nothing more than a minute speck. I had been a total dick, and what did she do? She saved me. She held on and ensured I walked away from this with my life intact. That woman made sure I could spend another day with my brothers. Doesn't it figure that I'd stop thinking of her as a ghost now that she's gone, but even I have to admit that what she made me feel was as real as anything I've ever known. How will I ever forgive myself after this? It's my nightmare all over again, except this time it's much, much worse.

"Cole, man, were you out here when that thing exploded?" Macklin asks quietly.

It doesn't escape my attention that Knox has gone eerily still and silent. No doubt, he's feeling something, but I'm too afraid to ask what.

"She told me to run," I whisper.

"Who told you to run?" Thad demands, a warning in his tone.

"Fate."

He's on me in a second, his hands wrapping themselves in my shirt. He lifts me off the ground, my toes just barely touching. Rage is simmering in his eyes, and I've known him long enough to recognize the danger there.

"What did you do to her?" he asks menacingly.

"Bro, calm down. We don't..." Levi begins.

"No! He just said he was out here with her. Look at that tree! Look at *him*," Thad shouts at his twin, then to me asks, "Where is she, Cole?"

The look on my perpetually playful brother's face is a new one. It registers that he's deadly serious, possibly for the first time in his life. I didn't even think the word was in his vocabulary.

I knew Knox had grown fond of Fate, obsessed really, but it wasn't until this moment and the look in Thad's eyes, that I realize he wasn't alone in his feelings.

Thad doesn't take his eyes off of mine when he asks, "Knox, do you feel her?"

No response. Knox has yet to utter a single word, and his silence is telling. His eyes are locked onto the debris like it can tell him what happened.

"Dammit! Someone tell me where the fuck Fate is, or I

swear to God you won't like what happens next," Thad growls, his fury close to boiling over.

"Thad, let go of Cole. He'll talk. Just give him a minute," Mack soothes.

Thad's still staring me down, and I give him a small nod. As much an acknowledgement of the terms as a promise to abide by them. I could simply command him to release me, but I understand his worry. I also know things are about to get worse before they get better, and I don't need my powers to compound the problem.

Slowly, he lowers me to my feet and yanks his hands free. "Start talking," he demands.

I run those last few moments around in my mind.

She fucking saved me, and I didn't deserve it.

"Last warning," Thad growls impatiently.

His twin comes up to his side and places a hand on his shoulder. Recognizing how short Thad's fuse currently is, I know I need to start explaining myself.

"We were talking, and things got pretty heated," I begin.

"She came to you?" Macklin asks.

"Yes. She wanted answers, but I wouldn't give them to her."

Dammit, why didn't I just give her something? Anything. What harm could it have done? Why did I let my damn pride get in the way? Fuck!

"And then what?" Thad barks.

Shifting my gaze to the ground, unable to meet their eyes, my shoulders slump from the intense weight of my regret. "I said...some things I shouldn't have said."

"Some things like what?" Levi jumps in, placing a hand on his twin's chest to stop him from coming at me again. They share a heated look, doing their damn twin speak, and I watch as Levi's jaw clenches and he shakes his head, giving his brother a warning. *Fuck, hope he's got a good leash on Thad because he's really not going to like this. None of them are.*

"I told her you guys should give her a personal demonstration of your powers. That I'd rather see her gone than for you guys to be hurt."

"You said *what*?" Thad explodes.

With great power, comes great responsibility. I fully understand the wisdom behind those words. My brothers don't realize the burden I bear. They don't understand it's my duty to keep each and every one of them safe - or the effect the potential consequences have on my decision-making.

"Look, I can't let anything happen to you guys. You're my priority. You were all so wrapped up in her and her ass that you were blind to the very real danger she represented."

"How could we have possibly realized there was danger if you didn't fill us in?" Levi mutters, clearly exasperated.

His twin barks out, "News flash, dickweed. None of us are mind readers."

"I realize I was wrong to keep the details of my nightmares from you, especially after Fate came into our world. I'm sorry," I murmur, my hand snaking up to run through my hair, messing it up even more than it already was. I'm frustrated and pissed. Not at them, at myself.

"Sorry isn't worth jack shit. Not when one of our lives could have been in danger. Not that I think they ever were. And if I find out you harmed one hair on her ghostly head because of some perceived risk, I'm gonna..."

I shake my head, annoyed despite myself.

"Are you even listening to the words coming out of your mouth? She's a goddamn ghost. How could I harm a hair on her head when my hand would just pass right through it?"

"Oh, so you've got jokes now, do you? Let's see how funny it is when my fist rearranges your teeth!"

And with that, Thad's big ass fist comes flying at my face. Anyone else would've been knocked out, or possibly worse. Lucky for me, I've lived with these fuckers much too long, and they're predictable. Even so, I barely manage to duck and dive, narrowly missing a punch that would've hurt like hell.

By the time I've righted myself, his twin has him in a headlock.

"She better be okay, bro, or you and I are going to have problems," he mutters, half out of breath.

"She didn't..." I pause, knowing there are no words that will make this any easier on them.

"She didn't, what?" Macklin asks, an urgency in his tone that tells me things are about to go from bad to worse.

I hesitate, growing just as frustrated as they are at my inability to find the right way to say this. I know they need to hear it, but I'm unable to form the words. Knox is the empath of the group, able to discern and deal with high emotion. Macklin is the resident peacekeeper, knowing how to handle tricky situations in the most calm yet effective way possible. Either one of them would be more capable of handling this than me. Chalk it up to one more thing that falls on my heavy list of thankless duties.

"She said to tell you guys thank you for making sure she didn't spend these last few days alone."

The blood drains from Mack's face. It's at that moment, I know I've made a huge miscalculation. This *thing* between them all goes a lot deeper than a simple fondness. Even for Macklin. It's also in this moment that I know this could very well break them. It's already broken me, and I didn't think I could be broken any more than I already am.

Shit. How did I not see this sooner?

"Why can't she tell us that herself?" Levi asks, obviously confused.

"Because she's not here anymore," Mack falters, his voice quivering slightly at the end. The look on his face is one of disbelief and denial.

Fuck! This is worse than I thought.

Levi drops his hold on Thad, and as if that's all he's been waiting for, Thad lunges, taking advantage of my distraction.

"You son of a bitch! I'll kill you!"

He's on me before I can outmaneuver him, knocking me to the ground and landing a solid punch to my jaw. I block the next one and manage to buck the big fucker off me. Rolling quickly to the side, I jump to my feet. He's slower to stand, so I'm ready for him, but I don't want to fight. I need to explain what happened.

"Just hold on a damn minute!" I shout, holding out both hands with the hope that my giant of a brother recognizes the universal symbol for stop. "I didn't do anything to her! Her power went crazy when she touched the willow tree's trunk, and she couldn't move away. There was light everywhere and this humming power that made my ears ring. She knew she wasn't going to be able to hold on to it much longer, and she told me to run. She fucking saved my life."

It hits me again, the sacrifice she made for me. All of the sorrow and guilt and regret that has been building up inside me for years suddenly assaults me. Overwhelms my senses and shatters my control.

"She saved my life, but I couldn't save her," I rasp as I let my head drop to my chest and close my eyes so I don't have to look at the slivers of wood and clumps of dirt. My voice wavers as I whisper, "I had just found her, and now I've lost her all over again."

No one speaks. The soft chirping of crickets and a toad's croak out in the distance are the only sounds breaking the silence.

"What's the last thing you remember?" Mack asks gently.

"I remember seeing lightning start to streak out of the connection between her and the tree. That's when she begged me to go. There was nothing I could do, so I ran as fast as I could back toward the house to get you guys. I heard the blast and got hit from behind with a punch of power, and then it was lights out."

"Do you think there's a chance she survived it? I mean, she's a ghost. Maybe she just got blasted back to the house. Like a reset or something?" he asks hopefully.

"She knew, Mack. She knew whatever the hell was happening was the end. I could see it in her eyes."

"But we have to check. Thad, Levi. Run back to the house and..."

"She's not there," Knox cuts in, his voice flat, without a hint of the emotions he has to be overwhelmed with.

"What do you mean? Is she out here somewhere? Can you sense her?" Mack questions.

"I feel her. It's like she's...everywhere. The ground, the sky, the air surrounding us all."

Mack and I share a quick look of concern. Knox was closest to Fate, and this has surely hit him the hardest.

"Knox, that doesn't make any sense. She can't be..."

"I think her essence engulfed everything when the blast went off. Her power soaked into the surroundings when she wasn't there to contain it any longer," he says quietly.

The entire group goes silent again at his words, reality

sinking in. Our potential missing piece, the one we had only just found, is gone. I have another nightmare to add to my collection, except this time I won't be suffering it alone.

I'm not sure how long we sit there, silently processing all that's happened while the moonlight plays with the remains of what was once a large beautiful tree. When I finally snap out of the internal battle raging inside my mind, I take a deep breath before slowly lifting my head. I look around at my brothers, all grieving in their own way.

Levi has a hand on the back of his twin's neck, while Thad stands with his fists and jaw clenching, staring angrily at where the willow once stood tall.

Knox has both hands on his head, his fingers tightly gripping his hair. His face is etched with agony. Not only is he dealing with his own emotions, but all of ours as well.

When I look at poor Macklin, my heart breaks all over again. For the first time in our fifty years together, his attention had been captured by something other than his research. Wait. Not something. *Someone.* Knox may be the empath of the group, but Mack is the heart, and now, that heart has been broken. A single tear leaks from his eye, which he quickly wipes away with the back of his hand.

Setting my own feelings aside to be dealt with later, I figuratively put my leader hat back on, though it's sitting slightly askew now. Not exactly comfortable, but that suits me just fine at the moment.

"Come on. Let's get back to the house. I need a shower, and you all could use some rest."

Levi wraps his arm around his twin's shoulder and leads Thad away, murmuring softly.

I walk over to Macklin, asking a silent question when our eyes meet.

"I'll be fine," he manages before turning and heading toward the house.

I watch the three of them go, wishing there was more I could do to help them. Glancing at my remaining brother, the despair that's rolling off him is so thick I can practically grab it with both hands.

"Knox, you too."

"I'll be just a minute. I need...space."

I know he means from the emotions we're all projecting, so I give him a nod.

"Don't be long or I'll be back to drag you in."

I slowly make my way toward the house, the night's events playing in a continuous loop in my mind like a movie on repeat. My head is still pounding, but that pain has nothing on the regret pooling in what remains of my heart, eating away at it like a flesh-eating disease.

Levi is holding the door, waiting for Mack and me. When my boot hits the stone patio, I hear Knox's shout.

"Wait! Something's happening!"

Mack looks back at me, and we both turn and race back to the tree where Knox still stands. Levi yells for Thad, his voice desperate, and I know they won't be far behind.

"What is it?" I ask.

Knox is still staring at the debris like it holds all the answers, and I have to tamp down my impatience. Just as I'm about ready to lose it, Thad and Levi come running up.

"I don't know. All of a sudden, that feeling of her being everywhere slowly started to recede, almost like it was being sucked down a drain. Power is growing again, somewhere in this rubble, but I just can't pinpoint where with everything else going on."

"What does that mean?" Thad rasps.

"Everyone quiet," I command. "Let's give Knox a minute so he can figure out what's what."

The seconds tick by while we all wait. My hope is soaring even though I try to tamp it back down. Hope is a dangerous thing.

A soft moan echoes through the night.

"Did you hear that!" Mack says excitedly. "Which direction did it come from?"

"Everyone split up," I command, ready to put my restlessness into something productive. "Search everywhere. It's not like we can find her by touch, so we'll have to use our other senses in the dark."

Everyone but Knox takes off. I know he's seconds away from emotional overload. It's only happened one other time, and he was unconscious for three days. We can't afford to have him out of commission right now, and I don't have time to talk him through the worst of it. Walking over to him, I put my hand on his shoulder.

"Brother, can you hang in there just a little bit longer? If it's really her, you might be the only one able to find her. We have to know for sure. We need you. *Fate* needs you."

His head slowly turns my way, and I see how desperate and on edge he is.

"Please?" I murmur.

He takes a deep breath, knowing I don't use that term often, and releases it as he straightens his shoulders. A small nod is all he manages before he walks away to join the others.

"Grid formation, everyone. We don't want to leave a single inch unchecked."

As we all get into position and start the search, I make a promise to myself that if we find her, I'll do everything I can to make up for my behavior. She may never be a fan of mine, and that'll have to be okay. As long as she sticks with us and makes my brothers happy, I'll learn to be content with that.

As the minutes pass, the little sliver of hope that had worked its way past my defenses is starting to waver. Doubts fill my thoughts, souring my already dark mood. Maybe it wasn't a moan. Maybe it was an animal or the creak of the wood after the blast. Maybe it was simply the wind.

Then I hear Knox shout, "Guys! Over here!"

We all turn and run toward him, all the way to the far back corner of the blast site. Not even the moonlight is enough to break through the darkness here.

"Is it her?" Macklin asks as we run up.

Knox is facing away from us, his shoulders hunched and his head down. He has something in his arms, but it's so dark it's hard to make it out.

"Knox, man, come on," Thad grates out.

Knox turns around, and I hear a swift intake of breath. It may have been one of my brother's, but it very well could've been my own.

We all watch in stunned disbelief, our eyes glued to the sight in front of us.

A few feet from where we stand, Knox is staring down at the face of the flesh and blood woman passed out in his arms. When his eyes come up and meet mine, I see the shock and relief and confusion there.

"It's her," he whispers. "She's alive."

Chapter 13

Fate

Ghost Girl Fact #6: Being alive is way harder than it looks.

*W*armth surrounds me. Like I'm nestled into the world's most amazing bed, and I never want to leave. Whispered conversations full of urgency and confusion seem to bounce around the room, or wherever the hell I am, but I can't quite make out the words. I'd love to see what all the fuss is about, but opening my eyes seems like an awful lot of work at the moment. Honestly, my whole body feels sluggish and heavy, as if the entire force of Earth's gravity is pushing down on me. But that's not possible. Gravity doesn't even know I exist.

I'm not going to complain though. This is quite possibly the best first dream ever, because...I *feel*...so many things. Solid. Whole. Alive. I'm hoping it lasts just a little bit longer. I want to soak up as much feeling as I can.

As I slowly pull myself out of the mental fog I found myself in, the muddled voices gain clarity.

"How did this happen?"

The voice is low, rich, and masculine. Cole. He's close enough that his words shoot a spark of heat through my already sensitive body. Apparently even in dreamland my body is a traitorous bitch where he's concerned.

A ghost of a touch slowly brushes hair off my face. The slight roughness of skin trailing across my forehead and the silky softness of hair sliding across my cheek sending tingles throughout my body. No way in hell the blue-eyed asshole would touch me that reverently. My money's on Macklin.

The wonderfully comfy bed shifts beneath me, and I suddenly realize that it's not a bed at all. I'm on someone's lap.

Fuck. This dream just gets better and better. Pretty sure I'd moan from the pure pleasure of a hard male body beneath me if it didn't require energy I just don't seem to have.

"I honestly have no idea. This shouldn't be possible."

The soft rumble of uncertainty somewhere in front of me is most definitely Macklin. I want to give him a giant hug to make that hint of vulnerability go away, but my body is still not cooperating, which is beyond inconvenient. I'm apparently a real girl in this dream, and I want to take full advantage of my change in circumstances while I can. There are so many things I want to do in my dream body. These guys are at the top of that list.

A male chuckle rumbles beneath me.

"What is it?" Cole questions.

"If I wasn't sure this was truly her before, I am now. She's gone through a plethora of emotions in the last few minutes. Desire being the primary one."

I'd recognize that deep, husky voice anywhere. Knox.

It's his lap I'm snuggled up on. It's then I feel his arms wrapped around me, cocooning me in the safety of his embrace.

Hell yes! Now we're talkin'.

"She must be regaining consciousness slowly. We should dim the lights and keep our voices low. Everything will probably seem amplified when she finally wakes up."

Aww! My sexy nerd is so thoughtful. He just earned himself some extra lovin' if I can manage to kick this body into gear.

I attempt to open my eyes, move my fingers, wiggle my toes, but nothing is happening. It's damn frustrating. I can feel my power moving through my body. Starting at my head, lingering in random areas, then moving on to the next. What it's doing, I have no idea, but the tingling sensation would probably make me giggle if my body wasn't on lockdown.

It reaches my pinky toes, and I'd sigh in relief if I could. I'm ready to give this being alive and alert thing another go. I try to open my eyes once more, but my power chooses that moment to kick it up a notch, rolling back up my body like a wave. Just when I think it's finally over, an intense burning flares to life in my mid-section.

What the fuck now? I whine silently.

It slowly expands out to my extremities until there isn't a single centimeter of me that isn't engulfed in fiery pain. The room beyond my eyelids is flickering wildly from bright to dark. Over and over again.

"The fuck? This is her, right?"

Even though my ears are ringing and every sound has a tin can quality to it, I recognize that sexy, naughty voice. Thad.

"It's her. I can feel her power growing. We thought she was strong before, but that was nothing compared to what I feel within her now," Knox answers, sounding worried.

The marks on my bicep pulse twice before I'm suddenly jolted with what feels like a bazillion gigawatts of electricity, causing my back to arch and my jaw, fingers, and toes to clench tight. I would make a puckered asshole joke right now if everything didn't hurt so damn bad. The guys start cursing and shouting, but there's nothing I can do to stop it. I can't breathe, can't see, can't do anything but ride it out. I can't even focus on the panic and fear bubbling up inside because everything just hurts too damn bad. When it finally begins to recede, my body slumps back down into Knox's lap.

Shit! This dream could sure as hell be a lot less painful, thank you very much.

"What in the hell just happened? Is she okay?"

The concerned and reasonable yin to the naughty yang. Levi.

"Don't look at me. This is beyond even my level of knowledge and understanding." Sounds like Macklin isn't all that happy about his power failing him at the moment.

It's then I feel Knox's hand rubbing soothing circles on my upper back with a firm yet gentle touch. His other hand is lightly stroking up and down my outer thigh, sending a different kind of tingle straight to my very real, very excited vagina. And damn, does it feel good.

A moan shatters the quiet in the room, and then I realize it came from me.

"Come on, little ghost. Open those eyes for us."

The rumble from Knox's voice close to my ear adds tingles on top of my tingles.

I can do this. I *will* do this.

Body, do you hear me? Cooperate and I'll make sure these guys take full advantage of you as soon as possible. Deal?

Slowly, I open my eyes. It takes me a second to focus, but when I do, the first thing I see is Macklin's worried face over the shoulder of the gigantic man directly in front of me. I try to lift my hand to soothe him, but my limbs feel like they weigh a ton.

"You're okay. Don't try to move yet," he says quietly.

"What..." I try to speak, but my throat is as dry as the Sahara, and my voice is nothing but a wisp of sound.

"Let me get you some water."

Macklin turns and heads over to the side table to grab one of the bottles there.

When my head drops down a bit - *who knew heads were so damn heavy* - my gaze is caught by eyes the color of the most beautiful seafoam green sea glass I've ever seen, with only hints of gold and brown around the edges. They're staring into mine, and the concern and worry within them takes my breath away. I'm not ashamed to admit I have no idea which blond giant is currently making my heart skip a beat - *wait, it's beating! Oh my ghost, that's heady stuff* - or making my head spin from the emotions I can sense coming from him. But I know the serious look he's giving me is loaded full of things I can't even begin to comprehend right now.

"Here." Mack hands the water bottle to his brother but directs his instruction to me. "Let him hold this up to your mouth for you. Try to take a couple of small sips. Not too much or too fast."

We're still in a staring contest, the twin and me, as he raises the bottle to my lips and slowly tips it up. It's then I notice the tattoos covering his right hand and arm. Thad. I wouldn't have guessed he could be this gentle or this serious. The playfulness I've grown so used to is nowhere to be found. The intensity in its place is potent enough to cause my newly solid lady bits to sit up and take notice.

The moment the cool water hits my tongue, I close my eyes and release another moan as I swallow because it tastes and feels amazing. Which is the absolute craziest thing. It's water, but it could be the finest wine for all I care at this moment. I can *taste,* and I can *feel.*

"You keep making sounds like that, woman, I'm not sure I'll be able to restrain myself."

My eyes pop open. I'm relieved, and maybe just a little disappointed, to see the familiar naughty gleam has returned, along with his trademark smirk. With our gazes locked, he slowly reaches up to brush more hair out of my face. So it was him before, that first gentle touch.

Huh. Will wonders never cease.

"Let her have one more sip, and that's enough for right now," Macklin asserts, bringing my attention back to him and off the giant wall of sexy man meat in front of me. "We'll let you have more once you've acclimated a little." His calming voice soothes the restlessness inside me.

"This is the best dream ever," I whisper shakily.

I see the side of Mack's mouth quirk up and one of those damn dimples appear. That's enough to send my freshly beating heart into overdrive.

"Put that dimple away, Sexy Nerd. I'm in no condition to lick it yet."

His eyes widen, and his cheeks turn a deep shade of pink.

"Yup, definitely her." Knox chuckles, the vibrations doing pleasant things to my very sensitive, very female body.

"Woman," Thad growls out, "what are we going to do with you?"

"Oh, I can definitely think of a few things. Just have to wait for this dream body of mine to get with the program, and then we're golden."

Groans sound off around me.

"What'd I say?" I ask innocently.

"Fate."

The sound of his voice saying my name sends another surge to the girly bits. Cole may be an ass, but this body doesn't seem to give a damn. I glance to my right and see him moving closer. When he sits down in a chair across from Knox, Thad, and me, elbows hitting his knees and stretching that black shirt across his wide shoulders, I take him in. He looks tired, I realize. Those blue eyes of his have lost their angry gleam and are bracketed by worry lines that make me do a double take.

He's worried? About me? Does this dream take place in the Twilight Zone?

His clothes are dirty and tattered, and his normally pristine faux hawk is a haphazard mess. He has some dried blood above his cheekbone, and some part of me wants to go to him and soothe the pain and guilt and worry I feel emanating from him, but I tamp that down quickly. He's not interested in a truce. I know that now. *Wait, I know that? How?* Then it hits me all at once.

He was an ass. We argued. The tree. Blackness. Now I'm here. Solid. *Alive!*

"What the fuck?" I mouth the words because my voice has left me.

Our eyes lock, and I'm sure the look on my face is one of both surprise and horror. Bet that's an attractive mix. Now, normally I might be a little concerned about my appearance, but I just don't have it in me at the moment.

"You remember," he murmurs softly.

I can only nod as the night replays in my mind. It gets a little hazy toward the end, but everything up until I released the tight hold I had on my power is crystal clear. This isn't a dream. This is *real*.

I. Am. Real.

"The tree..." I let the explanation trail off as another realization hits. That hint of a memory I had of the ancient willow has me reeling. I wasn't a ghost at all. I'm something...more. Just like them. And something seriously fucked up happened a long, long time ago. I just need to remember what.

"What about the tree, Fate?" Macklin probes gently like I'm a live wire about to whip around and spark against anyone who comes too close. "Cole mentioned you couldn't move away from the tree. Do you know how or why?"

I'm still looking at Cole when I respond.

"The tree and I. We shared a connection. Our power. It was the same. It was one. I recognized it the second my power started to surge during our argument. It called to me. When I..." I pause briefly to figure out how to explain what I somehow just know, but the situation is too complicated to express or sum up with simple words. "It was like a flashback. I remember being buried, alive but severely injured. The dirt being flung on top of my broken body. I could only lay there as I was slowly covered inch by inch. Dying, I guess, is the closest word that's accurate. My power knew what it needed to do. It harnessed my life force, my soul if you will, and from that energy the willow tree grew. It housed the other half of my power until I was strong enough to take it back."

The room is still and silent. The look on Cole's face is blank, closed off once again. No emotion or hint of what he's feeling is seeping through. I'm sure he doesn't believe me. *I* barely believe me. I mean, I sound like a nutcase, but I know with every fiber of my very real body that it's true. They still haven't uttered a peep, so I continue, verbal diarrhea spewing from my mouth because I can't seem to stem the flow no matter how hard I clench my jaw.

"When the fragment of memory hit, it was like a portion of my brain was unlocked. The portion with the understanding of what happened to me. My old body was nothing more than a vessel, though I'm not sure what that means exactly. So when the tree took half of my power to sustain my life force, the other half was able to maintain itself. To wait it out in the ether until it was replenished enough to gain form again. Only, it took awhile, and even then it could only manage a fraction of its usual state. Hence...ghost girl. During our fight, my power recognized that I was finally strong enough to rejoin the two halves, but something went wrong. Something is still missing. I just don't know what. There's this..." I pause, bringing my hand up to my chest. "Heaviness that sprang to life when you guys showed up. A pull or draw or whatever the hell you want to call it. Something inside me is pushing me to get close to you. Hell, you're all lucky I wasn't alive until now, or it could've gotten awkward really damn fast. Even sitting here, in Knox's lap, it's somewhat pacified, but I still feel this tug toward the rest of you. I'm probably not making any sense."

With a deep breath, I take a look around. Cole is silently assessing me, face blank as if he doesn't have a care in the world. No real shock there. Macklin and Levi have found a seat on the sofa next to us and are staring at me with varying levels of concern and uncertainty. Like they think I'm a fruit loop short of a full bowl. One look at Thad's face and I can't tell if he's confused or constipated. Possibly both. I can't see Knox since I'm still in his lap, but I sense a distinct feeling of excitement that surprises me. His body is tense, and his grip on me has tightened, but I don't need those physical signs to tell me what I feel. It's flowing through me. *What the hell?*

We're in the study, their favored meeting room. The blinds are drawn, and the lights are dimmed. Macklin's doing, which I appreciate tremendously.

Cole shares a look with the man over my shoulder, then looks at the others. They're silently communicating in brospeak, or whatever the fuck it is, and I'll be damn if I'm left out anymore.

As much as I don't want to leave the comfort of Knox's lap, I need to show these guys that I'm okay. I'm here. And I'm strong enough to help them figure this shit storm out. Also, that I'm strong enough for anything else they may be interested in. You know. Like sex. Lots and lots of sex.

Tentatively, I try to sit up, and that's enough to set the guys into motion. Macklin and Levi both jump to their feet, and Knox's arms tighten ever so slightly around me.

"Whoa, little ghost! Where do you think you're going?" Knox murmurs close to my ear.

"I need to move. Stretch. Something. I've got a real damn body, and it needs to start understanding just who's boss around here."

His chuckle is like a zing to my overcharged libido.

"That's not helping," I pout, crossing my arms over my chest.

"What's not helping, little ghost?"

"I think we can stop with the 'little ghost' stuff now, don't you?"

"Nope," he says, adding a little extra emphasis on the 'p' before continuing, "it just feels right."

I contemplate that for a minute, realizing he's onto something. It does feel right. Like he's always called me that. Strange. When I try to grab hold of the sliver of a memory, it slips out of my grasp faster than a heavily lubed up dildo.

"Alright. Help me up if you ever want another Fate-induced orgasm."

"Just take it slow, Knox. Her muscles probably aren't ready to support her weight yet," Macklin interjects.

"Are you saying I'm fat, Sexy Nerd?"

"N-no! I didn't mean...I wasn't implying..." he trails off.

God, I love it when he blushes. It's like a whole body experience, and it's fascinating...and a total turn on.

"I'm kidding, Mack. Relax," I tell him and give him a little wink.

Knox slowly pushes me to a sitting position. I can feel his hard thighs underneath my ass and try really hard not to think about what else might be hard down there...it doesn't work. It's like the mental image I've constructed of his dick is on a mental loop in my brain. The size of him. The heat of him. And that's from a simple touch over his jeans. The real thing is probably a work of art. *I might finally get a look at Thor's hammer afterall. Hot Damn!*

"If you don't knock that off, I can't be held responsible for my actions."

The whispered warning is enough to have goosebumps breaking out across my overly sensitive skin.

"Knock what off?"

My head turns, the action putting us nose to nose. Staring into his hazel eyes, my heartbeat thump-thumps a little harder, and a distinct dampness gathers in those tingling girly bits I'm so fond of. He leans in slightly, and my newly developed breathing stutters.

"Knox! Back off," Cole orders.

I'm not sure if I should thank him or throw something at his cranky ass. My head may be swirling and my body weaker than a newborn foal, but dammit...he just fucked up my first kiss.

I turn to give him a piece of my mind with a glare in his direction but stop when I see the worry and need in those blue eyes of his.

He stands and stalks toward me. I'm not sure what to expect, so when he offers his hands to help me up, I stare at them for a moment like they're snakes ready to strike. When I lift my eyes to his, the look he gives me erases any unease I have. *This is his olive branch,* I realize. I can either slap him upside the head with it, like he did me, or I can accept his version of a tentative truce.

I place both of my hands in his, and I swear my soul sighs at the connection. There's a sense of rightness that sparks to life inside me, and I wonder if he feels it too. He slowly pulls me to my feet. Macklin was right, I discover quickly. My muscles aren't quite strong enough to support me yet, and I start to collapse. Cole's arms are suddenly around me, supporting my weight and pulling me back up and into his chest. When my feet are underneath me once again, I risk a glance at the man that is suddenly over-whelming my senses.

His hold on me is strong and sure, our bodies fitting together like they've spent years in this position and are molded to the shape of the other. He's looking at me with a longing in his eyes that seems as familiar as the feel of his heart beating in time with mine.

This. *This* is the man my subconscious remembers. The man my heart longs for and my brain insists I know better than any other. But I need to remember that this man isn't him. He's changed, and despite what my heart and body want, I need to maintain a certain distance where he's concerned.

His blue eyes seem to take in and understand the look on my face. With a resigned sigh, he slowly pulls his arms back, allowing me to stand on my own, albeit a little unsteadily.

"Thank you," he whispers, soft enough only I can hear him.

"For what?"

"For saving my life."

As I look into eyes that, for the first time, seem to hold something other than total disdain, the ice around my heart melts just a little where he's concerned.

Olive branch, I repeat to myself.

"I'd never let anything happen to you."

His beautiful blue eyes widen ever so slightly before warming with an intensity that is both alluring and terrifying. He leans in just a fraction of an inch.

If he kisses me, I'm not sure if I'll kiss him back or knee him in the balls. My multiple personalities are in a heated debate over the matter.

Just when his lips are a hair's breadth from mine, a new voice has us jolting apart.

"What's up, bitches? Did you miss me?"

Chapter 14

Fate

Ghost Girl Fact #7: Give us a real body, and we become horny bitches. Eh, maybe, hornier bitches. Sorry, not sorry.

"Who the fuck are you?" Cole growls at the apparition staring at us from the doorway while simultaneously shoving me behind him. He pulls out a wicked-looking knife faster than I can blink.

Where the fuck was he hiding that thing?

My legs still don't want to support my gravity-affected body, and I almost crumple to the floor. Luckily for me, Thad reaches out and hauls me up before that becomes a reality.

I peek out from behind Cole, still cuddled up to Thad's side. His warmth infuses me with comfort. He smells like campfire and marshmallows, smoky with a hint of sweetness, which sends my newly developed sense of smell into delirium. Telling myself to behave, I look over at our ghostly visitor.

Her thick eyebrows furrow, almost like she's confused by

the question. Her hair is short, hitting just above her jawline. I can't tell exactly what color it is since she's nothing more than a white-gray mist, but I'm guessing blonde or a really light brown. She has a septum piercing and a labret in her bottom lip. Another on the bridge of her nose. Her ears sport large gauges.

She's dressed in jean shorts with fishnet stockings underneath. Her dark, long-sleeved Slipknot shirt is hanging off one shoulder, her bra straps as much a part of her outfit as her neatly laced combat boots that hit mid-calf.

"You're joking, right?" she asks, her head tilting to the side.

"Does it look like I'm fucking joking?" Cole snarls.

Her eyes jump from Cole to Knox to Macklin and back to Cole.

"That's not funny, Cole. A hundred years is a long time, granted, but c'mon..." She risks a quick glance at the man by his side. "Knox. Help a sister out."

Knox continues to stare at her, not uttering a word.

"What do you mean, a hundred years?" Macklin steps forward, his natural curiosity already engaged.

"And how in the hell do you know our names?" Cole adds.

She rolls her eyes and huffs in frustration.

Yeah, I so feel you, girl.

"What the hell, dudes? You left me by my lonesome, and now you pretend like you don't know me. Am I on *Punk'd* right now?"

Cole's eyes narrow on our new visitor. "How about you tell us who you are and we might not force you into the afterlife...yet."

Her eyes widen, and she takes a nervous step back. The fear I see causes a twinge in my chest, and I bring my hand up like I can rub away the sensation. I somehow know her, just like I know the guys, but I'm not going to tell her that yet.

"You wouldn't," she whispers nervously. Her eyes quickly find Thad and Levi before darting back to Cole. So she knows about their powers. Interesting.

"Oh, but we would. Now start talking," he demands.

"It's me. Reggie. Assistant to the queen."

"Queen? Queen of what?"

Macklin is like a little kid with a new toy. His excitement is contagious, and I find myself propped forward, totally invested in what she's going to say next.

"Shit, Fate! The fact that you aren't nagging me about the title tells me you don't know who I am either," she mutters to herself. "What the fuck happened to you all?"

The guys all spare a glance my way. I stand up straight...or at least attempt to. These legs are as wobbly as a young kid on a bike without training wheels for the first time, but I attempt to pull up my big girl panties and be the badass I hope like hell I am.

"You sure look awfully modern for someone over a hundred years old."

It comes out a little raspy and wavering in a way that doesn't go unnoticed.

Her eyes narrow, and I feel a hint of anger firing up inside her. Her glare finds all of the guys before landing back on me.

"If they did this, whatever *this* is, to you, so help me, I'll find a way to kick all of their asses. I promise."

Cole growls and takes a step forward, the knife in his hand starting to glow. The move has Reggie's eyes widening, and she jumps back. I don't have time to question him about the seemingly magical weapon because our new ghostly friend starts to ramble.

"Fine. Fine. Um...so, I'm Reggie, the queen's assistant. But I just told you that. Fate pulled me out of the judgment line hundreds of years ago. Being her loyal advisor and trusted friend earned me some perks. Things like being able to adapt my look to the current times." She pauses and waves a quick hand at her outfit.

When no one speaks, she continues on in a voice so soft I almost don't hear her. "Do you guys remember anything?"

"Knox?"

The single word out of Cole's mouth is a question and command all in one. I can sense the power now like a zing through my already hyperactive body.

"I'm not picking up on any hints of deceit or dishonesty, so she believes what she's saying. She's also confused and really concerned. I don't feel any threat."

"Awesome. Then I'm gonna sit my shaky ass down. I'd rather not become a heap on the rug in front of our...guest. Kind of ruins the whole badass ghost girl vibe I had going for me."

"Are you okay?" Reggie starts to take a step forward until the sight of Cole and his knife blocks her path.

The concern lacing her words hits me, along with a distinct sense of protectiveness that isn't at all faked.

"Cole," I murmur. "Put the knife away. She's not here to hurt us."

His eyes land on mine, and there are so many emotions swirling in their depths, but we don't have time for that right now. She may be our best chance at getting some answers, and her comment about changing her look rings true considering I could do the same thing when I was in my spectral form.

He seems to consider his options before nodding, the knife disappearing as quickly as it came. He doesn't back away though, keeping his sentry position like the stubborn ass he is.

Watching us, Macklin's eyebrows go up. Probably as surprised as I am that Cole took an order...from me. Maybe today is the day pigs fly.

Before I can argue, Thad picks me up and walks over to the sofa. He sits, settling me on his lap. I'm tucked into his arms, and since he's roughly the size of an oversized chair, it's rather comfy. I discreetly tuck my face into the space between his neck and shoulder and inhale his smoky, campfire scent again. A small moan escapes my lips before I can stop it.

"Well, apparently some things haven't changed in a hundred years, eh, boss?"

I guess I wasn't as discreet as I thought. Warmth floods my cheeks, and I briefly wonder what's wrong with me. *Do I have a fever? Is it getting warm in here?*

Thad's chuckle rumbles beneath me.

What the hell is so funny?

Clearing my throat, I turn my head toward Reggie and see the laughter in her eyes.

"That blush looks good on you, woman," Thad whispers in my ear.

Oh my ghost! I'm blushing *right now?* I choose to ignore him, the warmth spreading down my neck and chest. I'm probably as red as a lobster. *So not attractive, Fate.* "So...um...you must know a lot about these guys and me."

She hesitates like I'm trying to lure her into a trap.

"Yes. Of course I do."

I carefully word my next question to avoid giving away the extent of just how damn clueless we are at the moment.

"What do you know about what happened a hundred years ago?"

"Not a whole lot. You went missing. The guys went into a panic trying to find you. Then they showed up at the Gateway, unconscious. I watched over them for about fifty years until one day they just vanished again, but it wasn't like there were really any threats. The doors have been sealed shut. Until today, that is."

"Wait a minute. You mean to tell me that you watched over our unconscious bodies for fifty years?" Cole grounds out.

"That's some fucking creepy ass shit," Thad mutters so low only I can hear him, causing me to giggle. That earns me a glare from Cole. I simply stick my tongue out at him, and he rolls his eyes in response, though I swear I see a slight tilt to his lips that wasn't there before.

"Well, yeah. I mean, Queen B over there would've had my ghostly ass on a pike outside the compound if anything happened to you all. Plus, we're friends, right? That's what friends do when shit hits the fan," she ends with a shrug.

A quick glance at Macklin tells me he's barely containing himself. He's practically bouncing in his seat. A grin twists my lips, and I give in to the urge to hide my face in Thad's neck again before he can notice. Thad gives me a squeeze because he knows exactly what I'm doing. My sexy nerd just loves a good Q&A session. When I finally pull my face free again, I see Mack look at Cole who just gives him a quick nod.

"What's the Gateway?"

Reggie gasps. "Wow! So it's not just me. You've forgotten the whole shebang!"

A growl comes from the direction of the two angry-looking men standing guard. Cole and Knox are both strung tighter than a trapeze highwire, vigilantly blocking the path to me. Their protectiveness is absolutely adorable...and admittedly hot as hell.

Behave. There is a time and a place, and this is neither of those. Patience, body. Patience.

"Reggie, is it?"

At her nod, I continue. "How about you pretend we know nothing and tell us everything you can."

"Ok. Well. You're Queen of the Gateway Realm. Actually, hell...let's back up a step. You're not actually a queen. But I call you queen. Or Queen Bitch. Or Queen B. Or boss. We share a mutual love of sarcasm and busting these guys' balls."

"Ooh. You're my new favorite person already. Please proceed."

That earns eye rolls from Cole and Knox.

"So...these guys are your handpicked team. Cole was first. He's your right hand man. No one gets to you unless they go through him."

Cole's heated eyes find mine, and I have to push back the whimper I feel building.

That explains a whole helluva lot, but don't let those pretty blues distract you!

"Then Knox came along. He's the Gatekeeper, weeding out the good souls from the bad before they get through your door."

It's Knox's turn to watch me from under heavy-lidded eyes that promise all sorts of things that I get to uncover later.

"Macklin is the info hub or Keeper of Records. He's your most trusted advisor."

Mack's serious expression catches me off guard until a small smile tilts his lips. I smile back. Cue blush.

Eek. He's adorable. I could just eat him up.

"The twins were the last to be added. They're the Key Masters."

"What is this? A bad *Ghostbusters* reboot?" Levi scoffs.

"Actually, they used those terms in the movie because of you guys. Your legend precedes you. Fate would've thought it was hilarious. Damn, we would've had a good chuckle over that," Reggie says, a wistful look on her face.

"Zuul was a helluva lot hotter than Knoxie boy over there," Thad jokes.

"Fuck off, Thad," Knox grumbles.

"Now, now, boys. Let the girl finish."

"As I'm guessing you've ascertained, there's more than just the professional side of your relationship with them."

"Um...care to be a little more specific?"

"She means we fuck, woman." Thad's low growl in my ear has me shivering...and not from a chill.

"I mean, you do a helluva lot of that, sure, but it's more complex too. You support each other, love each other, would die for each other. I've never seen a bond like yours in all my years." Her voice drops to a mere whisper before she adds, "Can't you feel it?"

I chance a glance at each of the guys and find five hungry looks staring back at me.

"So...we're in a...relationship? Me and all of them?"

"Yup. Lucky bitch!" she says, but I can sense she isn't jealous. Just amused.

"Well, thank God. That explains so much."

"You mean like why you're always so damn hot and bothered every time you're near us?" Levi whispers from behind me. When he sat down next to his twin, I'm not sure, but his breath trailing across the back of my neck has my shivers turning into full blown goosebumps. I squirm slightly and feel a distinct wetness between my legs. At least now I know I'm not a total nympho. Only for these guys apparently. That I can live with.

"Better stay still, sweets. Otherwise, you might find yourself in between a rock and a hard place." I look over my shoulder and see the naughty gleam in Levi's eyes. Pretty sure I know exactly which rock and which hard place he's referring to, and my lady bits pulse in full agreement.

"Seriously, guys? Can you three knock that shit off long enough for us to finish getting our answers?" Knox reprimands.

I glare at him briefly, my anger surging. I know he's right, but everything is new and feels amazing.

Can't he just let me have my moment?

"Sorry, not sorry, Knox. Can't let a fairly decent, *alive* body go to waste. Never know when life might take it away from me again."

"Oh...it's so much more than decent. Don't you agree, brother?" Levi croons as his fingers leave a trail from my shoulders, down my spine. Stopping right above the curves of my ass. Every nerve ending I have is on high alert, and that touch was *over* my clothes. Imagine if we were to remove them.

Speaking of, I take a second to glance down my body, noting for the first time that I'm in a pair of gray sweatpants that are definitely too big and a worn black t-shirt with their company logo. Also too big. I don't have on any shoes, and I'm fairly sure I'm not wearing underwear. This is definitely an interesting development.

"For sure, brother. More like hot. Smokin'. Sexy as sin," Thad purrs.

"For fuck's sake. Macklin, get Fate and take her to the

other sofa. Out of reach of those two imbeciles," Cole orders.

I pout slightly, but not for long as I see Mack walking over to me, a blush staining his cheeks. A chance to snuggle with my sexy nerd? Yes, please!

Thad grumbles as he lifts me up and places me in Mack's arms. Arms that are strong and lean and flexing underneath my body. He walks us over to the opposite sofa and sits down. It's like a game of pass-the-Fate, and I can't say I'm all that upset about it. As he gets comfortable, I snuggle into his solid chest, and his arms tighten around me.

"Whose clothes am I wearing?" I ask low enough the others don't hear as they continue their discussion.

"They're mine. Yours were in tatters, and we had to make sure you didn't have any injuries."

When he notices my arched brow, he turns a deep shade of red.

"B-but we kept you covered as much as possible once we cut your old stuff off...and it was only for a few moments. Long enough to make sure you didn't need medical attention. Then I dressed you and gave you back to Knox."

"Back to Knox?" I question quietly.

"Yeah. He's the one that found you. He had a hard time letting you go long enough to clean you up."

I ponder his words. Poor Knox. He had to be overwhelmed with all those emotions. I make a mental note to talk to him alone as soon as I have the chance.

"Ten years?" I hear Reggie ask.

"Look, you don't need to worry about her. We have it under control. How about you explain the Gateway to us now?"

Knox's statement brings us all back to the topic at hand

but earns him a narrow-eyed glare from Reggie. He's still standing, his arms crossed over his chest with Cole by his side.

"The Gateway Realm is the plane in which all spirits must pass before judgment. You all are the sole proprietors. For the last hundred years, while the place has been on lockdown in your absence, no spirits have been allowed to cross over through the realm. My guess is...there's a huge backlog."

Knox and Cole share a quick look I can't quite decipher before turning back to our ghostly guest, and I make another mental note to ask them more about that look later. My mental to-do list is getting rather long at this point. I might need to get my Keeper of Records to help me compile a hard copy. Before anyone can ask another question, a loud rumble draws everyone's eyes to me.

"What was that?" I ask quietly.

"That would be your stomach," Macklin chuckles. "You must be hungry. Let's get you some food. That should help build your energy back up."

"Mmmm...food. Bring me all the foods. Oh, and coffee. Lots of coffee. Or wine! Wine would be good."

"How about we start with something simple. Maybe a turkey sandwich and some water?"

My eyes find his, and a whole different type of appetite surges to life.

Leaning forward, I whisper in his ear, "Or maybe I could just get a taste of you."

I expect the blush that stains his cheeks a light pink. What I don't see coming is the look in his eyes that is far from innocent. It's full of longing and fire and promise. My eyes widen as he leans in to me, our lips a mere inch apart when Knox and Cole shout in unison, "Food!"

Mack jerks back and turns as red as a tomato, adjusting his glasses.

I just turn my glare on the two smirking and infuriating yet sexy-as-all-hell men who just fucked up another first kiss.

Fucking cockblocks, the lot of them.

Chapter 15

KNOX

EMPATH FACT #2: I LIKE PINK, AND I CANNOT LIE.

I slice the second turkey sandwich in half and add some cottage cheese to the plate per Macklin's orders. Gotta feed our girl.

And now we know that's exactly what she is. *Our girl*. I knew she felt like she belonged with us. Turns out, it's more than that. We belong with her too.

Putting the finishing touches on lunch, I grab bottled waters out of the fridge.

As a self-proclaimed foodie, I can appreciate a gourmet kitchen, and this one is top notch even if I don't always get the chance to put it to use. Other than throwing together lunches or grabbing some prepackaged garbage out of the pantry, it usually sits empty. Being on the road three hundred and sixty five days a year, give or take a day or two, lends itself to takeout and drive-thru burgers. I'd love to try out the new, state of the art appliances that were recently installed by the current owner. White cabinets with elaborate crown molding line two of the walls with an eat-in dining area nestled into a cove on the far side of the room with a circular table and six chairs. Yes, if I had the time, I could really whip up some delicious home-cooked meals for us in here.

"Huh. Do we have some place we call home?" I think aloud. Wondering if home-cooked meals maybe used to be a thing for us.

Great. More questions for Reggie.

Picking up both plates, I carry them back to the study. The curtains have been opened, letting more light through, though that does nothing to dispel the tension in the air. It's so thick, I feel as though I could reach out and slice it with the knife I just used.

"Here you go, little ghost."

"Thank you, Knox."

The touch of her fingers against mine as the plate passes between us shoots an instant spark through my body. For the first time, I take her in and notice things about her that weren't visible in her previous state. Her eyes are a strange shade of silvery gray I've never seen before. They stand out against the darkness of her hair, which is a deep, rich brown. Her full lips are an enticing shade of pink. But it's her aura that's the most surprising. It's a shiny silver at the core, lightening as it expands out around her. I've never seen anything like it. Silver indicates a strong connection to the spirit realm itself, including the ability to communicate with spirits and traverse other realms. The very edge has a hazy rim of color that shifts faster than I can blink. Though at the moment, it has settled into a soft shade of yellow. She's happy, and damn, that brings a big smile to my face.

Before I can make a complete fool of myself, I set her water bottle on the table in front of her and head over to the other sofa with my own plate.

"What? You didn't make me one?" snarks Thad.

"Make your own, you lazy bastard."

He simply laughs in response.

Crazy dipshit!

The twins and Mack are scattered on the sofas, lounging like they don't have a care in the world, but I can sense differently. Everyone is coiled tight. Unanswered questions lingering out there - about who we are and what happened to us.

Cole paces in front of the bay window, not acknowledging anyone. His confusion and anger and sadness are like a battering ram against my subconscious. I push it aside for now, my own emotions already overwhelming me.

"Where did Reggie go?" I ask around a mouthful of deliciousness.

Levi takes a drink of whatever dark liquor he poured into the glass in his hand before responding, "She went to check on the Gateway. Something about wanting to make sure, now that the doors were unsealed, that the chamber wasn't flooded with misfits. Whatever that means."

A soft moan echoes through the room, and I glance at Fate. Her eyes are closed while she chews. She swallows and takes another bite, completely unaware that she's captured the attention of every male in here. It shouldn't be nearly as erotic as it sounds. She's only eating for Christ's sake. Her eyes pop open, and she catches us all staring, but that doesn't stop her from taking another large bite.

"What?" she asks innocently, her mouth almost overflowing with food.

On anyone else, the look would be borderline disgusting, but with her, it's somehow both adorable and sexy at the same time.

"You have no idea, do you, little ghost?"

Her cheeks pinken slightly, and the sight makes me

wonder what other parts of her would look like covered in that particular shade.

"What? It's good. Like...really good. You have no idea. My taste buds thank you."

"I'd rather *you* thank me later," I say with a wink. Her blush deepens.

"Spirits save me!" comes a voice from behind, damn near giving me a heart attack.

My plate almost tips off my lap before I manage to grab it and save my sandwich.

"What is it, Reggie?" Macklin asks, his sudden concern slamming into me and mixing with my already heightened sensitivities.

"Old Man Summers is back, making his demands again. I was kind of hoping the old coot would be one of the unlucky ones trapped in the ether. No such luck."

The pout on her face is enough to tell me how she feels about that. She perches her hazy form on the arm of the sofa, the bookshelves clearly visible through her body.

"So the spirits have returned to the Gateway?" Macklin muses.

"Not many, but word is starting to spread."

I take my last couple of bites, wishing I'd grabbed some cottage cheese for myself, my mind already mentally inspecting the cabinets for my next snack while I chew and consider what Reggie just said.

"That's a good thing, right?" I ask around the mouthful of food.

Before she has a chance to answer, the doorbell rings.

Not one of my brothers makes a move to answer it. Rolling my eyes, I place my plate on the side table and get up to answer the damn thing myself. Lazy bastards, all of them!

The bell rings again just before I open the door. Mandy is standing on the porch in a pair of high-waisted jeans and white button-down cropped shirt that's tied just under her breasts and unbuttoned enough for me to be worried about some form of wardrobe malfunction. With sky high heels on, she's damn near my height.

The aura surrounding her is a light green with an orange center. She's selfish and materialistic with a self-indulgent streak a mile wide. Doesn't take empath skills to figure any of that out. Her boobs are enough to give most of that away.

"Hiya there, Knox. I thought I'd drop by to make sure you all were settling in okay and ask if there was anything you need help with?"

She pushes her chest out and starts twirling her blonde hair around her finger. At one point in time, I may have considered what she is not so subtly hinting at. Now, it doesn't even register on my attention-worthy meter.

"Thanks, Mandy, but I think we've got everything under control."

"That's great! Then I can just make you guys dinner. I've brought everything I need with me," she says as she grabs the bags by her feet and pushes her way through the door.

"Knox, who was at the..." Cole begins, closing the study door slightly behind him, but he's cut off by our new guest.

"Cole. Hey! I was just telling Knox that I wanted to stop by to see if there is anything I could help y'all with, but he says you're all set. I did bring stuff to make dinner though. Hungry?" she asks, her eyes roaming over us both in blatant invitation.

"Thanks, Mandy, for checking on us, but we're pretty busy at the moment," Cole responds in a low voice.

"Nonsense. You boys need to eat, and I brought plenty of food."

She strides past Cole, down the hall into the kitchen. Sharing a panicked glance, Cole and I quickly follow to find her already unloading her bags onto the granite counter.

A home-cooked meal would be nice, but there's no way Mandy will be the one to cook it. She's gotta go...*now*.

I walk to the front of the large island that takes up a majority of the space, and Cole follows hot on my heels.

"Mandy, really, we were just on our way out to do some research. Rain check?" I practically beg.

"Don't worry, silly. You go do your research, and I'll just get this prepped and cooked, so it's ready for when you get back. Hope you boys like lasagna," she chirps, changing course and heading right for me. "Of course, we could always start with dessert."

I love lasagna...and dessert, but no way in hell am I telling her that, especially not when her breasts are like two heat-seeking missiles aimed directly at my chest. She stops with less than a foot between our bodies. Her fingertips start to trail back and forth along my waistline, pausing only long enough to fumble with the button on my jeans.

My dick refuses to rise to the bait.

Just as I'm about ready to step back, Fate's voice joins us from the doorway.

"Now, boys, you didn't tell me you were expecting company."

I swear I hear a muffled "Uh oh" come from directly behind her, but I don't have time to contemplate that because my eyes are locked on our little ghost. She looks stronger than she has all day, with a kind of fire in her eyes that I haven't seen before, literally. I can see a flame reflected in them.

Even in oversized sweats and a t-shirt three sizes too big, she looks amazing...and pissed.

"Why don't you introduce me to your...guest," she quips.

By this point, she's made her way into the kitchen, the whole time glaring daggers at the blonde who's still standing with her hand nestled awfully close to my cock. As Fate rounds the opposite side of the island, her fingers trail across the surface, leaving sparks in their wake. Those fiery eyes leave Mandy only long enough to send me a warning look. One that very clearly says, if I don't remove Mandy's hand, Fate will.

Sparing a glance at Cole, who admittedly looks more unsure than I've ever seen him before, I swallow nervously before taking a big step back and gently removing Mandy's wandering fingers. I briefly wonder if she noticed the power emanating from Fate, but she seems oblivious.

Mandy isn't looking at me though. Her eyes are locked onto Fate with a challenging gleam in them, obviously unaware of the danger, as Fate stops in front of the stove.

"Hi! I'm Mandy Caldwell. The agent who helped the guys get this rental," Mandy says, walking up to Fate and holding out her hand.

Fate ignores it.

Not the least bit affected by Fate's rudeness, Mandy rambles on. "I was just in the neighborhood and thought maybe they could use a home-cooked meal." She points at the food she's unloaded onto the counter. I silently pray for divine intervention. That's what we're all going to need to get out of this unscathed.

"By all means, just make yourself at home," Fate snarks. "I'm Fate, by the way."

Cole's eyes catch mine again, and a sense of mutual fear and panic floods the room.

"Oh...Macklin, Thad, Levi," Fate sing-songs loudly. "Your *friend* is here to make you dinner. You should really come say hello."

If those boys are smart, they'll hear the underlying danger in that request.

Of course, the numbnuts miss it.

Footsteps and grumbling echo through the foyer. Reggie suddenly appears next to Fate, the counter and cabinets wavering through the haze of her ghostly body, takes one look at our former real estate agent, and chuckles. It's not a happy sound either - more like a *shit's-about-to-hit-the-fan* kind of sound. That doesn't bode well.

When Macklin reaches the doorway, he stops abruptly. The twins, talking amongst themselves instead of paying attention, run into Mack's back causing him to stumble almost comically into the kitchen. Thad and Levi use that distraction to finally take in the room and immediately shoot worried looks at Cole and me.

"Hey, Mack! How's the research coming along?" Mandy simpers before turning to the twins. "Hiya, big guys."

I didn't think it was possible, but Fate's eyes narrow even more. That's when I notice she's standing precariously close to the knives. We're entering very dangerous territory here, folks.

"Uh...hey, Mandy. How are you?" Macklin mumbles.

"Oh, I think I'm doing much better now, Mack," she titters.

From the corner of my eye, I see Reggie whispering in Fate's ear, and I'm not sure if she's trying to calm the situation or incite violence. I could see it going either way. Luckily, Mandy seems to be oblivious to her presence - as the living tend to be.

The twins are uncharacteristically silent. For once, they're the smart ones here.

"So, Fate, how do you know these boys?" Mandy asks.

The kitchen has become a cesspool of emotions. Anger, jealousy, fear, even arousal - *that has to be the twins*. It's all swirling through the room, and I have to take a few deep breaths to keep myself steady. Cole shoots me a look, making sure I'm holding up against the onslaught. I nod to let him know I'm okay for now.

Fate's arms are crossed over her chest, her fingers drumming at a concerning pace. She's pissed and feeling extremely possessive. There's also a slight sense of irrationality, but I would never tell her that to her face. Nope. Not if I want to keep breathing...or keep my dick intact.

"Hmm...you can say we go *way* back," Fate responds simply.

Mandy seems to stand up straighter, rising to the challenge in the air, and I know the next thing out of her mouth is going to set all of this tension ablaze.

"An old friend. That's so sweet." Mandy pauses, and I wait for whatever disaster is about to leave her mouth. I'm not left wondering long. "Oh, Cole, darling, remember the *amazing* time we had at that small restaurant in town a couple nights ago? Maybe the guys can take Fate there. I'm sure she'd enjoy it."

Cole looks like he's been caught in the crosshairs, and his eyes lock on mine, both of us looking for a way out of this train wreck.

Fate grins. I'd be relieved if that grin wasn't completely sinister.

"It's so cute you think you can get rid of me that easily. As if you actually stand a chance. It's the boobs, right?" Fate ponders, finger tapping her chin as if she's in serious thought. "I mean, they *are* impossible to miss. I'll give you that. But those jeans gotta go."

Mandy just stands there, mouth wide open, stammering while she tries to think of a comeback. Fate doesn't give her the opportunity.

"Of course, I'm pretty sure the boys prefer something a little more au naturel."

We all watch in rapt fascination as Fate brings both hands up to her own tits, giving them a nice squeeze. Pretty sure I'm not the only one that has to adjust my junk. We all know she's bare underneath that shirt.

"Who the hell do you think you are?" Mandy sputters. "You honestly think you're better than me, standing there looking like you just rolled out of bed in those ratty gray sweats? Why would they want trash when they could have this?" She waves her hand up and down her body.

"Oh, sweetheart, I *know* I'm better than you. That's not even a question," Fate snarls. "You're no better than a blow-up doll. One poke and you'd deflate faster than the Goodyear blimp."

"You bitch!" Mandy shouts before lunging for Fate.

Before I can so much as twitch, Levi grabs Mandy from behind, halting her attack. The second Fate registers the touch, the atmosphere in the room changes, becoming heavier. Darker. Malicious.

Lights start to flicker, and the temperature in the room becomes frigid.

Levi seems to recognize his mistake a second too late and immediately releases Mandy, stepping back with his hands in the air.

"What the hell is happening?" Mandy asks nervously, her words coming out around a puff of air visible in the cold. She wraps her arms around herself and nervously looks around the room. Pretty sure I could feel her fear wafting off her even if I wasn't an empath.

"Mandy, maybe you should leav..." Macklin trails off as his eyes widen in horror.

My eyes find the source of his shock and quickly do a double take at the same time registering Fate's complete fury.

The knives inside the block slowly pull themselves free, hovering briefly in midair before steadily turning their tips toward Mandy.

Movement to my left catches my attention. The silverware drawer slowly opens, the forks and butter knives all ascending into the air.

I risk a glance at Fate, and the fun-loving, sarcastic girl we've all become entranced with is gone. In her place is a powerful, angry woman.

And my dick definitely takes notice.

"Uh oh," Fate whispers menacingly, the sound having a melodious echo to it. "Better run."

With one glance at the floating kitchen utensils, Mandy looks like she's ready to hyperventilate. She rushes past Levi and Thad, tears pouring from her eyes. She stumbles into the wall as she turns the corner but quickly rights herself and runs to the front door, throwing it open and hurrying out to her car.

We all stand, unmoving. A car starts, its tires peeling down the gravel drive. Those are the only sounds disrupting the utter silence of the room. With Mandy gone, the lights stop flickering, and the temperature slowly returns to normal.

"Hmm...guess she didn't want to make dinner after all. Such a shame," Fate tsks sarcastically.

"Butter knives? Really, boss?"

"It was effective, wasn't it?" Fate mutters. "That shit wasn't easy, you know. Cut a ghost girl some slack as she relearns everything, yeah?"

"Knox explained a few things while you were cuddled up with Macklin. I can't believe you've spent the last ten years as a ghost. Just wait until you get the hang of things again. We're going to have so much fun!" Reggie claps excitedly. "Damn, I've missed you!"

"I honestly expected to have to work a little harder to scare her off. That was kind of disappointing," she pouts.

"Maybe she has a fear of pointy objects?' Reggie retorts.

Fate smirks. "If she didn't before, she does now."

The two burst into laughter like a couple of loons. The rest of us just stand around in shock, not one of us having so much as twitched.

"Oh, c'mon, guys. Lighten up a little, would ya? I wouldn't have actually hurt her. At least, not a lot." Fate pauses, and then turns to us with a scowl. "But you all definitely have some explaining to do. Just how much time did you spend with that Barbie wannabe?"

"Um...Fate?" I murmur softly.

"Yes, Knox?" She blinks her innocent gray eyes up at me, and the distinct flame I saw earlier is gone.

"Think you can put all the sharp things away now?"

She looks around, startled for a second, before snapping her fingers. Knives and forks all slowly make their way back to their homes.

Looking a little chagrined, she mutters, "Oops."

Just like that our little ghost is back, and as she turns to us, the look on her face says it all. We're in deep shit.

A paddle suddenly appears in her hand. Out. Of. Nowhere. Even she seems momentarily surprised but recovers quickly.

"So...which one of you wants to explain yourself first?" she asks with a wicked glint in her eye, tapping her other hand with the paddle - the sound echoing through the space.

Macklin blushes. Cole pales. Thad and Levi quickly raise their hands. I simply smirk and give her a wink. I want to see someone's skin turn pink, but it sure as hell won't be mine.

Chapter 16

Macklin

Techie Fact #3: It's always the quiet ones you should watch out for.

"*How* ow is she?" Cole asks, seemingly calm. He's seated at the kitchen table, with an honest to god newspaper in his hands, which crinkles when his grip tightens on it. That's a telltale sign his nerves are getting to him. Bet he cracked his phone screen again, hence the reason he's going it old school.

"She's still sleeping. Peacefully." Walking up to the coffee pot, I pour myself a cup. I'm tired, and just feel off. My hand rubs my chest, like it can ease the weird sensation that's been forming there.

Knox is at the stove cooking breakfast, making the whole house smell amazing. There's a small radio on the counter playing some current pop tune, and he's humming along as he pops a bite of something in his mouth before dumping the rest into what looks like an omelet.

"How long is she going to sleep? That can't be normal, right?" Cole grumbles from behind the paper.

"The woman just rose from the dead less than forty-eight hours ago, found out she's tied to the lot of us, and had a confrontation with Mandy. All in the same day. Cut her some slack, mate."

"When the fuck did you become Australian?"

Knox just chuckles, shooting me a look. "Blame the Keeper of Records. He told me words."

"Fuck's sake, Mack. Didn't I tell you not to give that dumbass useless facts?"

I grunt, which earns me looks from both of them. I'm not normally a grunter. That's Cole's thing. But I'm suddenly tired of being the one responsible for keeping the peace between these crazy...fuckers.

Yeah. Crazy fuckers.

"What the hell is wrong with you?" Cole demands. Not with his power. With his dad voice. That just grates even more.

"What? Can't a guy grunt every now and then? You sure do a hell of a lot of that."

Cole's eyes narrow, and he sets the paper down.

Knox places the omelet in front of Cole, wiping his hands on the apron he's wearing, and gives me a look. "Since when do you cuss?"

"Sorry, *Mom*," I mock, eyeing the apron and the hands he's just placed on his hips. "Am I not allowed to cuss? Need I remind both of you that I'm an adult and can do whatever the hell I damn well please? Christ. Now I know what it's like to be a teenager." I'm working up some righteous, though highly irrational anger, and stalk over to the cabinet with my cup in hand, grab the bottle of irish cream off the shelf, and add a healthy dollop to my coffee mug. I'm not normally a drinker, but this isn't a normal kind of morning either.

Take that, shitheads!

"Uh oh. The resident nerd is drinking at seven in the

morning. Pigs must be flying," Thad snarks, taking a seat at the table. I didn't even hear him come in.

What is wrong with me?

Levi chuckles before adding, "Has hell frozen over? Sure would make our jobs a damn bit more difficult."

Glaring at the lot of them, I grab a donut from the counter and make my way to the table. Cole is still eyeing me while he eats his omelet, and Knox is throwing together food for the twins who are bouncing clichés back and forth like they're the funniest things they've ever heard.

Dumbasses.

Frustration hits me. Along with a slew of other emotions. I'm not normally the emotional one. I deal in facts. Facts and logic. All of these feelings must be short-circuiting my brain.

"Seriously. What is going on with you?" Cole demands with a little of his power this time.

"I..." Trailing off, I try to come up with an explanation, but I don't have one. "I honestly have no idea. Does anyone else feel...off?"

They look around at each other before their eyes all fall on me.

Surprisingly, it isn't Cole or Knox that respond. It's Thad.

"Yeah, I feel it too, bro. Like something in my chest is fighting to break free."

"Same here," Levi agrees.

"I've felt it since the very first day," Knox adds, setting new plates in front of the twins, with a bagel in his hand for himself.

Cole just stares at all of us like we're a few numbers shy of a full equation.

"Oh, come on, boss. Even you have to admit you feel something," Levi coaxes.

Cole takes a quick drink of his coffee before setting his cup down a little harder than necessary.

"Fine. I feel it too. It's the same feeling I've had for damn near ten years, except it's stronger now."

"So, let's put together the facts, shall we?" This is what I do best, putting the details together to get a glimpse at the full picture. Something inside me starts to settle with the familiarity of the action.

"Fuck, here we go," Thad grumbles around a mouthful of food.

My glare is enough to have him muttering out, "Sorry, bro."

Yes. The sky must be falling if Thad is apologizing. Oh hell, now I'm spouting clichés.

"It's safe to say Fate is the cause of these feelings. We know that before this all happened, she was an important part of our lives. *All* of our lives. How do we feel about that? Aside from the twins, sharing hasn't really been a thing for any of us."

Silence. *Bingo! Score one for the resident nerd, or should I say* sexy *nerd?*

"For the record, she makes me feel things I'm not sure I've ever felt before. Or at least not that I can remember. I've...uh...dammit, I'm just going to say it. I haven't been with anyone since I woke up in New York," I blurt out.

Their stunned faces lock onto me with looks of disbelief and wonder like I'm some mystical creature they didn't believe existed. Not sure why they're surprised. Even Levi noted they've never seen me with anyone. It just never felt...right.

"You mean to tell me," Thad begins, pointing his finger at me like he's having a hard time comprehending the words that are leaving his mouth, "you haven't had sex in over fifty years?"

"No fucking way. I call bullshit," Levi retorts.

"Believe whatever you want. There was just never anyone that excited me enough...if you know what I mean. And in reality, it's been one hundred years." *Fuck. I'm blushing again.*

"No, Mack. What *do* you mean?" Knox asks, a smirk on his face.

Bastard's going to make me say it!

"Fine. You want me to say it? I'll say it. I couldn't get it up for anyone. I tried over the years, but when things would get hot and heavy, it was like my dick just shut down. Now it makes sense why! It wanted her. *Only* her. At least I can proudly say that I never strayed. I stayed true to her without even knowing she existed. Can you all say the same?"

Another round of silence greets my statement, and it's my turn to throw a smug look around the table. "Now that we've found her again, I can definitely say that everything is back in working order. But there are five of us, and I know I'm not the only one that wants her or that she wants in return."

Cole shifts slightly in his chair. The man doesn't fidget. Ever.

"Even you, Cole," I say softly.

There's a look of hope in his eyes when they meet mine, and I nod in reassurance.

Cole shifts his gaze around the table. "I'm assuming all of us are interested?"

He receives four nods in confirmation.

"And we're all okay...sharing her?" he asks, a little less certain.

I'm not sure what the past looked like for all of us. If we

were confident in our relationship and easily shared ourselves, our *time*, with her, or if we had some sort of schedule, but something tells me things aren't going to be quite so easy this time.

"I'll take her any way I can get her," Knox confirms. "If that means I have to share her with my brothers, the men I trust above all others, then that's fine with me."

The twins respond in unison, "Agreed!"

"Considering the situation and all of the unknowns still lingering out there, I'm honestly a little relieved to have you all at her back. Between all of us, we can better watch out and care for her. Let's not forget that something happened to her one hundred years ago. There's a very real possibility that whatever that was, that threat could still be out there."

The level of seriousness at the table is honestly astounding. I'm not sure I can remember a time when all five of us had a conversation where someone, namely one of the twins, wasn't throwing snark at every opportunity.

"Then it's settled. We'll take things at her pace, obviously, but anything goes." Knox stands, clearing the plates from the table.

"I'm not sure I'd say *anything* goes," Cole mutters, his eyebrows furrowed.

"Oh, come on, so you might see my dick on occasion. There are worse things, right?"

"Knox, your dick isn't high on my list of things to see."

"I don't know. It *is* pretty impressive."

"Not more impressive than mine," Thad challenges.

"Or mine," Levi quips.

"That's not fair. Yours are probably identical, taint biscuits."

Thad eyes me a moment. "What about you, Mack? Want in on this challenge?"

I simply smirk in response. They forget...I know *everything*. Height, weight, shoe size...and other personal stats. As long as it's factual and somewhat static, it's safe to bet it's in my brain.

Thad and Levi's brows raise in surprise.

Knox just chuckles. "Dammit. The nerd has us all beat. I can tell. I'm not betting against him."

The twins share a look, doing that weird twin speak they always do that annoys Cole and Knox. When they look back at me, it's clear they think they've got one up on me. Little do they know.

"Alright then, let's see it. We're confident we've got you beat."

"You're all fucking *taint biscuits*," Cole mutters, rolling his eyes, clearly exasperated with the lot of us. "What? Are you going to whip out a tape measure and verify?"

"Good idea. I'll go grab one from the equipment room," Knox states before running off down the hall.

"Fuck's sake. I live with a bunch of imbeciles," Cole gripes, but there's a distinct undercurrent of amusement in his tone.

Knox comes running back in. "Alright, boys. Let's see what you've got. Wait, what are we betting?"

The twins walk over, Thad to my left and Levi coming up next to him. Since it's early, we're all in jogging shorts or sweats, making this task easy peasy.

"Winner's choice. No rules, no holds barred. You play, you pay," I suggest.

"Mack, you're really going through with this shit show?" Cole asks.

"Maybe it's time I live a little."

For the first time in years, I see a hint of a smile tilt his lips. "Fate really has twisted us right the fuck up, hasn't she?"

"Yup," Knox says, popping the 'p.' "And we all love it. Now stop stalling and drop 'em."

Grabbing the waistband of my shorts, I push the material down to my knees, hearing the twins mimicking the movement beside me.

The room is silent for a moment before Thad blurts out, "Bro, where the fuck have you been hiding that thing?"

The room bursts into laughter, and I start plotting my winnings. Sometimes it's damn good to be the nerd.

Chapter 17

THAD

TWIN FACT #2: WE MAY NOT EXPERIENCE EACH OTHER'S EMOTIONS, BUT I CAN STILL READ YOUR THOUGHTS, WANKSTAIN.

*I*f someone asked me to define 'sexy as fuck,' I'd show them a picture of Fate.

Even as she sits in the antique settee she had the guys haul down from the attic, curled up with her long, slim legs tucked under her, I can't help but stare. Her silky hair is up in a messy bun. Wearing a simple white tank and short shorts, her feet are bare. She's the hottest fucking thing I've ever seen.

It's been three days since the woman literally rose from the dead. Which, by the way, has me feeling so many fucked up emotions I can't even begin to explain them all.

In those moments where I thought that we'd lost her for good, losing my shit doesn't even come close to describing it. I was just damned glad we found her.

Now I get to keep her.

But we have to help her get back to her normally sassy self first.

It killed me to see the feisty, playful woman become quiet and withdrawn after the incident with that bitch Mandy. Knox said she was overwhelmed, or some shit like that, but I think she's unsure. Of us. Can't say I'd blame her. The girl's been alone for ten years, and then we show up, and it's been one clusterfuck of a whirlwind after another.

She chose a bedroom for herself that first night and locked herself away from all of us. We didn't see her for over eighteen hours. Macklin said she needed sleep, as her body was unused to expending so much energy, and I guess that makes sense. Doesn't mean I didn't itch to check on her every few minutes though. Levi kept saying I was acting worse than a mother hen.

Huh. That would be a first.

I'm usually the love 'em and leave 'em sort. Not the spend-the-night-cuddling, talk-about-our-emotions sort, but she makes me want things I've never even considered before. The woman is under my skin. No doubt about it.

Instead of joining us in the study once she surfaced from her room, she's been lounging in the overly feminine sitting room across the foyer, the one us guys avoid like the plague. With its antique tables lined with doilies — seriously, who uses fucking doilies anymore — an abundance of ridiculous pillows, and its fragile-looking chairs that couldn't hold a lap dog let alone a real man, it's like inviting a bull into a china shop. In other words, Levi and I should definitely steer clear.

From my spot on the leather sofa in the study, if I lean over far enough, I can see her sitting in her favorite seat. Having her in my line of sight comforts me. Yeah, Levi's giving me shit for that too.

What the fuck, right?

I find myself leaning against the door jamb, just

watching her, because spying on her from the other room wasn't enough. Another first. I act. I don't observe. I think she fucked with my DNA or something because I'm not sure I even recognize myself right now.

She fiddles with the small device in her hand, mumbling and grumbling the whole time. Macklin decided, in his infinite wisdom, that she needed a cell phone, so we can all get a hold of her when we need to. Yeah. No problem at all.

Dumbass!

Once she figured out how to turn the damn thing on, he had to explain the basics to her. That was an interesting conversation. Oh, sure, she's seen plenty of people using the devices, but when it came down to actually using one herself, without her powers, let's just say that it was pretty damn hilarious. It's kind of like checking out that Pincushion, or Pintacular, or whatever the hell it's called website. Sure, they give you pictures and detailed instructions, but the end result isn't always the gorgeous creation they achieved. More like an epic fail. Sometimes monkey see, but monkey can't do. Now that she's figured out texting and emojis, we're all inundated day and night. I mean, a guy can only take so many eggplant emojis before he's ready to show her the real thing, right?

As she bites her lower lip, intent on whatever it is she's doing, softly cursing every few seconds, my dick takes notice and insists it should be us biting that pouty pink bit of sweetness. My hand drops down to give our pal a little more room. It's getting a little restricted in there.

"Hey, woman. That phone still causing you grief?"

Any other person might startle at my sudden appearance, but not her. Our girl doesn't even so much as flinch.

"This game is ridiculous. How am I supposed to move all

of these little things across the screen when it's so damn small?"

"What game are you playing?" I ask as I enter the room and try not to cringe. The carpet is a pale, pale pink. The wallpaper is cream with itty bitty roses scattered all over it. In one word...hideous. No, I take that back. Two words...fucking hideous.

"It's something called *Candy Crush*," she mutters, face still glued to her phone.

And there goes my mind. Right into the gutter.

"I have something that can crush your candy, woman."

That makes her pause and look up at me out of the corner of her eye. A smirk appears, and I'll be damned if that isn't a welcome sight.

"You think you've got moves, do you? Think you can spread my jam?"

"Oh hell yeah. I can definitely fill up your soda."

"Gonna release my honey?"

"You know it, girl. I'll melt your ice so fast you won't know what happened."

"Are you two really flirting with *Candy Crush* innuendos right now?" my wankstain of a brother interrupts.

Fate just chuckles. It's one of the sexiest damn sounds ever.

"Hey there, Levi."

"Hi there, sweets. Hmm...guess that kinda fits with the *Candy Crush* theme, right? How are you feeling today?"

"Almost normal..." She pauses, tapping her chin with her index finger. "At least I think. Hard to know what normal is when I haven't been normal for at least...oh...something like a hundred years give or take."

She looks sad again, and the sight does funny things inside my chest. Levi and I share a look, one that requires no words because we can have entire conversations with our eyes alone.

"Your powers still giving you shit, babe?" I ask, walking over and crouching down in front of the settee. No way in hell will I sit my gigantic ass on it. It'd probably crumble to the ground.

My hand finds her calf, and my fingers begin absently rubbing circles lazily along her soft skin. She peers up at me, a sheepish look on her face.

"Maybe. I can't figure out what's wrong. Macklin's been researching potential causes, but so far no luck. Reggie hasn't been much help either."

"We'll work it out. Don't you worry that pretty little head of yours."

"You shatter a glass with a look or accidentally cause a vase to fly across the room all by itself, and it's like you've got the plague or something. Just what I didn't need - more things for Cole to grumble at me for," she huffs. "I swear. I don't know how I survived his moods the first time around without killing him."

"Don't worry about him," my twin says, walking into the room and making it feel ten times smaller than it did before. "We all know that you're feeling off right now, and damned well you should, all things considered. But I think I may have just what you need to take your mind off of it."

Her eyes leave mine and focus on my brother.

"Oh! Now I'm intrigued. Do tell," she says, sitting up a little straighter.

"Thad and I just got hired to clear a house about an hour south of here. Wanna tag along and see us in all our glory?"

Her eyes light up like we just offered her a million dollars. Or maybe coffee. Yeah, definitely coffee.

"Think Cole and Knox will let me go?"

"Who's the boss around here?" I challenge with a smirk, knowing just how to get her fired up.

The feistiness that's been missing the last few days once again sparks in her eyes. "That would be me," she declares with a confidence I find sexy as fuck.

"Hell yes, you are," Levi croons. "Don't you let them forget it. Go grab the boots Knox bought you and throw on a pair of jeans too. Not sure what shape this place is going to be in."

"Thanks, guys." She pauses, placing a delicate hand on my bearded chin, the touch sending the good kind of electricity straight to my junk. "I appreciate you so fucking much right now."

She leans forward and plants a soft kiss on my cheek before standing and doing the same to Levi. Still crouched in front of the settee, I watch her fine ass sway as she damn near skips out of the room. When she's out of sight, I look up at my twin and see him enjoying the same view.

"Bro, you sure it's a good idea to bring her along?"

"It's time she sees what we're about, Thad. Keeping her cooped up in this place isn't doing her any good. Those jackasses need to pull their heads out of their asses and realize that."

"Don't get me wrong, I agree one hundred fucking percent. Their excessive coddling is doing nothing but alienating her," I respond, pausing long enough to put my thoughts together. "Just want to make sure we know what we're getting ourselves into here."

"It'll be fine, brother. She needs to learn about us. About our abilities. Especially now that we don't have to worry about our powers hurting her. The more she knows, the better off we all are."

"You're right. Not sure why I'm so worried about it."

"Because you've become a regular fucking prick, that's why."

"Shut the fuck up, asshole!"

His laughter dispels my unease. He's right. It's time to show our girl what we can do. I trust my brother's judgment more than I trust my own most of the time. He's just as invested in Fate's well-being as I am. He would never jeopardize that.

"You get all of our stuff loaded up?" I ask as I stand and head out of the god awful room.

"Yeah. It's all in the SUV. Not sure if we'll even need it based on the conversation I had with the client, but better safe than sorry."

Cole walks out from the kitchen followed by Knox.

"You guys heading out to a call?" Cole probes.

"Yup. It's just south of here. Couple says their young daughter keeps talking to her 'imaginary friend,' and it has them freaking the fuck out," Levi responds.

"You need some back up?" Knox asks around a mouthful of pear. The dude is always fucking eating. How he manages to stay fit is another of life's great mysteries.

Levi and I share another look before I respond simply, "Nope. We're all good, bro."

Cole's eyes narrow slightly. "What aren't you telling us?"

"No idea what you're talking about, man," Levi mutters.

"You two are acting shifty as fuck, which usually means you're up to something, and that never bodes well for us."

"I don't know what the hell is up your ass," I reply. "We go on calls without backup all the time."

Just as Cole gets ready to open his mouth to command we tell him what the fuck we're up to, I see movement on the stairs.

My eyes lock onto her like a magnet to metal.

Her hair is falling loosely down her back, making my fingers itch to touch the silky waves. She covered the white tank with the cropped leather jacket I told Knox to add to the pile of shit he was buying. Her dark jeans look well-worn even though they're brand new, with holes on her thighs and across one knee, showing hints of skin. Her black combat boots are laced up with hot pink laces and make her look more badass than I thought possible.

Her eyes find mine, and the smile I see there tells me she knows exactly how I'm feeling right now. Here's a hint...it's not saintly.

"Where the fuck do you think you're going?" Cole demands.

The smile vanishes, and her eyes narrow.

"I'll go wherever I damn well please. You're not my daddy, Cole."

She walks down the stairs, every male eye glued to each of her steps. Her shoulders are straight, and there's a fire in her eyes that I would be leery of if I were Cole. That's not a figure of speech either. There's a hint of literal flames in her gorgeous gray eyes. Last time we saw that, Mandy almost got shish kabobbed by a bunch of butter knives.

As she reaches the last step, the candles on the table in the foyer all flare brightly. The flames are brighter than they should be naturally and seem to be growing larger by the second. Fate's eyes widen in panic, and the flames flare higher.

Levi reaches out and wraps his large hand around her smaller one. She eyes the connection, and, as if that was all she needed, the flames are immediately extinguished - both the literal and the figurative ones.

"That's exactly what I'm fucking talking about. You can't

control your powers and shouldn't be leaving the house yet," Cole snaps.

"How about you back the fuck off, Cole," Levi barks, shocking the hell out of Cole and Knox. Levi is usually the mellow to my harsh. The calm to my storm. The sun to my rain. For him to go against our leader shows just how much Fate is affecting him too. "That's exactly why I asked Fate to come with us. To get her out of this house so she can blow off some steam. Better to aim it at some ghosts rather than your cranky ass."

Fate's eyes tear up, and one fat drop spills over, rolling down her cheek. She looks so damn sad that I just want to hug the shit out of her. She gasps, bringing a finger from her free hand up to touch the wetness.

"What is it, babe?" I murmur softly, closing the distance between us and wrapping one large hand behind her neck, my thumb brushing another tear from her cheek. Her hand is still in my brother's, and something about the three-way connection just feels right somewhere deep inside my soul.

She looks up at me, another tear spilling free. "Ghosts can't cry. I haven't shed a tear in...God...I don't even know how long."

"You're alive now, babe. You're going to feel all the feels, and, as much as it pains me to say it, crying is part of that. But just for future reference, tears are more Knox's thing."

That brings a small smile to her face.

"But that's not what's really bothering you. Talk to me."

The smile falls, and her eyes well up again. Shit! Why'd I have to go and open my big, dumb mouth?

"What's wrong with me, Thad? Why does my power keep freaking out?"

"Nothing's wrong with you, babe. I'm sure your power is

just trying to balance itself out after everything you've been through."

"You really think that's it?"

She's silent for a moment, the hope in her eyes causing a strange fluttering in my chest as tears continue to slip down her cheeks. My heart is pounding, and everything inside me wants to fix whatever is causing her pain. *The fuck is this?* It feels familiar, but so has every fucking other thing lately.

"I do. You've been through hell, woman. Cut yourself some slack."

"What would I do without you guys?" she whispers.

"You'll never have to find out," I whisper back.

"We're leaving," Levi informs Cole and Knox. "We'll make sure to text when we arrivè and when we're on our way back."

I force myself to step away from the woman that's doing crazy things to my insides and turn to face my brothers.

"You guys make sure she's safe, yeah?" Knox murmurs.

Cole remains stubbornly silent, his jaw clenched so tight I'm surprised his teeth haven't shattered. He obviously wants to argue against this little outing but has realized how pointless that would be.

"You know we'll guard her with our lives," I say solemnly, earning a begrudged nod from Cole.

Knox moves toward Fate. Releasing Levi's hand, she steps into Knox's embrace, his arms wrapping around her and his cheek coming to rest against her temple.

"You listen to the twins, little ghost. Do as they say and don't do anything crazy. I expect you to come back to me, you hear?"

"I'll behave. I promise," she says quietly.

She steps back and spares a glance at Cole.

"Please understand why I need to do this," she pleads.

"I do understand," he mutters, "but that doesn't mean I have to like it."

She surprises us all when she walks up to him, stopping with only inches to spare.

"Thank you," she says before going up on her toes to give him a kiss on his cheek. I've never seen Cole blush. Almost wish I had a camera to record the moment.

"Alright, you two," she says, turning our way. The tears are gone, and our feisty girl is coming back online. "Let's hit the road. Assuming, of course, that I can actually leave the property now that I'm a real girl. Wouldn't that be shit luck."

"Right this way, woman." I bow, sweeping my arm toward the front door. "Your chariot awaits."

"Don't let him lie to you, Fate. It's a Denali, and a messy one at that. His lazy ass uses the floorboards as a garbage can for all his fast food wrappers."

"Why does that not surprise me?" Her laughter dispels the negative vibes crowding the room as I follow slightly behind her and Levi, risking a backward glance at our brothers. I can appreciate the worried looks on their faces even if I think they're unnecessary. They should have a little more faith that we'd never let anyone or anything harm a hair on her head. Playful and provocative we may be, but when it comes to the most precious thing in all our lives...being protective is the name of the game.

I give our brothers a small nod in understanding and rush out after our girl. She's waiting for me just outside the door, and when she places her small hand in my much larger one, I feel complete for the first time in this current existence.

Because that's what this last fifty years without her was – existing. With her by my side, her hand in mine...that's fucking living.

Chapter 18

LEVI

TWIN FACT #3: STAY OUT OF MY HEAD, DIPSHIT!

A look in the rearview has my heart stuttering in my chest.

Fate's head is sticking out the back window, with the biggest smile I've ever seen plastered on her face. She's practically bouncing in her seat, her excitement and utter joy overflowing now that she's successfully left behind the place that's held her captive for the last ten years. Standing up to Cole's asshole-ish ways was worth it for the simple pleasure of this moment.

"We're almost there. You ready, woman?" Thad asks, twisting around to watch her as she pulls her head back into the SUV.

"I'm totally ready!" she eagerly replies. "What should I expect once we're there?"

Thad looks over at me. He's still nervous about her seeing firsthand what we're capable of. Why, I'm not sure. It's not like him to worry so much. I still love the dipshit, and the fact that I know my twin possibly better than I know myself means that I understand why he's freaking out. His feelings for Fate are new for him, or at least new as far as this current existence is concerned, and Thad doesn't do emotions. I, on the other hand, want to feel all the emotions. The good, the bad, and everything in between. It's what makes life worth living.

I pull off the interstate and navigate onto Main Street which runs the entire length of the small town in Southern Illinois. I've got to admit, it's got a certain kind of charm. There's a grassy median running down the center of the street with old-fashioned street lights perched in regular intervals. The shops on each side have doors open in greeting and signs swinging in the breeze. Benches dot the sidewalk, so the weary can rest or neighbors can sit and chit chat.

"Oh my ghost! What the hell is that?" Fate gasps from the backseat.

Up ahead, I spot a crowd gathered around something very large and very orange.

"You've gotta be shitting me," Thad mutters.

"Is that what I think it is?" I ask.

Fate scrambles in between our seats to get a better look, having unbuckled her seat belt in her excitement.

"Can we stop? Please? I want to see what that's all about."

"It's the Wienermobile," I confess reluctantly.

Her eyes cut to mine. "I'm sorry. What did you just say?"

"The Oscar Mayer Wienermobile. It travels across the country promoting the Oscar Mayer hot dog brand."

"You mean to tell me that car is shaped like a giant wiener?" She glances back to the crowd, considering. "Now *this* I have to see. I bet it's epic!"

Thad rolls his eyes and looks back at her. "Mine is even more epic, woman."

"Babe, I have no doubts on that score. But it's not every day a girl gets to see a gigantic mobile wiener." She turns those gray eyes on me and sticks out her lower lip in a pout that is just too damn sexy to ignore. "Pretty please, Levi?"

"How the hell can I say no to that? Let's do it."

Thad groans as I pull into a spot in front of the local diner and throw it in park. Before Thad and I can even unbuckle our seatbelts, Fate's already opening the door and bolting out of the car.

"Come on, dipshit. We can't let her get into any trouble, or the guys will have our asses," I exclaim, quickly exiting the car and jogging after her.

She's right at the front of the crowd, staring in wonder like it's the most magnificent thing she's ever seen. Honestly, it probably is at the moment considering her unlife these last hundred years or so. In reality, it's a giant orange hot dog on a bright yellow bun. I don't get the allure, but others obviously do. People are asking the driver questions like he's some sort of celebrity.

He spots Fate and immediately does a double take. His short, five-foot-five-tops ass is going to try to hone in on our girl. I can see it written all over his ruddy face. Unbelievable. Like he even stands a chance. Wait 'til Thad gets a load of this.

"Hey, pretty lady. Want to sit in the driver's seat?" he walks up and asks Fate.

"Hell yes!"

Well, damn. Guess the little man has some game after all. Either that or our socially deprived girlfriend is just a little too easy to please these days.

She ducks through the door in the middle of the - fuck, I never thought I'd say this - wiener before I can stop her, immediately making her way up to the driver's seat and waving out the window.

"You let her go inside that thing?" Thad grumbles, coming up beside me.

"Have you met that woman? You think I could stop her from doing anything she wants to do?"

"Good point, wankstain." Thad's eyes narrow on the driver standing a little too close to Fate for our comfort. "Who the fuck is the douche canoe leaning over her shoulder?"

"That's the driver, and he's got about two seconds to remove his hand from her arm, or I'll be removing *him*...permanently."

At that point, a spark of electricity is visible through the window, and a loud yelp reverberates out the door. The driver clutches his hand and backs away from Fate, quickly shaking his head. We can't make out what she's saying, but the guy looks terrified.

She slowly makes her way back outside and over to us, the smirk on her gorgeous face doing nothing to ease my worries. In fact, it increases them.

Thad's fists are clenching by his sides. "What the fuck did he do?"

"He asked if I'd like to get a drink with him later. When I politely refused, he asked if maybe I just wanted to get a closer look at *his* wiener." She snorts, rolling her eyes. "Like I'm not already surrounded by enough wieners as it is."

"He fucking did what?" Thad bellows. "I'm going to kick his ass!"

I quickly grab Thad's arm and pull him back.

"No need," Fate adds a little too smugly. "When he went to slide his hand down my arm, my power didn't take kindly to that and shocked the shit out of him."

"What did you say to him before you walked away?" I ask.

"I told him I was actually pretty hungry and would be willing to look at his wiener if I could have a bite," she snickers. "Even snapped my teeth and licked my lips for good measure."

We both just stand there, gaping at her.

"Holy fuck! You're like a female version of us," Thad sputters, eyes wide.

"If the guys find out about this, they won't leave you alone with us. Ever," I reply with a grin, only partially serious.

"Then let's not let them find out, eh?" She simply shrugs and starts walking back to the car. "Come on, boys! We have a house to un-haunt. De-haunt? De-ghost? What's the technical term for removing unwanted spirits these days?"

"It's called clearing or cleansing the home," I tell her as we all climb back into the SUV.

"Got it! Now what else do I need to know?"

"Buckle up first and then we'll give you the rundown."

"Seatbelt. Right," she grumbles, eyeing the safety device like it's a snake that's going to bite her hand if she touches it. When everyone is in and restrained, I put the SUV in drive and head toward the residential section of town. The house we're driving to sits at the end of a long, gravel lane. The separation offers privacy without destroying the close-knit feel small towns are famous for, as the neighbors' drives veer off to the left and right with their own private entrances.

"Okay, so here's how we usually do this," I start, knowing Thad isn't going to be much help. He's become such a Nervous Nelly where Fate's concerned. "We talk with the family first, getting an idea of what we're dealing with.

Usually, we recommend they leave the premises to avoid any confrontations, especially with angry, aggressive spirits."

"They willingly do that? Just leave two strangers alone in their home?"

"By this point, they're usually willing to do whatever we say to get rid of whatever is causing them grief."

Thad adds seriously, "And you're here to observe *only*. If we tell you to do something, listen. Sometimes these spirits don't want to give up their current arrangement so easily, and they lash out. I don't want you accidentally getting caught in the crosshairs."

"I understand. I promise to listen and not get in the way," she replies with an innocent look on her face.

Something tells me to be wary of that look.

I don't have time to question it as we pull up to the house at the end of the drive. It's a seemingly well-maintained, older two-story with light gray siding and white trim. The large yard is mowed, with several flowering bushes lining the front. There are a couple of ride-on toys and a few dolls sitting near the sidewalk that leads up to the porch. The windows at the front of the house are open, the curtains fluttering in the breeze. A rocking chair and small table sit next to the screen door.

At first glance, everything appears completely normal, but appearances are often deceiving. I mean, just look at us.

"You guys aren't going to grab your gear?" Fate asks as we meet on the sidewalk and make our way up to the house.

"We usually wait until they're gone so we don't freak the family out any more than they already are," Thad states in a low voice.

"Plus, we might not even need it," I add before leaning forward to ring the doorbell. The sound echoes inside.

"Be right there," a feminine voice calls out.

"Just remember," Thad murmurs, his eyes locked on Fate, "do everything we tell you to do. No questions."

"When did you become such a worrywart?" Fate complains with a roll of her eyes.

"Since you exploded like a goddamned grenade," Thad snaps.

"Point taken," she whispers back just as a young woman approaches the screen door.

"Can I help you?" she asks as she dries off her hands with a dish towel.

"Hi there. I'm Levi, and this is my brother Thad," I greet her as I motion toward my twin before nodding toward Fate. "This is our assistant, Fate. We're from Valley Investigations and Paranormal Society. You called about a situation in your home?"

"Oh! Yes. Hi. I'm Paula. Please, come in. Have a seat in the living room, and I'll grab my husband from the backyard. Tricia is upstairs playing in her room."

We follow her into the front room of the house. A well-worn sofa and loveseat fill the space around the coffee table, which has magazines neatly stacked on top. Everything is clean and tidy. Pictures of the young family hang on the walls and adorn the mantel over a small fireplace.

We sit down on the sofa, Fate between Thad and me. It's a little bit tight with our considerable bulk, but Fate doesn't seem to mind. She silently takes in the room, a slight furrow between her brows. Before I can ask her about it, the screen door toward the back of the house opens and closes, and the sound of footsteps immediately draws closer. As the couple enters the living room, the wife looks excitedly nervous, while the husband looks like he'd rather be anywhere but here. That's pretty typical for most of our jobs.

"Um, this is my husband Frank. Frank, this is Levi, Fate,

and Thad. They're from the paranormal company I told you about. They said they can help us."

We stand and shake hands with the reluctant-looking man. The couple is in their early to mid-thirties. They both have mousy brown hair and tired eyes that speak of the struggles they've been having here.

"I don't know if y'all will be able to help, but at this point we're willing to give it a shot," he says, placing his hands in his back pocket. He won't look at us, instead maintaining eye contact with his wife.

"Why don't we all sit, and you can tell us what's going on," I suggest.

They shuffle over to the loveseat, sitting and sharing a look before he places his hand on her knee, obviously giving her comfort.

"We moved into this rental six months ago. At first, everything was great. There's plenty of space and lots of yard for Tricia to play in. She's six. The neighborhood is quiet, and everyone seems friendly."

I spare a sideways glance at Fate who's still slowly inspecting the room. Every so often, she'll tense up, but her face is as calm as can be.

Paula's voice brings my attention back to her. "Then about four months ago, we heard Tricia talking in her room. It sounded like she was playing with a friend, but I knew no one else was here, so I opened the door and peeked in. She was sitting on her rug, all her dolls and accessories scattered over her bedroom floor. When I asked her why she'd made such a mess - because she's almost always obsessively neat - she said Abigail wanted to play dolls. I asked who Abigail was, and she said it was a little girl she had made friends with. But there was no one else in the room." The tears start falling, and she quickly tries to wipe them away.

Frank reaches over to the end table, grabbing a tissue for his wife. They share a brief look before he turns to us, taking over the explanation and giving his wife time to compose herself.

"It went on like that for a little while, and we just chalked it up to an imaginary friend. We'd left behind family and everyone we knew when we decided the city wasn't for us, and Tricia took it pretty hard. She's struggled to make friends at school, and since it seemed to be pretty harmless, we didn't worry much. All kids have imaginary friends, right?" He sighs and rubs his forehead with his free hand.

"I'm guessing things changed," I solicit.

"Yes," he answers gruffly. "Instead of harmless playing, she started wandering off in the middle of the night. We'd wake up to the sound of the door opening and find her outside in the backyard with her stuffed animals. Or down the gravel drive in the middle of the day when we'd been looking for her everywhere. She just keeps saying that Abigail is trying to keep her safe, but we're worried that one of these days she's going to walk off, and we won't be able to find her."

"Have you ever noticed anything that felt negative in nature?" Fate asks suddenly.

I peer at her at the same time Thad does. I'd give anything for Knox's ability right now. Something is going on with her, but I'll have to wait until the family is gone to ask.

"Around the time Tricia started wandering off, we started hearing random footsteps upstairs when all of us were down here. Doors slamming shut. We've had dishes fly off the table and shatter against the wall when we turn our backs. Lately, Tricia refuses to go into her room. She said

Abigail has told her not to because the 'bad man' is in there," Paula stammers.

Just then, we hear the pounding of little footsteps on the stairs, followed swiftly by doors slamming shut.

Paula jumps up as a little girl carrying a floppy-eared bunny hurries into the room.

"Mommy, Abigail says we should go now. The bad man isn't happy that these people are here."

Paula and Frank share a look and then glance back at us. Fate stands up and walks over to Tricia before crouching down in front of the little girl. "Hi, Tricia. My name is Fate. That's a cute bunny you have there. What's her name?"

"Her name is BunBun."

"That's pretty. Does Abigail have a bunny too?"

"No. She said she lost hers a long time ago, but it looked a lot like BunBun."

"Is Abigail here now, Tricia?"

"She's waiting at the top of the stairs, keeping an eye on the bad man for you. She says she knows who you are and that you'll help her."

Fate peeks over her shoulder, eyeing Thad and me before turning back to the little girl.

"Abigail's right, Tricia. We're here to help. Why don't you go wait on the porch while these guys behind me talk with your mom and dad."

"Okay," the little girl agrees before walking toward the door. Just before pushing it open, she turns back to Fate. "Abigail says she has to go away now, but that she'll always remember me. Will you tell her I'll miss her and to be safe?"

"I can definitely do that," Fate whispers.

The little girl nods her head and walks out the door. Fate stands up and makes her way back over to the side of the sofa next to us.

"Don't worry," I reassure the nervous parents, "we'll take care of the problem, and hopefully you'll be able to get back to normal life."

"Thank you. We're going to the park. Just text me when you guys are done," he says, nervously looking at the ceiling. He grabs his wife's hand, pulling her behind him as he snags her purse off the entry table and heads out the door without a backward glance.

"Fate," Thad says before grabbing her hand, "what's going on?"

Fate takes another look around the room. Her brows are furrowed, and I notice goosebumps break out along her arms.

"I don't know. There's something strange happening here, but I just can't sort out what it is I'm feeling. I'm a little out of practice, guys."

Thad's big hand engulfs hers, his thumb rubbing back and forth.

Just as I'm about to suggest that we go grab our gear, a small ghostly figure appears in the doorway. Thad and I jump up, and Fate takes a step back toward us. We're in a line, looking at the figure standing a few feet away, her long hair nearly down to her waist with a big bow sitting on the top of her head. Her dress is tattered and stained with dirt and blood, pieces of the material missing in random places. Judging by the style, I'd guess she was alive some time in the late 1800s.

"You're from the Gateway," her little disembodied voice says.

"You must be Abigail," Fate says quietly.

"Yes. And you are Fate, the one the Gateway chose as its own."

"Yes. But how do you know that?"

"We all know who you are. You've been gone a very long time."

"I have, but I'm back now."

"I know. Everyone knows. Some are more happy about it than others."

"Others like the bad man?"

"Yes. And there are lots more like him. They know you're here now, and they're coming for you."

"Why are you warning me?"

"Because I don't like to see people get hurt the way I was hurt," Abigail states simply.

"Is that why you stayed with Tricia?"

"Yes. I didn't want the bad man to hurt her, so I'd lead her out of the house whenever he was around."

The room is quiet at the admission that the ghost of a little girl would protect her living counterpart. We don't see much good in this line of work, and it makes me want to step in and do whatever I can for this little girl who died much too young.

"Abigail, would you like us to help *you*?" I ask gently. "Maybe make it so you can see your family and friends that are waiting for you on the other side?"

Fate's eyes are on me, and I wish I knew what she was thinking.

"I'd like that very much, but you have to make sure the bad man crosses over too. I can't leave here until I know he's gone and Tricia's safe."

"Where is he?" Thad asks.

"He's in Tricia's room. Up the stairs, the only door on the right."

Thad and I share a quick look, both stepping away from Fate. My twin acknowledges what both of us are thinking.

She's not coming up there with us. The guys will have our asses.

Who's going to tell her?

You tell her, bro.

Hell no. You do it, dipshit.

Rock, paper, scissors?

Fine. On three.

One, two, three...

I push through a mental image of a rock. Thad sends paper, then immediately does a silent celebratory dance.

Fuck!

My eyes swing over and lock with hers.

"Sweets, I need you to listen to me, okay?" I whisper.

She nods.

"Stay here with Abigail. No matter what, do not come upstairs, got it?"

Her eyes narrow, but she nods again.

"Fate, I need you to say that you promise to stay right here. I'm not falling for that innocent look," I insist. "You forget...Thad is my twin."

The side of her pouty pink lips tilts up, and I've never wanted to kiss someone as badly as I want to kiss her right now, but we have business to attend to first.

"I promise to stay here," she vows.

I wrap my large hand around her neck, pulling her to me, and kiss her forehead, desperate for any connection.

"Good. We'll be back in just a minute."

Thad and I head over to the stairs and look up.

"You go first, and I'll cover you," I tell my twin.

He glances over his shoulder to where Fate is standing. When he turns back, he tilts his head all the way to the left until an audible crack is heard, then repeats the motion on the other side.

"She's not going to freak out, brother. Give our girl some credit."

A large Gurkha blade appears in his hands. It's long and slightly curved but wicked in battle. My hand lights up from the bright white orb that appears.

A gasp behind us draws our attention, and I see Fate's wide eyes as she takes in my twin's weapon and my palm. It's not fear or worry in those gray depths, but appreciation and pride. Thad releases a breath at the sight and takes the first step up the staircase.

"Told you," I quip.

"Shut up, wankstain."

We hit the hallway outside the bedrooms and make our way a few feet down to the only door on the right hand side.

"On three?" he asks.

"On three," I confirm.

"One," he whispers.

"Two."

His hand grabs the doorknob.

"Three!" he shouts.

Throwing open the door, we burst into the room and stand back to back.

"You see him?" I ask.

"No. You?"

"No."

The room is icy cold, the window frosted over with little snowflake imprints covering the panes. In the middle of June. A blast of cold air whips around us, our hair flying in the current.

"Where the fuck is he?" Thad shouts over the noise.

Before I can answer, the cold stops and rushes past us and out of the room.

"Fuck! He's headed for Fate," I yell, a lead weight sinking in my stomach.

We rush through the door and run back down the stairs to find Abigail cowering against the wall outside the living room.

Walking up next to her, we stand in the doorway, and see the aggressive spirit behind Fate. His arm is around her throat with the talon-like claw of his opposite hand digging into her neck. The fact that I can see her swallow through the transparency of his arm does nothing to calm the whirling anger and fear in my gut.

The motion has his grip tightening ever so slightly, and a small drip of blood runs down the creamy expanse of her neck. My eyes meet hers, but instead of the fear I expect to see, she looks as steady as ever...but a lot pissed off.

What fresh hell is this? Thad urgently sends over through our connection. *How is he touching her right now?*

I have no fucking idea, bro.

"Now, here's what's going to happen," Bad Man says.

"Yeah, you're going to let her go, and we're going to send your ass to the fiery depths of the other side where you belong," I growl.

The dickhead smirks. Seeing the wall behind him through his creepy as fuck face does nothing to detract from the sinister feeling he's projecting. "Oh, I don't think so. You're going to go back and tell your little crew that their days of ruling over us are over. The queen is coming with me."

"Are you fucking mental?" Thad asks the demented apparition.

"Like you two douchebags can stop me. Without your queen at full power, you two are as dangerous as a couple of toddlers with diapers full of shit."

"That is oddly specific," Fate notes.

"Shut the fuck up!" Bad Man snarls, though Fate just smirks.

Thad and I take a step forward, but he catches it. A blast of icy air throws us back against the wall in the hallway.

Scrambling to get up, Thad moans and clutches his shoulder. A trickle of warmth makes its way down my forehead. *Fucking for real right now?* I wipe the blood out of my eye and rush back to the living room doorway.

The sight in front of me has me pausing, Thad coming up beside me.

"What the ever-loving fuck?" Thad murmurs.

Fate is standing in the middle of the room, her gray eyes alight with ghosted flames. Her long, brown hair is swirling through the air, and Bad Man is kneeling in front of her, terror etched on his face. A rope made of what could only be described as electricity is wound around his body, tying his arms to his sides.

"Never touch what's mine," Fate fumes, her voice low and full of menace.

The sound has a slight echoing chime to it, sending a shiver through my body, and I see my twin shiver next to me. I'd be lying if I said something about her possessiveness doesn't turn me right the fuck on.

Suddenly, I see her standing in front of me, but not here...somewhere else. Some*time* else. She's wearing a fancy black dress that trails on the floor behind her, and she's berating a spirit that's kneeling on the ground at her feet for giving us shit. Thad's next to me and we share a look, rubbing the bulges in our pants in perfect unison, grinning wildly at our hot as hell woman.

The memory evaporates as quickly as it came, and I find myself wishing for more of those little snippets from our past lives. Every hint of familiarity seems to fill up an empty space inside my soul.

Bad Man whimpers, cowering in front of her, bringing me back to the present. Completely unconcerned with him, her eyes lock onto us and flare again at the damage she can see. The rope tightens around the man at her feet, and he cries out in pain.

"We're okay, sweets."

She considers that a second, the flames in her eyes diminishing ever so slightly, and the rope on the pissant in front of us loosens a bit. Obviously, whatever she sees in my eyes is enough to calm her rage. Looking at the apparition kneeling in front of her, she tilts her head slightly, considering something.

"Oh, Thaddie Poo, wanna take care of this piece of shit for me?" Fate sing-songs in a malevolent voice. The melodious chime from the encounter with Barbie was obviously her *playful* voice. This one is just creepy as fuck.

"Uh…" is my twin's reply. Master linguist, he is not. Pretty sure he's standing there with a hard on he can't hide, drooling over the sexy as fuck, completely badass woman in front of us.

"What he means to say is…yes, sweets. He'll take care of this shithead for you."

Thad's brain finally catches up with his dick, and he steps forward. Clearing his throat, and running a hand over the bulge in his jeans, he huskily spits out, "I got this, woman."

His Gurkha reappears and begins to glow as he slowly approaches Bad Man.

"What was that about toddlers with shitty diapers?" he retorts, stopping a couple feet away from the ghost that is now trembling in fear. The blade's red flames flare brightly.

Heat emanates off it, but it's harmless to us. Spirits are another story. I feel it's power inside me, the other half of my own. The opposite of my pure light.

Thad eyes Fate. Her normally gray eyes are still shrouded in ghosted flames while she locks eyes with my twin. She nods, and that's all the permission he needs.

He swings the blade right through Bad Man's midsection.

The apparition screeches loudly while his entire ghostly body is engulfed in flames that don't burn anything but the piece of shit spirit. We all stare while he slowly vanishes in a cloud of black smoke.

"It's safe now, Abigail," Fate says quietly, her hair slowly falling to once again rest against her back.

The little girl apparition pops her head around the archway leading into the room and releases a pent up breath, walking right up to Fate.

"Thank you, Queen. I can finally rest now that I know he's not going to hurt anyone."

With that, her little ghostly arms wrap around Fate's legs in the biggest ghostly hug I've ever seen. Fate just smiles and runs her hand through the ghost's long hair.

"Old me might not have liked being called Queen, but new me is kind of liking the sound of it."

We all chuckle slightly, the air in the room growing lighter with each passing second.

"Levi, I think you can help Abigail now," she murmurs.

I reach my hand out, my palm glowing with soft white light. "Abigail. Are you ready?"

"Yes, I am," she says, walking up to me but pausing a foot away. "Tell Tricia that I'll miss her very much."

"Of course. She told us to tell you she'll miss you too and to stay safe."

She takes another step closer to my hand and eyes me seriously for a second.

In a voice so low only I can hear, she says, "Take care of our queen."

"I will. I'd give my life for hers," I vow.

She studies me for a minute before she places her tiny hand in mine.

"Bye, Levi," she says, and then she's gone in a wisp of white smoke.

My hand drops down to my side. There's a peace inside me when I can send one of the deserving to meet with the spirits waiting for them on the other side. I look up, and my eyes lock on Fate's. They're once again the gray I've grown so fond of. God, she's fucking beautiful.

Her eyes sparkle with all sorts of things I can only hope to rediscover one day. She takes a few steps, stopping with only inches to spare between us, and my forehead drops to hers while my hands find her hips.

"I thought we were going to lose you again," I whisper.

"You'll never lose me, Levi. I'm here to stay."

"I sure as fuck hope so, sweets. I'm not sure what I'd do if anything happened to you."

"Here's to hoping we don't have to find out," she says as she goes up on her tiptoes and lightly touches her lips to mine.

I stand there, frozen in place. Her lips are softer than I imagined and feel like heaven against my own. Her hands snake up my chest, her touch waking me up and sending me into action. My hand comes up and wraps around the back of her neck, pulling her face into mine. I kiss her like she's my last breath of air, running my tongue along her lower lip, begging her to open up for me.

It's like coming home. The warmth of her mouth and the

touch of her tongue on mine as her body leans into me. My hands slide down to her ass, pulling her against me, eliminating even the tiniest space between us like my body wants to become one with hers. I groan through the kiss, all of our important parts suddenly lining up.

She pulls back, and I try not to mourn the loss of her taste. Then I realize Thad has come up behind her, pinning her between us, and the fire in my blood soars with the three-way contact. Our connection, already strong, comes alive. Suddenly, their thoughts are inside my head.

God, she's so fucking hot.

I can't lose this, *can't lose* them, *again.*

I shut the connection down before I'm overwhelmed by the intensity of the moment. She tilts her head over her shoulder, kissing my twin the same way I was just kissing her, while my mouth finds her ear, licking it and trailing kisses down her neck. I grind my erection into the softness of her and a low moan escapes her mouth. I wish like hell we were anywhere but here so I could take advantage of what I know we all want.

But we're not. We're in our client's house, and the guys are probably having mini heart attacks since I forgot to check in when we arrived.

Dammit! Being the responsible twin really has its disadvantages sometimes. I pull away from Fate slowly, the sight of her playing tongue twister with my twin sending more heat through my blood.

"Guys, as much as I want to see this thing through to its obvious conclusion, we can't. Not here."

"Goddammit, bro!" Thad curses as he pulls himself back from Fate. "Sometimes I hate your realist ass."

Fate chuckles even as she groans slightly while removing herself from between the two of us.

"Rain check?" she asks, a wicked smirk tilting her swollen, pink lips.

"You know it, woman," Thad promises, lifting his hand to push her hair out of her face.

"Oh my ghost! Look at that!" she exclaims, pointing at my brother's wrist.

"What the fuck?" I murmur, seeing the solid line dotted with four dots in the center.

Thad eyes his wrist and smiles broadly. "Bout damn time I got mine."

Fate eyes me, a little bit of hope mixed in with a hint of fear. "You?" she asks nervously.

I glance down to my own wrist, seeing the solid black line with five dots in the center, and hold it out for her inspection.

"Yup. Me too. You?"

She shrugs out of her leather jacket and eyes her left bicep.

Just above Knox's and Macklin's lines are two lines that match ours.

Her fingers ghost over the marks before her eyes come back up and connect with mine.

She smirks, shrugging her bare shoulders that are just begging me to lick them. "Looks like you boys are stuck with me."

"Wouldn't want to be stuck anywhere else, sweets."

Chapter 19

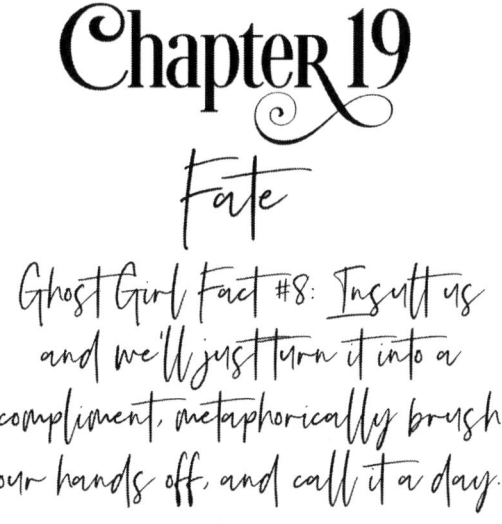

Fate

Ghost Girl Fact #8: Insult us and we'll just turn it into a compliment, metaphorically brush our hands off, and call it a day.

The SUV barrels down the two-lane road, back to the estate. The guys are on the phone with Cole while my head hangs out the window, feeling the sun and wind on my face. It's one of the best feelings in the world. Next to being sandwiched between two totally drool-worthy guys, of course.

Hot damn! That was worth every added little bit of frustration. I make a promise to myself that one day soon, I'll grab one, or more, of my guys, find an empty bed, and put it to good use. It's been too damn long, and it's way past time I get a little TLC.

I hear my name and reluctantly pull myself back inside the vehicle. The guys keep telling me it's not safe, that I'm not a dog, but I just can't find it inside myself to care. I've already come back from the dead once. I say bring it on! Well, okay. Maybe I need to talk myself off the ledge that leads to crazy town. Don't want to do something stupid and miss out on all those orgasms I keep promising myself, right?

"How mad were they?" I ask, biting my lower lip. Nothing flares my ire up faster than the blue-eyed devil that is Cole, and we can't afford to let my emotions get out of control right now. Crazy fucking powers. Ugh!

"Well, they weren't fucking happy," Thad mutters.

Cue eye roll. "No shit, Sherlock."

"Better learn my name, woman. You'll be screaming it out from beneath me soon enough."

"Whoa! You sound pretty confident in your abilities, big guy."

"Never had any complaints," he croons, a smirk plastered on his way too kissable lips.

But that's all it takes to set off my temper - so much for keeping my powers under control. Throw a sprinkle of jealousy my way and *Bam*! One irate ghost girl coming right up. My hands start to spark, and the car starts to shake, a little smoke seeping out of the inside vents.

"Bro! What the fuck?" Levi growls, nervously eyeing me in the rearview mirror. "You better calm her down. Now, before she makes the car go boom!"

Thad swiftly turns in his seat, casting me a nervous look once he gets a glimpse of my pissed off expression.

"Babe, I didn't mean..."

"Don't you 'babe' me, Thad. I know exactly what you meant," I growl. "A ghost girl can't even leave her men alone for a hundred years without them going off to find somewhere else to stick their willies."

"Ok, first off. We don't call them willies. We call them dicks. Or cocks. Definitely not fucking *willies*. Secondly, might I remind you that we had no memories. Of anything.

Not even *you*. I can promise that none of those girls meant anything even close to what you mean to us."

I know he's right. I know I'm being slightly irrational. But I. Don't. Care. I look at the hunky piece of twinsie in front of me and narrow my eyes. Time to prove a point.

"You're right," I murmur thoughtfully.

I watch as his smirk makes a reappearance. Poor man. He thinks he's won this round.

"I mean, I guess since we have no memories of each other, then I shouldn't feel guilty for all those daydreams about hot men with all their muscles and sexy ass smiles. Guess it's totally okay that I wondered how they'd feel above me, and beneath me, and behind me. All the while wishing they were touching me. Licking me. Thrusting their big, yummy cocks into me while I come like I've never come before. It's okay, right? I mean, since I had no idea who you guys were and all. You want me to detail out some of my more naughty daydream sexcapades, *babe*? Wanna hear *all* about the one where some Scottish guy with a killer accent ate me out like I was his last meal? Or what about the blond surfer who could bend my body in ways I didn't know I could bend, all while he fucked me senseless? I mean, I could detail it down to the size of each guy's *cock* and how good it made me feel? Hmmm?"

By the look on his murderous face, I think he gets my message. If he doesn't like imagining me with some fictional guy, then he definitely wouldn't want to hear even the tiniest hint of me with someone real. I can't deny they had a life before they found me again, but I'll be damned if they'll get to parade it in front of my face. I tend to get a little stabby just thinking about them with anyone else. Maybe now he gets that.

He ends our silent staring contest with a small nod.

"Message received," he grumbles.

The sparks disappear, and the ride smooths out now that the vehicle isn't under duress. Fucking wonky powers. From what Reggie has explained to me, they shouldn't be so reactive to my emotions, but so far no one can figure out how to fix it. Story of my life.

I catch Levi's eye in the rearview mirror and realize he's looking pretty stabby himself. Good. Hopefully they pass the message along to the others.

"You hungry, sweets?" he murmurs cautiously.

"Mmm...yes. Find me some yummies!"

"You're pretty yummy, woman. Wouldn't mind getting a bite of you."

I cock my eyebrow and look at the naughty twin in the passenger seat.

"You're not forgiven yet. If anyone is getting my yummies, it's Levi. He's been a good boy."

"I'm not sure if I should be appalled at being likened to a well-behaved toddler or excited because...hell yes, I want your yummies."

"Mmm...you're right. I'm not really the *call me Mommy*, sort. Ew..." I trail off as I suddenly feel my mark flare up with the itchy-tingle I've grown to recognize as that damn ghostly summons. "What the hell?" I mutter.

"What is it?" Thad asks nervously.

"I think Knox is trying to summon me. I don't even know if it will work now that I'm in this form. Shit!"

"You think he's trying to pull you back to the house? Why not just call us?" He pulls out his phone. "No bars."

"It's gotta be important for him to be trying this right now. He and Macklin agreed to wait until I felt stronger."

"We're only about fifteen minutes out," Levi says as the car picks up speed.

"Good," I say nervously, bringing my fingers up to run over Knox's mark. I can actually feel the tug from his line specifically as I brush over it. As I start to pull my hand back, my fingers slowly start to fade, wisps of smoke trailing off where my fingertips once were then out the window as my hand begins to disappear.

"Uh...guys..."

Thad looks back, and his eyes widen in fear. "Fuck! Levi. Hurry."

Levi looks back at me in the rearview, but by this point, the fade is picking up speed, smoke flying out the window faster than a smoker dragging on a cigarette.

It doesn't hurt, but it's damn disconcerting.

"Guys. Get to the house as fast as you can. Something tells me shit's going down." I glance at my bottom half and watch as my belly fades away to nothing. I look at my twins one last time before it begins to consume my chest, crawling up my neck. "And hurry! Son-of-a-..."

I don't get to finish the word before I'm whisked through the vortex. It's only seconds before I start to materialize in the foyer of the estate. The wisps of smoke slowly gain solidity until I'm whole again and clutching the table in the middle of the space to keep me upright.

"Bitch!" I cry out. "Knox, you better have a damn good reason for..."

"Well, well, well. If it isn't the self-proclaimed Queen of the Gateway." A raspy voice with a distinct New York accent cuts off my well-deserved rant.

I look up, and my eyes catch on an apparition standing in the doorway to the study. He's tall and gangly, with deep sunken eyes and cheeks. He's dressed in an old-fashioned suit from the twenties, complete with pinstripes and that weird little pocket handkerchief. His hair is slicked back, and his whole look screams mob. Though the badass effect is lost since he's totally see through.

He's holding my new friend with an arm wrapped around her front and a ridiculously slender hand wrapped around her throat.

To her credit, Reggie doesn't look afraid. Just worried. And she'd only be worried for one reason.

"Who the fuck are you?" I eloquently ask the mystery man while I try to force myself to stand up straight. Traveling via the ether is not for the faint of heart - or ghost girls who don't have their shit together yet.

"Ah, ah, ah...you're not the one askin' questions here. I am. And you're gonna tell me what I wanna know, or I'm gonna end your little weirdo friend here."

I narrow my eyes and place my hands on my hips. "Hey! That's not very nice. No name calling."

The slimy man looks at me like I've grown two heads.

"They said you were different."

"Who's they? And how am I different?"

"You're..." he waves his hand around in the air like he's trying to come up with the right words, "significantly less intimidating."

"I'm not sure if that's a compliment or an insult."

"Definitely not a compliment," Knox mutters.

I glance back to see him, Cole, and Macklin standing side by side, forming a wall behind me.

I hadn't even realized they were there. Good God. Am I that easily distracted?

Turning back to Mob Man in front of me, I eye Reggie. She shakes her head, ever so slightly, and looks even more nervous than before.

"And tell me...why should I be afraid of you?" I sneer.

The evil glint in his eye gives me pause.

"Because I know how much you value your friend here, and I can send her to the other side faster than you can blink if you don't gimme what I want. You with me? And I'm not talkin' 'bout the pleasant side either."

My temper starts to rise, and with it, my powers. I force myself to take a steady breath, knowing I can't afford to lose my shit and let my powers go haywire. Not now. I need to maintain control for Reggie's sake.

"You, a measly spirit, can send her to the afterlife?" I ask doubtfully.

His eyes narrow and begin to gleam red. He brings one of his translucent hands up, and it's then I notice a large signet ring on his bony finger. Right in the center, inlaid in the metal, is a glowing red ruby. Something tells me it isn't just a fashion statement.

"How the fuck did a ghost like you get a ring like that?" Cole demands from behind me.

I don't turn around, though I want to. It sounds like he has some idea what that ring is, but I've learned my lesson while out on the call with the twins. Never give your enemy your back.

"Friends in high places, my boy. You best remember that. Now..." He glances back at me. "Where is it?"

I study him for a second. Am I supposed to know what that means? Do they not know we don't have our memories? There's that mysterious *they* again. What the hell is really going on here?

"Where is what?" I ask.

"Don't fuck with me, girl. Where is the book?"

"Oh. The book," I repeat slowly and pretend to fidget nervously. I have no fucking clue what he's talking about, but he doesn't know that. Let's see just how distracted I can make him. "I've placed the book away for safekeeping. Can't let insignificant spirits like you get their greedy little hands on it."

His hand tightens on Reggie's neck, and she lets out a soft squeak. Ok, guess that answers one question. Spirits, or at least *this* spirit, can hurt other spirits. Good to know.

"You'll tell me where the book is right now, or you can say goodbye to your little friend."

One of the guys snorts behind me, and I hear a muttered, "Someone thinks he's Al Pacino."

Before I can show off my awesome impression skills, he brings his free hand up, makes a fist, and aims the ruby right at Reggie. She looks at me with resignation in her ghostly eyes. She knows that I have no idea what book he's talking about or where it might be.

Can't a ghost girl catch a break? I mean, as if ten years of solitude weren't bad enough, then I find out I've been deadish for the last hundred years and have absolutely no memories of anything or anyone. Now I don't even have time to acclimate to this solid ass body I'm sporting because Mob Man over there has to go and fuck with my friend. Why do the bad guys always want to touch what's mine?

I feel my powers come alive, my fingers starting to spark.

When Mob Man notices, I sense his hesitation as his nerves kick in. He wasn't expecting me to be able to do this. Obviously, *they* aren't fully informed, or he would've been a little more careful who he was threatening.

An idea begins to take shape. He doesn't really want Reggie. He wants me. Isn't that what Bad Man wanted too? Things are starting to make a little more sense.

"Fate," Knox angrily whispers from behind me.

I smirk. My empath already has an idea of where my mind has gone, and he is not happy. Cole's going to lose his shit in three...two...one...

"You don't really want to hurt my lovely friend over there. What you really want is me, right?"

I see a calculating gleam in his eye. Perfect. Just what I'm going for.

"Like hell," Cole growls. "Don't you even think about it, Fate."

"Oh, she's thinking about it alright," Knox scoffs.

"Oh, ain't this cute? Your ridiculous little male menagerie is concerned for you. Big Bad Queen of the Gateway can't even make decisions on her own anymore? Such a pity you've been reduced to this. Guess my *friend* was right afterall. You're of no real concern to me. Gimme me the book, and I'll leave you all to do...whatever it is you all do."

My eyes narrow, and my power surges to life inside me, but I tamp it back down. This guy has no idea what he's in for, and I want to keep him complacent.

"How about an even trade? You take me and let her go, and I'll lead you to the book."

He considers me for a moment, the hand with the ring twitching slightly. Then he considers my guys. Apparently making a decision, he drops the hand with the ring but doesn't let Reggie go. "Okay."

"Fuck no, little ghost!" Knox snarls.

"Fate, what the fuck?" Cole shouts.

"Fate, you can't do this," Macklin pleads.

They all talk simultaneously, but I can't let their worry and fear distract me. Something in my brain starts to fissure, a small crack becoming a narrow opening where a memory slips out. Not only should I have five marks on my bicep where I currently only have four, but I should also have one on my wrist. One that I share with Reggie. They call me ghost girl for a reason. I can do things no normal person can do. Being able to affect and be affected by spirits is one of them. With the good, always comes the bad. You know - a yin and yang kind of thing.

Latching onto the idea forming thanks to my wacky memories, I know exactly what I need to do and trust that Reggie knows the old me well enough to know what she'll need to do next.

"Okay, Mob Man. On the count of three, I'll give you my hand, and you let her go. If you try to screw us over and take us both, let's just say my guys have full permission to take you out by any means necessary."

"God dammit!" Cole mutters behind me, but out of the corner of my eye I see the glow from that mysteriously large knife he has hidden somewhere on that delicious body of his.

I risk a quick glance over my other shoulder, and I'm stunned to see Knox's eyes glowing, shifting from color to color, while his hands are holding luminescent orbs that match the color shift in his eyes. First red, then blue, yellow, then green, and on and on they change. It's hypnotizing.

Macklin's eyes are also gleaming, but his are a pretty blue, like the color that flickers in a flame from a gas fire. He doesn't have orbs like Knox. Instead, his entire body is encompassed by a faint glow similar to his eyes.

Well, damn! My guys are always hot, but with their powers out and at the ready, they're sex personified. Desire unfurls throughout my body faster than a lit match thrown on a trail of gasoline.

Down, girl! Now is totally not the time.

Why do I feel like that's the story of my life these days? *Ugh. #GhostGirlProblems.*

Mob Man's voice is suddenly pulling me out of my little desire bubble. "On three then."

Time to get this show on the road.

"One...two...three..."

I reach out my right hand, and his bony fingers grasp mine. Reggie releases a totally undignified yelp as she's pushed toward the guys. "Hey, watch it, you brute," she mutters.

As she rights herself and begins to pass me, my left hand comes up and snags her ghostly left wrist. Out of reflex, her hand clasps mine in return. Our eyes meet, and the connection is instantaneous. But the moment is quickly over, and we're yanked apart faster than I can blink. I only hope that was long enough.

Mob Man's arm is now wrapped around the front of my shoulders and pulling me into him so my back hits his front, his coldness seeping into my being. Gross! I don't want his tainted spirit germs invading my new body.

The guys look ready to lose it, but I stay as cool as a cucumber. Honestly, that phrase has never made any sense to me, but whatever. *No time for rambling thoughts, Fate. Keep it together.*

I give them a slow nod, letting them know it's okay. That this is exactly what I wanted to happen. They each nod back reluctantly, and a shaken Reggie is standing next to Cole with a determined look on her ghostly face.

See you there, she mouths before giving me a small nod. Since Mob Man's gaze is fully locked onto the guys, he doesn't notice.

"Now. Your queen and I are going to leave. You don't follow, or she's dead." He brings up the signet ring, making a show of running it down the side of my face.

The guys all snarl. Even calm, peacekeeping Macklin. I kind of dig it.

I roll my eyes at Mob Man. This dude is so clueless. And fucked. *Definitely* fucked. And not the fun kind either.

Slowly, I bring my hands together in front of me, hoping he misses the movement. I can't really see them since my face is tilted slightly toward the ceiling, but I say a small prayer that this is going to work. Otherwise, I'll look like the loser he currently thinks I am. Only one way to find out.

My right hand grips the inside of my left wrist. The guys' eyes dart down to my hands, then quickly away, as if they know I'm up to something but don't want to attract Mob Man's attention. They're looking at me with varying levels of curiosity, anger, and fear. I'm totally going to get disciplined for this little stunt later. Might need to lend them my paddle.

"Alright!" Mob Man growls. "Take me to the book. Now!"

"You got it, Mob Man. I'll see you guys soon. Don't freak out."

With that, I close my eyes and think, *Gateway*.

Before I even finish the word, our bodies start to dematerialize. One quick look at the guys tells me they are, indeed, freaking out, and I can feel their all-consuming panic. Hell, I'd be lying if I said I wasn't a little nervous myself. I *will* see them again. Reggie won't let me down. I somehow know that down in the depths of my soul.

The last thing I see is Thad and Levi bursting through the front door, both with matching looks of horror on their identical faces as they take in me and Mob Man slowly turning into wisps of smoke. I shoot them a quick wink before the smoke completely consumes us, sucking us into the vortex.

Chapter 20

Knox

EMPATH FACT #3: TO HELL WITH THE FACTS. I'M COMING, LITTLE GHOST. JUST HOLD THE FUCK ON.

Gone. Her and the slimy *Scarface* wannabe vanished right before our eyes. I search inside myself, that spot I've reserved just for her, but it's just a small spark. Wherever she is, she's too far out of reach.

"Where the fuck is she?" Cole growls. He's on the verge of totally losing his shit, and I don't even have to be an empath to sense that.

"She took him to the Gateway," Reggie offers quietly, looking at Cole like he's an enraged bull, ready to charge.

"The fucking *Gateway*? How the hell are we supposed to get to her? What the fuck was she thinking?" He's pacing now. Never a good sign. "I should have tied her to the damn bed and left her there."

"I think she would've liked that actually," Thad retorts.

Cole just growls at him. Literally.

Reggie eyes him warily as he continues to mumble to himself. "Is he going to be okay?"

"Don't worry about him. How can we find her?"

"I can get you there, but first I need to mark all of you."

"Mark us?" Macklin asks. Not even Fate's spectacular vanishing act or the fact that she could be in danger can quell his eternal curiosity.

"You know, with the mark of the Gateway. It's similar to the marks you all share," she replies simply.

"Only two of us are marked," Macklin responds.

"Bro, make that four of us," Thad says proudly, lifting up his wrist and showing it off as Levi does the same.

"Wait, only four of you share her mark?" she asks, and I can sense her steadily growing concern.

"Why? Is that a bad thing?" I question.

"That's a *terrible* thing!" she exclaims. "How did I not realize that? It explains so much."

"Explains what?" Cole snaps.

"It explains why her powers are acting all crazy and why she's not at full strength yet. She had to sacrifice pieces of herself to tie you all to her. Those pieces were gifted to you and sealed with a mark that each of you wore. Through those marks, your commitment to each other was sealed and the bond created. Those powers of yours, they used to be hers. Only residual bits of each one remain within her. Without that bond in place, she's..." Reggie trails off, searching for words while we all stand back and wait in stunned silence, "unbalanced, for lack of a better word."

"You're telling me this is our fault?" Cole says quietly. "That she went off to the Gateway, with a man that could very well kill her, missing integral parts of herself because she doesn't bear all of our marks?"

"*Your* mark," I add softly. I'm trying really hard not to blame him right now, but I'm fucking pissed. His eyes cut to mine, and the regret and despair I feel pouring off him are enough for me to temper my next words, even if my soul is seething inside. "She doesn't bear *your* mark. You hesitated. Don't get me wrong, I understand why, but she's ours. Even you have to admit that now. She's lodged somewhere deep inside our souls, and there's no getting her out. I wouldn't want to even if I could."

The room is silent while we all process those words. She's ours. We're hers. Now it's time we go get our girl.

"Do it." I look at Reggie and stick out my wrist. "Give me the mark."

"Are you sure?" She looks around at the other guys.

Macklin steps up next to me, holding out his wrist. "We're sure."

Levi steps up next. "Let's get this done. We need to save Fate."

Thad follows his twin. "Do it. I need to get to my woman."

Reggie looks at Cole. He's standing in front of us, head hanging down, shoulders slumped, guilt and blame flowing off him faster than raging rapids.

"Cole, man, I know we don't say this enough, but we appreciate all you do for us. We respect your judgment and understand why this entire situation has been hard for you. We'll discuss your hard-headedness later. First, we have to do this. Now."

Cole raises his head, his eyes connecting with mine. "I've let her down. I've let all of you down."

"And you can make it up to her, right now."

He glances around the room, meeting the eyes of each of our brothers. Walking up on my other side, he holds out his wrist.

"We need to save our girl. I can't let her down again."

Reggie smiles, looking at each of us. "You all may be a bunch of douche canoes, but, for the record, I love you like brothers. Damn glad to see you again." Walking up to Cole, she clasps his left wrist with hers.

"Do you swear your allegiance to the queen and promise to protect her from here on out with your life?"

Without hesitation, Cole responds, "I do."

"Good. We have witnesses in case you forget that again." She snickers and walks up to me.

"What the hell?" he mutters.

As she clasps my wrist, I feel a slight warmth before she's moving on to Macklin.

"Why didn't he have to say the oath?" Cole asks.

"The oath wasn't a required part of the transfer. I just wanted to hear you say it."

"Fucking temperamental spirits," he grumbles.

We all chuckle as she moves on to Levi and Thad. Once we're all staring down at the new marks on our wrists in the shape of a small solid star, she stands in front of us again.

"Okay, quick crash course on how this works. Let's call it Gateway Dynamics 101. The mark on your wrist is what ties you to the Gateway. To move to and from, all you need to do is touch your wrist with the intent to go there. The intention part is important. Right now, since it's your first time - or at least your *second* first time - you'll need to actually say the word in order to move through the vortex. Damn. Bet non-virgins everywhere are jealous of you five right now. Not everyone gets a second first time."

"That's totally not helpful," Cole scoffs.

"Now...Fate is likely trying to stall until we all come to save the day. She's not familiar with the Gateway, but the Gateway will be familiar with her. Hopefully, she's still got her mental link in place even if she doesn't know it, so the Gateway knows to keep her secrets."

"That's reassuring," I deadpan.

"I know, right?" she quips. "Ok. I guess I should've asked this before, but you all do have your powers, right?"

"Yes," we all say in unison.

"Thank fuck for small miracles. Then light 'em up, boys."

On both sides of me, my brothers let their powers free. Reggie steps back, next to Cole.

"Now that's what I'm talkin' about. Nothing like showing up to a fight with all this glowing man meat. Good thing we don't need the element of surprise on our side. Everybody ready? On the count of three?"

We all mumble our agreements.

"One..." Reggie starts.

"Two..." I say.

"Three..." Cole adds.

"Gateway," we all say in unison.

As our bodies all start to dematerialize, I finally understand just why Fate hates this part. The lack of control. The disconcerting notion that your body is spreading out into the unknown and you can only hope and pray it all gets put back together the same way it came apart. There are certain parts of me I'd rather not lose if you know what I'm saying.

I send all of my thoughts across the ether to my little ghost, telling her to hold on tight. That we're on our way. Hopefully, it's enough. Hopefully, we're not too late.

∾

Fate

Ghost Girl Fact #9: Blades through a metaphysical body still hurt like a motherfucker.

The Gateway is not what I expected. In my head, I had concocted this image of some ancient castle, all stone walls and cold stone floors. Drafty windows and bad lighting.

This place is...none of those things. It feels warm and inviting with its white and black damask walls covered in photos that I have not had the opportunity to explore because dickhead has me backed into a corner, literally. I finally give up on standing and slide to the floor. The tile under my ass is sparkly and totally something I would've chosen myself. Though, I guess I did.

Huh. Good to know old me and new me share the same sense of style at least.

The main room is like a large conference room, mostly empty except for the totally amazing chair sitting up on a raised dais along the far wall. It's slightly ornate, with a white frame and black tufted back and seat. A red runner flows from the chair straight out the door.

Damn, I've got good taste.

Mob Man is pacing the space in front of me, waiting for his crew to show up. Every once in a while, he'll pause and aim that ring in my direction as if to remind me who holds the power here. When we first arrived, he contacted his *friend* who assured him he had nothing to worry about but insisted he wait for reinforcements.

His friend sounds like a dumbass to me.

"Do they not trust you to do this yourself?" I ask, sounding bored. Probably because I am. We've been here for what feels like hours but has realistically been thirty minutes. I'm hungry and tired and honestly starting to get a little worried. My power isn't cooperating - again. I've tried to shoot some of those electric sparks at the turd-waffle, but do you think anything happened? Nope. I've got nothing. Static electricity is more powerful than I am at the moment.

"She trusts me. I was told to wait here for back up, so that's what I'm doing."

"She? Who's she?"

"None of your damn business."

"Well, I mean...it kind of is my business since it involves me and my book."

"Just shut the hell up. Where the hell have you been for the last hundred years anyways?"

"That's none of *your* damn business. Unless you're my thong, don't be up my ass."

He side eyes me like he can't believe the words that are coming out of my mouth.

"Dude, no one is coming." Even I can hear the whine seeping into my voice. They should've been here by now. Unless Reggie and I weren't on the same page like I'd thought. Or maybe something happened to Reggie and the guys. Or maybe the guys didn't want to get involved. I mean, one command from Cole and they'd be forced to stay put. Lord knows Cole and I aren't on the best terms.

As the minutes tick by, hope diminishes. Mob Man becomes increasingly agitated while I sit with my back against a wall, a numb ass, and a bad attitude. Out of nowhere, five apparitions appear, startling the dead mobster.

Quickly recovering from his shock, he growls at the men, "Where the hell have you been?"

"Do you have it?" asks a gravelly voice. It comes from the one in the hoodie and baggy jeans that are about ready to fall off his ass. I mean, he's wearing a belt, but it's doing a piss poor job of keeping them in place. How do they get those damn things to defy gravity like that?

"No. I was told to wait and not to attempt to retrieve it myself."

Hoodie Man rolls his eyes. "Dude, she doesn't even trust you enough to get a simple book?"

"She trusts me," Mob Man sputters, glancing at me.

I just shrug my shoulders. "See, guy. She totally doesn't trust you."

"She just wanted back up with me in case anything goes wrong."

"Bro, she doesn't trust you," Hoodie Man says. "And I don't have time for this shit. Let's get the book and get the hell outta here."

As I watch the interaction, I feel a weird tingle inside my brain. Like someone's trying to get in. Are one of these guys a telepath? Is it my guys? Am I developing a brain tumor?

Hoodie Man glances my way and snorts. He's totally mature, I can tell. "So *this* is the Queen of the Gateway. You're sure? She doesn't look like much to me." He eyes me up and down, disbelief written all over his ugly ghost face.

"Yeah, it's her. How else would she have brought me here?"

Hoodie Man crouches down in front of me, his forearms resting on his knees.

"You don't look as badass as stories would have people believe. Maybe we've all been worried for nothing."

"Here's a tip," I say, leaning forward to place my forearms on my bended knees, mimicking his position from the ground. "You might want to pull up your pants because when my guys get here, it's going to be impossible to run in those things. And you *will* want to run."

"Oh, Sugar Tits, your guys aren't coming or they'd be here already."

"You lookin' at my tits? That's your second mistake. My guys won't take kindly to that either."

"How about you just tell me where the book is so we can all be on our merry way, yeah?"

"How about you eat a dick?" I reply, throwing in a head tilt for good measure.

"Okay, boys, she wants to do this the hard way," he says to his cronies in the back while getting to his feet.

"I like it hard, just not from you. Or at least I think I do. It's been awhile. But I do know I've got enough hard things of my own," I retort, really just trying to keep stalling in the hopes my damn men actually do come for me.

As all of their eyes start to glow red, I get to my feet and back myself against the wall. Right before they lunge for me, all the doors around the room start opening and closing. I now fully understand just how creepy that shit is because this time it isn't me. Though, whoever it is has good timing - a ghost girl can appreciate another, right? I'm all about solidarity.

The cronies pause, all looking at each other nervously.

"What are you waiting for? Grab her already!" Mob Man orders.

That tingling is back in my head, and I tap it a couple of times with the heel of my hand. The cronies haven't moved an inch and look even more worried now. Oh, right. Queen of the Gateway. Tapping her head like an insane person. I'm totally going to roll with that. With my evil smirk firmly in place, I take a step forward and twitch my head for good measure. They take a step back.

"What's the matter, boys? You aren't scared of little ol' me now, are you?" I ask with a little more confidence than I'm feeling.

Hoodie Man throws his arm out, halting his crew.

"No. Not really. All you've got is a couple parlor tricks from what I hear. We're not afraid of you."

The tingling is becoming an incessant buzzing in my brain. It's like the feeling you get in your hands or feet when the circulation has been cut off for way too long and then you try to use them. It's a strange mix of constant tingling with pinpoints of pain.

"Oh my *ghost*! Can you *stop* it already?" I yell out, smacking the heel of my hand against my head a couple more times, and a little harder, for good measure.

Hoodie Man shares a look with Mob Man. "She's out of her damn mind, bro. You sure she even knows where the hell the book is?"

"Well, I mean..." Mob Man responds, looking as nervous as the other guys now. "She said she hid it somewhere."

"Well that's fucking great," Hoodie Man states, throwing his arms in the air in frustration. "We're all going to have our asses handed to us if we don't get that book."

As they start arguing amongst themselves, I try to pay attention, but the constant brain buzz is driving me crazy. All of a sudden, the buzzing stops, and a wealth of information floods my brain. It comes so fast, I grab my head with my hands, bending over as the room spins - or at least it feels that way as my stomach does a flip.

It's over as fast as it began, and I stand up straight and shake my head back and forth to make sure there was no permanent damage. Mind melding is not for the faint of heart. Oh wait, that's a Vulcan thing, right? Well, whatever the hell that was, it was probably a lot like that.

But now I *know* things. Like how to navigate the corridors to get to my bedroom. Or how to lock the doors to keep the spirits out during the off hours. It's like I've been given the remote to a smart house, the Gateway being the smart house, and it's bluetoothed directly to my brain.

The room has gone quiet, and they're all staring at me again.

"What? You act like you've never seen a real woman before, boys," I snark, placing my hand on my hip.

Hoodie Man looks at his cronies, then Mob Man. "Get her!" he shouts.

I dive out of the way just as his ghostly hand brushes my arm, sending an involuntary chill through my body. Fucking ghosts. Always so damn cold. A room along the far wall catches my eye, and I race toward it. Throwing the door open, I'm just about over the threshold when my hair is tugged from behind so hard that I'm flung backward.

"Stop playing games, Sugar Tits," he snarls in my ear, his cold breath sending goosebumps down my body. "Give me the book, and I won't have to hurt you."

"Let me go, and I won't have to hurt *you!*"

He tugs me by the hair to the center of the room and pushes me to my knees. My eyes water from the burning in my scalp, and my knees throb from the fall. This being a real girl shit hurts something fierce, but I'll be damned if I let one tear slip free in front of these bozos.

"Now, that's a much better position for you, Sugar Tits."

"Ew! As if," I sneer.

The malevolent look on his face would break a normal girl, but I've got Cole, and he's a helluva lot scarier.

"Where. Is. The. Fucking. *Book*?"

"Up your ass and around the corner," I deadpan.

A ghostly backhand smashes across my face, whipping my head to the side, blood spurting out from my busted lip. Guess he didn't appreciate my charming sense of humor.

"I'll ask you one more time. Where is the book?"

"It's with Yomama."

"Dude, did she just cut a Yo Mama joke?" one of the cronies snickers.

Hoodie Man is obviously not amused, earning me another backhand across the face. This one hits me square in the eye, the force hard enough it sends my body crashing to the floor. My head bounces off the pretty tile with a loud thunk, and the room spins for a moment before the world rights itself again. I slowly push myself back to my knees. *This real girl shit is honestly turning out to be a huge pain in the ass,* I think as I take a deep breath, cursing the fact that my head is throbbing in sync with my rapidly beating heart. *Wonder just how much this body of mine can take? Pretty sure I'm going to find out.*

Warmth trickles down my chin thanks to the blood seeping from my lip. My eye is slowly swelling shut, and I'm pretty sure the sight of me would scare most small children. And these days, those little shits don't scare easily. The guys, however, are going to freak the fuck out when they get a good look at me. Assuming they actually show up. My stomach rolls, and I have a feeling whatever's in there will be making a reappearance on Hoodie Man's sneakers real soon.

"Last chance. If you tell me where the book is, I'll let you live. You don't, I kill you once and for all. But first, I'll go grab those useless guys of yours and kill each one of them in front of you."

And with that, I feel my power surge slightly for the first time since we've arrived. But it's still six against one, and those aren't good odds.

"How about you all go to Hell?"

He grabs me by the throat and pulls me off the ground until my feet are dangling in mid-air. For a ghost, he's got some impressive strength. My hands wrap around his translucent wrists, but no matter what I do, I can't relieve the pressure that's slowly cutting off my air supply.

"You should've just given me the book while you had the chance," he snarls, inches from my face.

"And you should let her go right fucking now," growls a voice from behind me. A voice I've grown to love and hate, sometimes both at the same time.

Hoodie Man doesn't even flinch. He looks to where my guys must be standing, and shouts out, "Get them! Maybe one of them can tell us where the book is."

As the sound of fighting breaks out all around me, Hoodie Man's hold on my throat never eases up. If anything, his grip tightens, and I know I'm going to pass out within seconds. Or worse.

"Maybe you misunderstood me?" Cole asks in a low, deadly voice that somehow still manages to do things to my semi-conscious body. Contrary bitch. Love him or hate him. Just pick one already.

"I'll give you the same offer I gave her. If you tell me what I want to know, you can have your pitiful excuse for a queen back, and we'll leave."

Things are going hazy, spots dancing in my vision as the room grows slowly darker.

With the last bit of awareness I have left, I hear a grunt

from behind me and a body hitting the floor. I recognize that grunt. It's been aimed at me enough times.

That's all it takes for my powers to flood through me. A threat to one of my guys. Even the asshole.

Hoodie Man whimpers as my power sparks against him, and the hand that's around my throat releases its hold, dropping me to the floor. I take a few deep breaths, desperate for air, but this is no time to be weak. My guys need me. I stand, admittedly on shaky legs, but my hands are alight with my pretty pink orbs, which are brighter than ever. The light in the room begins to flicker, and I glance behind me to see Cole picking himself up off the ground. Blood oozes from the wound in his shoulder, while his attacker is nothing more than a wisp of smoke behind him.

Our eyes meet, and in the space of a few heartbeats, all of his fear and regret and longing floods me, and my heart swells with an emotion I really don't have time for. Stubborn ass. Took him long enough. It's enough that he came for me. That they all came for me. I'll have to remember to thank them later.

Cole's eyes widen in terror a second before he shouts, "Fate!"

In that second, an image appears in my head and is gone faster than I can blink. With intent, I grasp the Gateway's mark on my wrist and spin to face Hoodie Man just as a magicked, ghostly blade slices right through my middle. I gasp.

"No!" Cole's guttural scream reverberates through the room. All fighting ceases, and I can hear the sound of footsteps running in my direction.

The entire room is focused on the blade sticking out of my mid-section, and I'm inundated with the feelings of disbelief and horror flooding off my guys.

I glance down at the translucent metal sticking right through me, then look up and meet the eyes of my attacker.

We stand there, a premature celebratory grin crossing Hoodie Man's face.

"Remember when I asked if you wanted to go to Hell?" I whisper, grimacing theatrically, though it really does hurt like a motherfucker.

My fingertips glimmer, the electricity pulsing off them in bright pink wisps of color. His grin morphs into a look of shock as I thrust my hand right into his chest. "I wasn't asking hypothetically, dumbass."

His eyes widen as a loud screech leaves his mouth. The blade simply slides through the rest of my body and disappears before it hits the floor. Meanwhile, I send a silent thank you to the Gateway for that little tidbit of information. Apparently all it takes is a little intent to shift between forms, my corporeal and incorporeal state bendable to my will, along with some strange new mix of the two. Thank fuck this ghostly body isn't quite as weak as the previous one - or as see through. Though the power required to maintain it is a bitch at the moment.

Flames engulf him, a chorus of screams echoing through the room before he disappears in a cloud of black smoke. I turn and face the rest of the astonished men in the room.

"Who's next?" I ask, realizing I'm floating slightly above the floor now, each of my hands holding bright pinkish orbs. Even my orbs are pretty. *#GhostGirlFTW*

The remaining cronies all make a run for the exit. I mentally connect with the Gateway, and the doors slam shut, sending them all to a screeching halt.

"Take care of them, would you? I think I might pass out," I mutter to the guys before I give up the hold on my power.

My body, once again returned to its solid form, reels from its injuries. The pain is too much to bear, and I start to collapse.

Strong arms catch me before I hit the floor, and the smell of soap and something earthy and alluring surrounds me. I manage to open my eyes and find myself staring into Cole's icy blues. His hand comes up to brush a stray piece of hair off my face.

"You came," I whisper.

"I'll always come for you."

I smirk. "There's a dirty joke in there somewhere."

He chuckles, and it's one of the best sounds I've heard all day.

"You can tell it to me later."

"The guys?" I whisper. I can't seem to keep my eyes open any longer.

"Don't worry about them. They're fine."

"Thank you."

"Shhh. I've got you now, love."

And with that, I pass out.

Chapter 21

COLE

ASSHOLE FACT #3: EVEN ASSHOLES CAN SAY THEY'RE SORRY.

Despite everything she just went through, the look of utter peace on her face should settle me, but it doesn't. Her eye is swollen shut and already turning black and blue, and she has a puffy bottom lip, though the blood has stopped seeping from the split. Even in this state, she's the most beautiful woman I've ever seen.

My guilt is practically a living thing, churning in my gut. If I hadn't been so stubborn, she might be sitting here giving me shit right now instead of lying unconscious.

When she passed out, I carried her away from the chaos. With Reggie leading me through the maze that is the Gateway, we made it to her bedroom. Placing her on the enormous bed that could easily fit our entire group - I had to stop my brain before it could dive too deeply into *that* thought - she didn't so much as flinch when her body touched the cool silk sheets. Reggie pointed me to the bathroom so I could find clean washcloths before racing back out to check on the others. I gently washed the dirt and blood off her face, wincing at each new mark I came across.

Then I cleaned myself up, bandaging my shoulder well enough that blood was no longer dripping down my body.

I've been lying here for the last hour, praying that she'd wake up soon so my heart would stop its frantic beating. My soul is restless, being this close to her and not being able to tell her how sorry I am. That I think she's one of the strongest women I know. That my feelings for her are so deep and complex that I couldn't put them into words if I tried. If I did, her contrary ass would probably just give me shit for it anyway. Then I'd get pissy, and we'd start arguing. I'm not going to lie, there's nothing hotter than seeing her cheeks flush with anger and those gray eyes of hers ignite with fire. Not the ghost kind. The female kind. And damn...I can't wait to see that look aimed my way again.

Now, as I lie here with my body next to hers, watching the slow rise and fall of her breathing, I know it's going to take time. I know she's likely never going to forgive me for being such a stubborn jackass. And that's okay. We have nothing *but* time for me to prove to her that I can be different. I make a promise to never put myself in a position to have to say I'm sorry to this woman ever again. She deserves more from me, and I'm going to give that to her. Starting right now.

∾

Fate

Ghost Girl Fact #10: Even injured, our bodies are insatiable bitches. See also Fact #7. (Side note: It's about damn time!)

My body is wrapped in a comforting warmth, surrounded by the scent of earth and sun and soap, which does miraculous things for my weary soul. It seems oddly familiar, though I can't seem to place it.

The pounding in my head and the sting from my lip as I take a deep breath tell me I'm most definitely still living. I'll consider that a win.

As I slowly open my non-swollen eye, a quiet gasp leaves my lips.

Inches from my nose is the one man I never would've expected to see. In sleep, his features have softened, looking almost innocent in their boyish charm. For the first time, I can appreciate how long his eyelashes are when his piercing blue eyes aren't distracting me. A small mole sits near his nose on his left cheek. His breathing is even as he sleeps, and I take a moment to catalog his features. It will help me remember the total innocence he's got buried deep down the next time he aims that grumpy scowl my way.

With his peaceful expression committed to memory, my eyes continue their exploration and land on a very impressive, very naked chest, minus the bandage criss-crossing over his shoulder and under his arm. The sight of the bandage does little to stop my gawking. Perfectly symmetrical chest muscles, an eight pack that is evident even in sleep, and tanned skin that is just begging for my tongue to trace every line and groove. For a moment, I forget who I'm drooling over.

But let's be honest, even when he's pissed off and scowling, my traitorous body still wants him. The man is hot. Both figuratively and literally. With his arm thrown over my body, I'm slowly overheating and not really in a good way considering my pulse is pounding and that pounding is reverberating through my injured skull.

I ever so slowly lift his heavy ass arm up and off my body, setting it gently on the bed in front of him. He doesn't so much as twitch. Making my way off the opposite side of the bed, I wonder just how big this thing is when it takes at least three or four good shimmies of my hips to even reach the edge. Setting my feet on the floor, I slowly attempt to stand, and I'm proud of myself when the room only spins once. Alright, maybe twice.

As I head for the only open door in the room, I glance back at the half-naked man still sleeping peacefully. Every ounce of my soul wants to climb right back in and take advantage of this situation. See what that chest of his feels like all up against my own. But every ounce of my sore body thinks that is a very bad idea.

Since when did you become such a realist? I ask said body. She's usually such a horny broad. Not sure why she's getting all shy now. Pretty sure she just rolled her eyes at me. And now I'm talking to myself. Maybe I hit my head harder than I thought.

From where I stand, I notice just how ginormous the bed really is. With its cream silk sheets that are now covered in my blood, it's easily big enough to fit, oh...say, five massive guys. Just imagining what we could get up to on that thing is enough to have me wishing I had all my memories back. Bet the highlight reel is epic!

The massive bathroom calls to me, and my injured body slowly makes its way across the room. The sparkly, dark gray floor tile warms my feet as I step in, marveling at the elegance and sense of serenity that engulfs me. Lighter gray mosaic tiles line the walls, with two large gilded mirrors placed above the double vanity on the right hand side of the space. The counter is lined with enough shit that you'd never guess we've been gone a hundred years. Makeup and lotions - *is that massage oil?* - all sit near the closest sink, with razors and cologne and all kinds of guy shit by the other. The shower easily takes up the entire wall on the opposite side of the room, enclosed completely by glass walls with a glass door at the center. This thing makes the bed look small. A tiled bench sits in the middle of the large space, with a small recessed shelf above it dedicated for towels. At the far end, it has one of those amazing showerheads on the ceiling and at least three more on the wall. Plenty of room for group showering. *Sign me up, please!* At the other end, still within the glass, is a large bowl-shaped tub that could easily fit three or four people.

First the bed, now the shower. One might think I had a need for spaces that could easily accommodate multiple people. My mind, though still scattered and pounding, has gone straight to the gutter. Even after discovering the uniqueness of our relationship, it never really occurred to me that these guys would be into a group thing. I've suddenly flipped from fantasies about sandwiches to fantasies about one big, heaping, man meat casserole. Ooh...and Jello. I mean, the tub *is* shaped like a bowl. There's always room for Jello, right?

Did I have a food fetish in my past life?

But the second I catch sight of myself in the large mirror above the sinks, my raging libido dies an instant death.

Even with the lights on low, I can see the utter devastation that is my face. I walk up and place my slightly shaking hands on the pretty white granite countertops and lean in a bit to get a good look at the damage. My left eye is swollen so much that you can barely differentiate between my upper and lower eyelids. It's a lovely shade of blackish purple. My bottom lip is puffy with a large split near the middle, and my neck is sporting a very unattractive necklace of finger-shaped bruises in varying shades of hideous. In other words, I look like hell.

That's only compounded by the fact that while my leather jacket and boots have been removed, I'm still in the white tank and holey jeans that are now dirty and stained with my blood.

I stare at myself a moment. Not only am I unused to seeing myself so battered, but also at seeing a face that is still so unfamiliar. I look back at my reflection, wondering what the old me saw when she looked in this mirror. Did she have the same doubts and worries that I have? That I'll never be powerful enough, or strong enough, or...hell...let's be honest...*me* enough to keep five guys interested?

"I'm sorry," comes Cole's low, deep voice from the doorway, startling me out of a brewing pity party.

I glance his way and am once again shocked by the sight of his bare chest. He takes my silence as a sign of my being upset, when in reality I am just struck mute by the way his abs and pecs flex as he shoves his hands into his back pockets.

"I know you and I didn't get off to the best start, and that I've been an ass to you since day one, but I never would've let you intentionally walk into danger if I had known."

Those last words break me out of my trance, and I finally bring my eyes up to meet his.

"If you had known what?" I ask, confused. My brain is *not* firing on all its cylinders.

"That not having all of your marks was the reason your powers were unstable. Reggie told us you need us to help balance them." He pauses and takes a couple of tentative steps toward me. Pulling one hand from his jeans, his fingertips skim over the four marks on my bicep. "You have my brothers' marks, but not mine."

"And whose fault is that?" I snap, angry despite myself.

"Mine. I know that."

I sigh, not wanting to fight. I get why he kept his distance. I would've done the same thing in his place. But it still hurts. Especially now that we know what he is to me. *My first.*

A sigh escapes me again as the weight of all of this strife between us slowly starts to dissipate. With understanding, comes a certain level of clarity which allows me to see things in a way I hadn't been able to, or *wanted* to, before. "Look, I don't blame you, Cole. In fact, I should probably be thanking you."

At that, his blue eyes widen. "Whatever the hell for?"

"For keeping them safe when I couldn't. For protecting them and making sure you all got back to me."

We stand there, staring at each other - both of us realizing we're at a sort of crossroads. I'm the first to look away. My own emotions are battering my defenses and his aren't helping.

"I need to take a shower," I say softly, turning to walk away and only wincing slightly as the room tilts a bit.

His hand reaches out and grabs my elbow, steadying me.

"Why don't you let me help you?"

I look at him like he's out of his mind.

"You can keep your bra and panties on, just let me help you get the dirt and blood off."

I study him for a moment, surprised to still see this helpful, open side of him. Another olive branch. One I can't and don't want to refuse.

"Okay."

Slowly, he reaches for the hem of my tank top and gently lifts it up, taking extra care when it has to go over my battered face. My eyes are locked on him as his finger comes down to trace a small, dark bruise on my abdomen where the blade impaled my ghostly form.

"I was struggling to keep myself from going solid. It's only a little sore," I whisper.

He sucks in a deep breath and releases it carefully, like he's trying to calm himself down. Nothing about the interaction is in any way sexual, but it stirs something in my belly that feels distinctly familiar.

I reach down and unbutton my jeans, working them over my hips. He shocks me again by dropping to his knees before me and helping me push the tight material down each leg and over my feet. I stand before him in nothing but a white lace bra and matching panties. He doesn't ogle my body or make any suggestive comments, but my body blazes to life like a bonfire regardless.

Standing again, he takes my elbow once more and walks us over to the large shower, through the glass door, and down to the far end. I swear, it's at least a mile long walk. Or at least it feels that way with my body battered and Cole's hands on me. Letting go long enough to reach over and turn on the water, making sure it's the right temperature, his eyes once again meet mine. There are unspoken words reflected in them, telling me a story that I don't think he even realizes he's written. One that would probably send us both up in flames if we were to read the words out loud.

"I'll leave the jeans on," he says quietly.

"Why would you do that?"

His face flushes with heat, which catches me off guard. He brings one of his large hands up and runs it down the back of his head and neck. His eyes won't meet mine, and there's something about his nervous energy that I find completely irresistible.

"I, um...don't really care for underwear."

My brain just about explodes with the implications of that simple statement.

"It's up to you," I say softly. "I mean, we're both adults, and I promise to behave."

His eyebrow quirks up like he doesn't quite believe that last part, and he continues to stare down at me, reading something in my expression that tells him what he needs to know. Unbuttoning his jeans, he pushes them down his muscular legs.

By some miracle, I manage to keep my eyes above his waist. I mean, I *want* to look. I really, really do. But I'm not sure my brain can withstand another hit at the moment.

With his hands on my shoulders, he gently guides me back until I'm partially under the flow of water. I close my good eye, letting the warmth roll over me, rinsing away the chaos of the day and soothing my ridiculously sore body. His large hands begin to softly massage shampoo into my hair, eliciting a moan I can't seem to stop from escaping my lips. It's not a sexual sound, though I'd be lying if I said his touch wasn't affecting me at all. When he's done, he lets the water rinse the suds away before combing the conditioner through the strands with his fingers. There's a shuffling somewhere beside me, bottles moving around with a thud here and clang there, like he's moving them around, looking for something. The noise halts when he's made his choice. The first touch of his hands as they begin to caress my body has me sucking in a gasp.

"I'm sorry, did that hurt?" he murmurs.

I shake my head and whisper, "No. It didn't."

He pauses for a moment, gauging my words, before his hands return to my neck and shoulders, working his way down and under my arms, over my chest and stomach, around my hips, and the inside of my thighs before carefully washing each foot. He doesn't linger on any one area, carefully working his way back up.

His touch is all business, but my traitorous body doesn't give a damn. My breathing has become erratic, and I'm drenched, *not* from the shower. I open my good eye and see his gaze is locked on me. I'm not sure I've ever felt so safe and cared for. Maybe in my past life, but definitely not in this one.

We stand there for a beat, taking each other in, neither of us making a move or speaking.

Finally, it's too much. All of the anger and sorrow and fear and regret and longing built up over the last however many years finally burst forth.

We step into each other at the same time, our lips connecting with a force that would probably shatter the moment between mere mortals, but just stokes the fire between us even higher. The distinct tang of copper hits my tongue, and I know that my lip has busted open, but I can't find it in me to give a damn. His large hand wraps around the back of my neck, pulling my face closer as if even the air between us should know better than to get in the way.

His tongue licks the blood off my lip before forcing my

mouth to obey his command and open for him. Our kiss is frantic. Manic. Out of control.

He pulls back slightly, and I groan, hating the little bit of space separating us.

My eyes open, and I see his widen in surprise as his thumb gently brushes underneath my black eye. The swollen one that suddenly doesn't seem so swollen.

"It's healing," he gruffly responds to my silent question. "So is your lip."

My tongue darts out to lick the cut but encounters nothing except smooth skin. Our eyes connect, and the barely banked heat in those normally icy blues is enough to have me melting on the spot.

"How?"

His fingers drop down and skim over the marks on my bicep. All *five* marks on my bicep. Our eyes meet again, and the tilted smirk on his lips even makes my inner bad girl swoon.

"You're all mine now."

"I think I always have been."

That's what sends him over the edge of his control. Reaching behind me, he grabs my ass and hauls me up, my legs automatically finding their place around his waist. Before I can ask about his shoulder, my back is hitting the cold tile and his mouth is on mine again. His very large, very hard dick rubs against my panties, and I move my hips, trying to get enough friction to ease the ache that has been haunting me for so long.

"Don't tease," I murmur as I come up for air.

"Wouldn't dream of it," he responds as his hand comes up to push the cups of my bra down, my breasts resting on the material. He just stares for a second before he's diving in with a groan and swirling his tongue around my nipple, sucking until my head tilts back, hitting the tile. I don't even feel it. He lavishes the same attention on the other one before he pulls back slightly. "I just needed a taste of those first."

"This is not a taste test. This is a feast. Devour me. Now!"

His chuckle is dark and delicious as his hand wraps around the leg of my panties and pulls. The threads snap, and the offending garment is sailing through the air behind him. We both moan as skin meets skin. His dick slides back and forth through my wetness, once, twice, three times. Granted, it feels better with the panties gone, but I still need him *inside me.*

"Please," I beg.

"What do you want, love?" he whispers.

"I need you. Now. Please."

His hand slides between us, grabs a hold of his dick, and lines himself up. He pushes in slightly and pulls back. In and out. In and out. I feel my power surge to life. Suddenly the feeling of him moving against me, teasing me, seems more than familiar. My body is remembering every touch, every caress of his skin against mine. The dueling sensations are vying for recognition, the phantom touch from a memory coming back into focus. We've been together like this before, entwined around each other, the cool tile against my back and his warmth enveloping me everywhere else. Every slip of him against my wetness feels amplified by its counterpart from my past, and I'm almost desperate in my need for him, two distinct sets of feelings coalescing inside me.

"Now, my alpha," I command in a voice huskier and deeper than my own.

"Yes, my love," he replies simply.

The next time our eyes meet, mutual flames are reflected there.

In one thrust, he's filling me where I've been so empty for so long. He's big, and I'm out of practice, but the little hint of pain is swept away by the pure pleasure of having him inside me. His warmth floods my soul and shatters the remaining barriers around my heart. With each thrust, he builds me back up, making me whole again. I can feel my body tightening, need and want coiling rapidly. His steady rhythm becomes erratic. His body joining with mine. Harder. Faster.

"Fuck," he moans. "You feel so damn good. I'm not sure I can…"

"Don't hold back. I want your cum. Now!"

"Fuucckkk!" His groan is all it takes, and I'm flying over the edge with him. Soaring into the ether. Together. He's still holding me like he'll never let me go, the blackness surrounding us, almost caressing us, as our souls are reunited. It's a place where no one can touch us or come between us. A darkness that only our light can dispel. His hips are continuing to thrust, slower now, dragging every last ounce of pleasure from both of our bodies. His mouth meets mine, but this time it's slow and gentle and says without words everything he's feeling. Time seems to pause, though I have no idea if that's how this works. I just know that this place is special. And it's ours. All of ours.

When he finally pulls away, we're back in the bathroom, both of us a little dazed and a lot exhausted. He slowly lowers me to the ground, holding on to steady me which I appreciate. I'm not all that sure I wouldn't just crumble into a heap at his feet.

"Let's wash up and go get some rest," he says quietly.

We wash quickly, and he steps out to grab us towels. His

goes around his waist, then he holds mine out for me. Stepping into him, his big arms wrap me in a brief embrace over the towel, and I take a moment to just enjoy the peace I feel. My face is squished into his chest, and I can barely breathe, but I don't think I've felt this safe since...hell, probably since old me stood on this amazing warmed tile. He carefully dries me off, kissing my forehead before picking me up, the towel falling to the floor. Walking into the bedroom, he lays me down softly on the plush mattress. The sheets have been changed, the cream exchanged for a deep navy blue.

"You changed the sheets?"

He blushes slightly and shrugs. "They were ruined."

"You going soft on me, alpha?"

He drops his towel, but this time, I don't even attempt to keep my eyes above the waist. I take him in. Every long, thick, *hard* inch of him, before he climbs in next to me.

He smirks. "Do I look soft to you?"

"No. Nope. Definitely not," I say, licking my lips. His dick bobs in response.

"Uh uh. None of that look. There will be plenty of time for that later. Now, you need sleep."

I pout, but he refuses to be swayed. He lies down inches from me, once again face to face. His hand comes up, and his fingers softly trace over my neck.

"The bruises are gone now."

"How's your shoulder?"

He rolls it a couple of times and moves his arm.

"Good as new."

I grab his wrist and turn it toward me, finding the mark that matches mine. A solid line with a single dot in the middle. Because he was my first in our past life. And now he's my first in this one. It feels destined.

With one finger, I trace the mark of the Gateway just below my mark on his wrist.

"Sounds like there's a lot Reggie hasn't told us."

"I don't think she realized just how much we didn't know."

"You're right. We'll have to ask her specifics."

"Later. Right now, we need to rest." He pulls me closer, his hand resting on the space just above my ass. My head is tucked under his chin, my hand absently stroking his chest. With every breath, I inhale his earthy scent, with underlying hints of sunshine and soap. I didn't know sunshine even had a scent until this moment, but it does, and it soothes me like few things can.

"We should check on the guys," I whisper, which is immediately followed by a yawn.

"Reggie said she'd make sure they were okay and would only disturb us if anything went wrong. I think she wanted to give us some time alone."

I make a mental note to thank Reggie later.

My eyes refuse to stay open a minute longer. Right before I drift off, I feel him place another soft kiss on my forehead. For the first time in a hundred years, my soul feels complete.

Chapter 22

KNOX

EMPATH FACT #4: SOME THINGS ARE BETTER LEFT UNFELT.

*T*he room is shrouded in black smoke from all the asshole ghosts we just sent packing. The back of my hand swipes across my forehead, collecting sweat and dirt along the way. I'm on edge. The emotions in the room slowly start to dwindle now that we've taken out the garbage...but not fast enough. Anger, hostility, fear, the need for revenge. All still swirling around, creating a powerful cocktail of negative energy. Even my usual breathing technique is struggling to keep it all at bay.

Then there's the worry I can feel from all the guys and the pain and guilt I can still sense from Cole. Fate is remarkably at peace, though there are muted traces of pain and worry as well. The sight of her dangling from that piece of shit's hands will haunt me for a long time. Our little ghost just can't catch a break.

Where the fuck did they go, anyway?

Glancing around the room, a scuffle near the door catches my attention. The twins have some poor schmuck of a ghost backed up against the wall and are taunting him with their powers.

Rolling my eyes, I shout, "Hey, numbnuts! Stop dicking around."

"How about you make us?" Thad jeers.

"Ignore them," Mack says, coming up beside me. "At least it's keeping them occupied."

"True that. Where the fuck are Cole and Fate?"

"She passed out. Cole carried her out of here with Reggie guiding him. I really think we need to check on them."

"I'm sure Cole's got it under control. Let's make sure everything is cleaned up in here, and then we can figure out where he's taken her."

"You're right. I'm sure Cole would let us know if anything were wrong," he murmurs, staring at the door like a dog whose owner just left for the day. His fear and worry are damn near suffocating me.

"She'll be okay, mate."

"I know you're right. I just keep seeing her impaled by that damn blade, and it's making me all...itchy."

"Itchy? That sounds like a personal problem."

He turns to me and glares. "Shut up. You know what I mean. It's like something inside me needs to see her to confirm she's still alive."

"I feel the same way, Mack. A part of me is desperate to go to her, but luckily for me, my empath abilities are helping me keep it locked down. I can *feel* that she's okay, so I don't need to storm the castle to hunt her down."

His hand lifts to brush through his messy waves, which fall into even bigger disarray. He's got a black smudge across his cheek, and his glasses are smeared with...god only knows what. "Cole was hurt too. What if..."

"Mack, they're *both* fine. I promise. I'll know if anything changes."

A sigh escapes as he struggles with his growing panic.

My hand grips his shoulder firmly, letting him know he's not alone. What he needs most right now is to be grounded. As much as I'm accustomed to being surrounded by emotions, Macklin is the opposite. Living his life with his head in cold, hard facts has left him unprepared for the vulnerability and emotional dependence that comes with this reignited connection to Fate.

"Right now, I'm pretty sure they're both asleep. Their feelings are muted, but still very much there."

"Okay. You'll tell me if you feel anything happening, right?" he asks, swiping a hand across his cheek, spreading the sooty mark even more.

"I will. I swear."

He nods, walking to a closet and grabbing brooms and a few rags along with some sort of cleaning spray.

"How the hell did you know that was there?"

"I..." he trails off. His brows furrow for a second, obviously trying to work something out in that big brain of his. "I just knew. Maybe the Gateway mark added to my knowledge banks or unlocked that portion of my memory. I'm not sure."

"Huh. Okay, then." He tosses me a broom, and we get to work cleaning up the dirt and overall grime from the slimy spirits. Amazing how much residue those fuckers can leave behind. The blood stains from Fate are another matter. I grab a rag and spray bottle and begin cleaning up the evidence that our little ghost is no longer a mere presence but a flesh and blood woman. What's more concerning is that she's able to be harmed by spirits. With that thought, I realize that the shroud of black smoke has been replaced with a blanket of worry covering the entire room. Now I'm the one with a prickly sensation crawling across my skin like an itch that can't be scratched.

"So, boys, you've got it all handled, yeah?" Reggie asks, sauntering into the room like she doesn't have a care in the world. Or at least she wants us to think that. I can sense differently. Her aura is a grayish yellow, giving away the concern she's trying to hide.

Mack rushes forward. "How is she?"

"She's still out. Cole was going to clean her up and watch over her. I made sure the rest of the entrances were sealed shut for now."

"And we're just going to let the asshole who's been a ginormous cock knob to her since day one care for Fate? He's more likely to argue with her or piss her off than coddle her. And we all know my woman deserves some damn good coddling at the moment," Thad grumbles.

My eyes narrow on him. "Don't forget, he's still the leader of this group, and we need to respect that."

"Yeah, yeah. Don't get your panties in a twist there, Knoxie boy. I get it."

"Plus, they need some time to...work through their issues. Don't you think?" Reggie asks.

Macklin nods. "She's right, guys. Fate needs Cole's mark to complete the bond."

"Fine. We can be patient. Right, bro?" Levi asks his twin, placing his hand on Thad's shoulder.

"I hate it when you all gang up on me," Thad mutters.

"So, it's settled. Let's get the rest of this shit taken care of, and then we can all throw our feet up in the office while we wait. There's a bottle of your favorite Macallan in there," Reggie states, lifting her hands and flinging brooms through the air at Thad and Levi with a smirk.

"You had me at whiskey," Levi quips and nudges his brother's shoulder toward the ash pile left from their little spirit play toy earlier.

By the time the chamber is clean and the tile once again sparkling, we're all exhausted. Mack leads the way to the office, and Levi heads straight for the bar to pour our drinks. Our resident nerd walks around the space, looking at items that haven't been touched in over a century.

Reggie walks in and pauses when she spots Mack inspecting a fountain pen and stack of papers on the lone desk in the room. "That's Fate's desk. That letter in your hand, you left it there for her the last time you were in here."

Mack looks astonished as he reverently runs his finger across the page. "We had something special planned for her."

"You did," Reggie agrees softly.

"What happened?"

Her despair hits me like a punch to the gut. "I don't know. I wish I did."

Levi walks over and hands out drinks, and the fact that Mack takes one says a lot about his emotional state. Along with women, he typically avoids alcohol since he says it impacts how quickly he can access information. We sink into the sofas with glasses of amber liquid in our hands. Reggie is staring off into the fire as if it can give her the answers to the questions we've all been asking.

"Think they're still okay?" Macklin asks, his voice hesitant like he doesn't want to ask but can't help himself.

"They're fine, Mack. Actually..." I trail off, sensing Fate is awake through our bond. She's tired and sore, but the hints of desire tell me that she's going to be just fine. "She's awake. And I'm pretty sure Cole's up now too."

Mack jumps to his feet. "That's great! Can we..."

Reggie cuts him off without even looking back. "Let's give them their space, Mack."

We all eye her a little warily for a moment. Her despair from earlier is growing, and if she doesn't knock it off, I'm going to have to do something about it.

Glancing at Mack, I quickly reassure him. "I can tell you that they're both feeling the effects of the fight, but they're otherwise totally fine."

His shoulders slump, and I feel like I just kicked his puppy.

"We feel your pain, Mack," Levi says, holding his glass up in solidarity, and Thad clinks the glass with his own.

A moment later, the room starts to feel overly warm. Glancing around, I note the fire is still fairly small, definitely not big enough to give off the level of heat I'm suddenly experiencing. A trickle of sweat drips down the side of my face, and I swipe it away.

"Is anyone else in here getting warm?"

"Nope," Thad responds.

Levi shakes his head.

Reggie mutters, "I wish."

Mack looks at me quizzically. "Are you feeling okay?"

"Yeah, I'm fine, " I mumble, though silently I question what the hell is going on. The emotion in the room, while high, isn't anywhere near the peak of my limits, but this feels remarkably close to that dangerous line. Something powerful is brewing.

"You sure? You're looking a bit flushed and are acting a little...shifty."

"It's just..."

The sensation floods me then. This isn't your typical kind of warmth. This heat is created when two people who share a deep bond start to become physically intimate. I've felt something like this before, but nowhere near as strong. With all of the fiery emotions between Cole and Fate, it's a wonder I haven't spontaneously combusted already. I flush for a different reason this time, trying to block out a bulk of the feelings before I'm coming in my pants again. Don't need a repeat of that any time soon.

Fuucckk!

"Knox? What is it?" Mack asks.

Suddenly, we're all hit with an intense blast of power that knocks us all back into our seats. Reggie ends up halfway across the room.

Levi's hand is holding his drink in the air, making sure he doesn't spill a drop of the precious liquid. "What the fuck was that?"

"Fuck if I know," Thad mutters, tossing back the last of his whiskey.

"Knox, what do you feel?" Macklin asks.

Sending my senses out, I suddenly know exactly what's happening and can feel the tension and relief and desire that's flooding the bedroom where Cole and Fate are holed up. "Um..." *Fucking smooth, Knox!*

All four sets of eyes turn to look at me.

Mack's nervously wringing his hands now. "Is it Fate? Is she okay?"

Trying again, I clear my throat. "I'm not sure."

Macklin's eyes narrow on me, and his finger points in my direction. "You're lying."

"What do you mean?"

"I can tell you're lying. Something inside me is..." He pauses, looking around the room. "Something is different. I can't pinpoint it, but I can *feel* it. Thad, tell me something. Let me see if I can figure out if it's true or a lie."

Thad's eyebrows shoot up. "Aren't we a little old for two truths and a lie?"

"Just fucking do it!" I growl.

"Fine. Calm down, bro. Okay. Let's see." He rubs his chin between his thumb and forefinger before coming up with what is sure to be a doozy. "Fate, Levi, and I got it on while we were out on that ghost call. Right in the front living room. Clothes hanging from the curtains. Sweat dripping down our bodies. Our dicks sliding in and out of each..."

"Okay...that's enough," Mack says, holding his hand out like that alone will stop the huge taint biscuit who's smirking on the opposite sofa. "That's a lie. Right?"

"Shit, bro! How did you know? I mean, it could've happened, but my wankstain of a brother put a halt to it."

Levi punches him in the shoulder.

"You know a client's living room is not the time or the place, dipshit."

"Fucking cockblock," Thad mutters.

Macklin interrupts their bickering. "I'm not really sure *how* I know. It's like that blast leveled up my powers. I can sort of...glean information from you and determine if what you say is true or not. Now tell me something else. Let's try it again."

Levi starts before Thad has a chance. "Fate shocked the shit out of the Oscar Mayer Wienermobile driver."

That earns him the side-eye from Thad.

"That's....the truth," Mack blurts out.

"Bro," Thad barks, "I thought we weren't going to talk about that."

"Too late," I chirp. "We'll discuss that little morsel when Cole returns."

"Ah hell," Thad grumbles.

"Your turn, Reg," Mack claps excitedly, earning a glare from the spirit.

"Fine. I'll play your stupid little game. I'm the one behind Fate's death and disappearance."

She says it with a straight face, and it's our turn to glare at her.

"Mack?" I hiss.

He studies her for a moment, his head tilting to the side like it might help him think better.

"That one's not quite as easy as the others. Mostly it seems like a lie, but there are hints of truth woven in. Maybe this new power isn't as reliable as I was thinking it was."

"*Did* you have something to do with what happened to Fate?" Thad snaps at Reggie.

Placing her hands on her hips, she stares him down. "She's my best friend. What do you think, you big oaf?"

Ignoring the silent glaring contest now taking place, Mack's disappointed eyes find mine again. "Guess I'll need to work out the kinks. What about you, Knox? Feel any different?"

"Don't think so," I say, getting up and heading to the bar in the corner. "Feelings all within normal parameters. Auras are still there with normal intensity, though now that you mention it, after that little blast, you've all gained a silver band around the inner portion of your auras. Much like the one our little ghost has. So yeah, just your average empath stuff here."

Thad walks up beside me and grips my shoulder with one hand while he holds his other hand out toward me for a refill. "It's okay to be average, Knoxie boy. We can't all be awesome."

He laughs like he's the funniest thing to happen since Jo Koy.

When our eyes meet, I feel my power surge in a way it's never done before.

Thad's face gets serious, then his eyes well up and tears spill over. Before I can figure out what's happening, he's sobbing like a baby, throwing himself into my arms and holding on tight. I reluctantly wrap my arms around him, awkwardly patting his back.

"What the fuck just happened?" Levi asks.

Not sure what's more odd, the fact that he doesn't seem the least bit worried about his twin or that he's got a hint of a smirk on his face.

"I honestly have no idea. He was laughing, and I just wanted to shut him right the fuck up."

Mack quickly gets to his feet, rushing over to us. Meanwhile, Thad is still sobbing in my arms.

"You just changed his emotions. You thought it, and it happened."

"I...I guess I did briefly think to myself that I wanted to make the big fucker cry, but I didn't want him to turn into a blubbering mess!"

"Well, maybe accuracy will come with practice."

"Fuck! How do I fix him?"

"Why fix him? I kind of like him like this," Reggie mutters.

"Imagine him calm and relaxed?" Mack shrugs.

"Super helpful, mate."

My hands are still patting the back of the giant man in front of me, but I close my eyes and imagine Thad calming down and getting just a little bit sleepy. I mean, it would be kind of nice to have him out of the way for a minute.

The crying slowly stops, and he stands, wiping his face with the back of his hand.

"Hey, Knox. 'Sup, bro?"

"Uh...nothing. Why don't you go have a seat next to Levi?"

Thad's face turns until he eyes his twin, gives the head nod that is in every man's silent vocabulary, then walks over and drops back into his seat.

Levi's eyes are as round as saucers when they meet mine. "Bro! What the fuck? That was *epic*!"

Mack claps his hands together. "We've all leveled up. Levi. What have you got?"

He looks at us warily as we both move closer.

"Well...uh...I'm not sure."

"Feel down deep inside yourself, in that place your power resides. It should feel different than it usually does," Mack spouts off, suddenly the expert in the crazy that has enveloped us all.

We watch as Levi's face scrunches up. He honestly looks constipated rather than powerful.

"Wait. I can feel it. It *does* feel different. There's this warmth and brightness to it I've never experienced before."

"Try to use that. Let's see what happens," Mack says excitedly. Dude really does cream his pants over a good mystery.

Levi closes his eyes, and suddenly the room is flooded with a bright light.

Covering my eyes with one arm, I shout, "Ok, shut it off...or pull it back in...or whatever the fuck. I don't want to be permanently blinded."

I peek out from behind my sleeve and see the room slowly returning to its normal state.

"That is *totally* badass!" Levi exclaims.

"Yay! You're a giant flashlight," Reggie deadpans, earning her a glare from Levi this time.

"So we can safely assume that if you have light, Thad has

something with darkness as he's your opposite." Mack is pacing back and forth, muttering to himself. "But wait, what caused it? Do you think Fate and Cole were affected as well? Are they okay?"

My eyes meet Levi's, and he must see exactly what I'm struggling to hide. "Oh, I think they're *just fine*. Right, Knox?"

Perceptive bastard!

"Um. Yeah. They're completely fine. More than fine, actually."

"Then what the fuck is going on?" Thad asks around a yawn.

I look at Mack, and his eyes go wide.

"Oh!" His cheeks steadily grow pink.

"No way! She's fucking the asshole first?" Thad groans, his eyes closing as he slumps further into the sofa.

Levi smacks him upside the head. Reggie tries too, but her hand sails right through.

"Hey! What the fuck, bro?"

"Could you be any more crude?" Mack says with a roll of his eyes.

"I mean, I could. Yeah." Thad shrugs. "But I'm a little tired at the moment."

Ignoring him, Mack says, "Well then. They're obviously okay, so we should just...let them be for a few hours."

"Sounds like a plan to me. Maybe I can play around with this light thing a little."

"Don't you dare! My eyes are still recovering." I shudder dramatically, but the bastard just chuckles.

"We could always play two truths and a lie," Mack suggests softly, a hopeful look on his face.

"Seriously, mate?" It's my turn to groan.

"I mean, I want to practice my new ability. Practice makes perfect, right?"

"Fuck! Fine. But it doesn't leave this room, understood?"

Macklin simply nods.

Levi drains his glass. "Count us in, after I get us refills."

Thad just yawns.

"Someone's gotta keep you all in line, so I'm in too," Reggie says, settling herself on the floor in front of the fireplace.

I glance at the clock and decide to give the lovebirds a few hours. If they're not out here by then, I'm going in after them. Can't let the asshole have all the fun, after all.

Chapter 23

Fate

Ghost Girl Fact #11: The universe loves to throw all of its shit at us in rapid succession. I'm on to you, Universe. You better watch your back.

I woke up in Cole's arms. Let me repeat that just in case the ramifications of that statement haven't hit home. I woke up in *Cole's* arms. Crazy, right? The asshole sure does like to cuddle. I know, color me surprised too.

Never in a million years would I have thought that this could be real life. Oh, sure, my body wanted the insufferable man, but my brain wasn't sold on the idea. Something about almost dying...again...changed that. Softened us both up to the reality of all of those complicated feelings swirling around inside of us - like a kid on a merry-go-round that's had one too many sweets, but as soon as the spinning stops and he vomits it all up, he feels so much lighter.

Cole and I are that kid. Now we're free of the mess that was holding us down. I know. I'm so awesomely dignified, it's no *wonder* the Gateway chose me. Cue eye roll.

Things can only get better from here. Right?

Turning, I watch my alpha cover that amazing chest with a black shirt he found in the massive closet. Apparently old me was a little bit OCD. All of the clothes were organized by guy, then by color. Shoes were organized by style and then, you guessed it, color. Accessories put away in alphabetical order by type. She was apparently a very well organized woman or, as I have started to refer to her, a total psycho. I swear, some days I wonder if the guys found the wrong girl.

He notices me perving on him from my comfy perch on the side of the bed, my arms braced behind me and my legs swinging off the side, and gets that smirk on his face that does lovely things to my lady bits.

"Knock that off, love, or we'll never make it out of this room."

"Hmm...I mean, that wouldn't be such a bad thing, would it?"

"It would if the others come crashing through the door to check on you."

"I repeat, that wouldn't be such a bad thing, would it?"

He just chuckles, walking over to me and wrapping those big arms of his around me as he pulls me up against him.

"I'm not sure how this used to work between all of us, but in this life, I'm not so sure I'm willing to share my time with you."

Resting my arms over his shoulders, my hands play with his hair as I study those blue eyes of his. His sudden possessiveness has me biting my lower lip, all the ways we could take advantage of our alone time playing on a continuous reel inside my mind.

He pulls my body harder into his, all of our important

parts lining up, his hard to my soft, and I can't stop the moan that escapes my lips.

Trailing his lips along my neck, he whispers in my ear, "I can see those naughty gears turning," he pauses, dragging his tongue around the rim of my ear, "but we really do need to check on the others. I need an update."

With that, he gives me a quick kiss on the lips and sets me on my feet before walking toward the bedroom door.

I stand there, hot, bothered, and confused about what the hell just happened. Along with the fact that I can actually *feel* the concern radiating off him. I'm staring at him for all of two seconds before a big, dramatic pout appears on my face.

"Nope. Save that pout for Knox or Macklin. It won't work on me."

"You suck."

"No, but I bet you do." He shoots me a wink as he opens the bedroom door.

"Hmph!" I narrow my eyes at the pain in my ass, or, more accurately, pain in my pussy. "It'll be awhile before you find out just how awesome this mouth is, you big tease."

He chuckles again, holding out his hand, and I all too easily relent and let him wrap his large fingers around mine as he guides us through the Gateway. We reach the set of double doors to the main chamber, and I mentally give them a little push. They slide open, revealing...an empty space. This feels eerily familiar. My stomach sinks for a second, wondering where in the hell the others are, before we hear low murmurs coming from a door off to the side of the dais.

I take a step toward the sound, but Cole tugs me back. He's still holding my hand and looking at me with that uber serious expression I've grown accustomed to. He glances down at our joined hands before meeting my eyes again. "I know things haven't always been easy between us."

"That's putting it mildly," I mumble.

His lips tilt up in a half-smile, softening his face for a moment before the serious Cole is back, his brows furrowing and his lips getting that tightness to them whenever he's stressing out about something. I note that his concern from before has morphed into intense worry now. For me. For us. Whatever it is he's struggling with, I want him to know that I can help. That we're in this together. Partners.

My hand comes up to cup his chin, my thumb running along his bottom lip. His tension eases, and with it, something shifts in my heart. Like a crack was just filled and repaired. I remember the first time I saw him outside the estate. The urge to do exactly this had scared the shit out of me. Now here we are.

Mind. Blown.

"I need you to promise me something," he asks softly.

"Anything," I respond without hesitation.

"Promise me you won't run. No matter what happens from here on out, you'll stay. You'll fight for us. For what we can rebuild."

"I promise," I whisper, too overcome by the depth of feelings I have for this man to say anything more.

"And I promise to trust you and support you and prove to you every day that I deserve to be by your side."

I can't help myself. I go up on my tiptoes and kiss him. It isn't the frantic meeting of mouths it was before. This is soft. Real. Heartfelt. A way to seal our promises to each other.

We pull apart, our hands still interlocked, and head toward the voices.

Finding the others in an office, they're sitting on deep

burgundy sofas that surround a lovely fireplace. A small fire is warming the room, and it settles something inside me. The total familiarity of this scene - right down to the seats everyone has chosen. It all just feels...right.

"They're aliiiivve," Reggie says, doing her best - which is terrible - Frankenstein impression. Then she pouts when no one pays her any attention.

The guys jump up and immediately surround us.

Knox is the first to get his hands on me, wrapping me up in a hug that barely allows me room to breathe.

"Are you okay?" he asks softly.

"I'm fine. Really."

He kisses my forehead before his eyes meet mine, gauging my words. I don't need words to know how he's feeling since his relief rushes over me like a gust of fresh air.

Before he can reply, I'm whisked out of his arms. I expect Thad or Levi, but my brows shoot up when I realize it's Macklin that has just stolen me away.

I don't get a word out before his lips touch mine in possibly the sweetest kiss I've ever had, telling me everything I know he's too shy to say out loud. When he pulls back, the familiar blush is there, and I can't stop myself from hugging the shit out of him.

"You gave us all heart attacks," he murmurs, and the fear and concern that he's been struggling with since seeing me almost impaled hits me with all of the force of a wrecking ball. The breath is briefly knocked out of me, and I try to stop my body from trembling under the sheer weight of his feelings. I manage to regain control of my own senses. Barely.

"I'm sorry. I didn't mean to make you worry. I should've checked in sooner."

"She was in no condition to do anything, let alone head

back into a potential battle," Cole grumbles from behind me. Like, *right* behind me. I can feel the heat coming off the guy just as well as I can feel the heat from the fire. Maybe he's part demon. It would explain a lot, actually.

"But you're okay now?" Mack asks as he backs away, letting his eyes survey my body. "I mean, you look pretty good."

My eyebrows shoot up. "Just 'pretty good,' eh, Mack?"

Cue blush. *Oh my ghost. It's just too easy.*

"You look amazing," Knox croons from my side.

"Wait. How *do* you look so amazing?"

"Jesus, Mack!" Knox slaps him upside the head.

Mack quickly grabs his glasses as they almost fly off his face from the force.

"I didn't mean it like that! She always looks beautiful. I'm just wondering how there's not a single scratch on her." He risks a glance at Cole. "Or you for that matter. Your shoulder wound was pretty serious. It probably needed stitches."

I point to the five marks on my left arm. Macklin's fingers run over the marks, and I shiver. The move was almost clinical in nature, but my damn body doesn't give two fucks. In all reality, she'd probably be happy giving more than two fucks. Horny broad.

Cole responds for me since I seem to have lost all ability to communicate effectively.

"The second my mark appeared on her arm, the injuries started to heal. Swollen and bruised eye. Split lip. Bruises around her neck. Bruised knees. A small bruise on her abdomen where the knife went through her. In a matter of seconds, they were almost totally gone."

"Wow! That's incredible. And your shoulder? The same thing?"

"Yup," he answers, pulling the neck of his shirt down

and showing the smooth skin that I may have kissed while he was sleeping. Yup. I was a total creeper.

"Are you fuckers done chit chatting? I'd like to hold my woman, now."

With that, Thad uses his substantial size to manhandle me away from the discussion still taking place amongst the others. The second I'm wrapped in his massive arms, I feel another body come up behind me and sandwich me in.

Mmm...twin sandwich.

"You really okay, sweets?" Levi whispers in my ear.

I nod, then let my forehead fall to Thad's huge chest, unable to speak due to the sheer amount of worry and affection I can feel emanating off these giant guys. Like an embrace within an embrace, our souls holding onto each other while their tenderness infuses me with warmth from the inside out. They may seem scary, but they're really just big, squishy teddy bears. Just don't tell them I said that.

They seem to sense my struggle and hold me tighter. This would probably suffocate any normal woman, but it just makes me feel cared for on a level I haven't known in too long. Like - at least a hundred years.

"We got you," Thad murmurs. "Don't ever forget that, babe."

"Thank you," I whisper back.

Then my stomach decides to end the feel-fest with a loud rumble, followed by a round of chuckles.

"You hungry, little ghost?" Knox asks.

"I'm starving. I don't think I've eaten since..." I trail off and try to think.

"It's been over twenty-four hours. Breakfast yesterday," Mack answers.

"Thanks, Mack."

Knox looks at Reggie. "Where's the kitchen? Mack and I will go whip some food up for the group."

"Take the main hall to the right and follow it until it ends. It'll be straight ahead."

"I think I knew that," Macklin states, a thoughtful look crossing his face.

"Any requests?"

Before anyone can respond, a voice from the doorway startles us all.

"Oh my gosh, Fate! It's really you. You're back!"

All eyes swing to the woman blocking our exit, the guys quickly forming a protective semi-circle around me.

"Who the fuck is it now?" I whine, throwing my hands in the air. "What's a ghost girl gotta do to enjoy some peace and quiet around here?"

"It's alright, guys. The Gateway let her in," Reggie responds before turning to our new visitor. "Destiny, what are you doing here?"

As if that's all my brain had been waiting for, the flood gates open and a sudden rush of memories is released, assaulting me with an intensity I struggle to contain. My hands grab my head as arms steady my swaying body. From somewhere in the room, I can hear the guys calling my name and asking if I'm okay. I attempt to respond, but the memory drags me under.

Chapter 24

Fate

One Hundred Years Ago

There is nothing more exhausting than a morning spent in the Land of Torment. It's hot there. Really, really hot. Think fire and brimstone and wisps of sulfur on the air. Then there are the screams. From everywhere. All the time. My body is wracked with shivers. Man, I loathe that place.

Every month, my sisters and I have breakfast together. We take turns hosting, but I just can't seem to find it in me to get excited about it anymore. It's not that I don't care for my sisters. I do. But Destiny has been absent more often than not lately. Her and Karma have been at odds the past few years. Karma is just...I release a loud sigh when I think of my eldest sister. I love her dearly, but the woman is a lot to handle on a good day, let alone a really bad one. Karma is like a cocktail of negativity and paranoia with a splash of vengeance thrown in. I'm not sure if the Land of Torment made her that way, or if she's always been a bundle of instability.

Karma was the first sister tested by the Gateway to take over the role of Guardian of the Spirits. It quickly became apparent that she was too darkly influenced, her balance tipped to the punishment side of the scale. She was given the Land of Torment, or sent there as retribution for the chaos she'd created, depending on whose story you believe, and became the Keeper of Darkness.

Destiny was the second sister to endure the test for the Gateway. She was everything innocent and pure, love and happiness, kindness and charity. Where Karma was the darkness, Destiny was the light. Pure, blinding light. When the balance tipped to the enlightened side of the scale too heavily, she was quickly given the role of Keeper of Light, on the Isle of Light - for obvious reasons.

Then, the Gateway tested me, more intensely than either of my sisters. It needed someone with the ability to remain neutral, rational, and unbiased. To fairly judge those who sought their path to the afterlife. When I was chosen, my sisters rejoiced. Though Karma, in true Karma fashion, seemed slightly jealous, which only grew worse once I cemented my balance through the bonds with my guys.

As I float through the Ether, I let my mind wander over today's topic of polite conversation, whether I should truly trust the guys. This seems to bother my eldest sister...a lot...as it comes up frequently these days. I constantly reassure her that they're totally dedicated to me and that I trust them implicitly, though, I will admit to having some doubts recently.

I'm sure that's common in every relationship that has weathered the years, right? Like the mysterious letters that the guys have been receiving that are whisked away before I get a chance to read them. Or the numerous last minute meetings one or more of them will head off to at all hours of the day and night. Then there are the low conversations they've been having when they think I'm not paying attention.

Karma thinks they'll leave me one day. Which is preposterous. We're all bonded. They couldn't leave me without severing those bonds and joining with someone else. But the little hint of doubt in the back of my mind grows larger every time she brings this up. I know I should just ask the guys, but it honestly seems so silly. *After five hundred years together, I know them. They would never do something to hurt me.*

Then there's Reggie. My best friend and confidant hasn't been around much lately either. I'll see her in passing, and then she scampers off saying she forgot to clean something. That woman hates cleaning as much as I do. Seriously, what is going on with everyone?

I shake the negative thoughts from my head and decide enough is enough. It's time I have a talk with everyone before my imagination gets the better of me. I'm the balance, afterall. I can surely be unbiased and rational when it comes to my five and my friend, right?

As I arrive back at the Gateway, I make my way to the great room. The doors are open, so I call out for the guys. It's quiet here. A little too quiet. There are always spirits lurking around, but even they seem to be absent right now. Strange.

Walking into my office, I see a note sitting on my desk, telling me the guys are at one of our favorite spots - a deep cavern with a large, natural spring-fed pool - and to meet them there as soon as I return. Maybe they've been planning something special for all of us. The thought cheers me up as I transition to my ghostly form and head back through the ether.

The humidity hits me the second I turn solid, heat flowing out of the mouth of the tunnel that leads to the cavern. I'm thankful for the flowing blue gown that is light and airy. It swirls around me as I walk down the path, cautiously excited to see my five, but I don't get more than a few feet in before I hit a veil of power. Something strong and different than anything I've ever felt before. I make a mental note to ask the guys about it.

Their voices reach me before I can see them, and I smile, warmth filling me at their playful banter.

Then I hear a distinctly female giggle. It sounds eerily famil-

iar. Almost like my own. My stomach drops, and my body goes cold.

As I round the bend that leads into the main portion of the space, I stop dead in my tracks. There, before me, is Cole. In his tan trousers and white button-down shirt with the sleeves rolled up, showing off the forearms that always manage to spark a tingle down deep in my belly. Except this time, it feels more like a lead weight.

In his arms, with her slender, pale hands clutching the front of Cole's shirt, is my sister Destiny. The curls of her long white hair are flowing freely in the slight breeze that blows through the cavern. Their eyes are both closed, and their lips are a mere breath apart from connecting. There's an odd shimmer around her, but I barely notice. My eyes are on the man that just broke my heart.

My book, which is always with me, falls from my hands, landing on the rough ground of the cavern with a loud, echoing thump. They jolt apart, confusion etched on Cole's handsome face as his icy blue eyes look at me like he's never seen me before. Destiny just stares at me, though I swear I see a slight smirk tilting her lips, her eyes mocking me. Something niggles the back of my mind when I look at her, but the scene in front of me is demanding all of my attention.

Cole's unfocused eyes shoot to Destiny and grow impossibly wider, then dart back to me with a dawning look of horror on his face.

"Fate? How did you..."he trails off, looking at Destiny. "Destiny?"

His large hand comes up and runs through his dark hair that has grown longer than usual, hanging down past his chin. "Fate, I'm not sure what's happening right now, but this is not what it looks like."

I can't speak. Can't move. Can barely breathe. I just stand here and let the tears fall while I look at my first. The one I chose before all others. With my sister.

"Destiny? When did you get here?"

I hear Macklin's words, and my eyes meet his as he walks up to our cozy little group. He takes one look at my expression, his glassy eyes shooting to Cole and Destiny, noting their closeness, and takes a step toward me. My body finally breaks out of its frozen state, and I take a step back. He pauses, glancing at the ground before picking up the book I dropped, his brow furrowing and his concern growing. He knows what that book means to me. Without it, my power would disappear, and so would theirs. The planes would be sent into chaos. At the moment, I don't even care.

Then I notice the others behind him. Knox, Thad, and Levi. Another step back. And another. They all have the same glassy eyes, their stares unfocused.

Were they all indulging in drink? Drugs? Those aren't usually things we enjoy, but others often do. Have they all changed so much while I sat here thinking everything was fine? Was I just not enough for them?

My mind whirls with the implications. The mysterious letters and late night meetings. Hushed conversations. Karma's insistence that they would leave me one day. My heart shatters into a million pieces, and a sob breaks free before I can stem the sound with my hand. They're all here. They all knew what was happening, and no one cared enough to stop it. Or they're all in on it. Together. Without me. With her.

"Fate? Please!" Cole begs. "Listen. I'm not sure what's going on here, but we'll figure it out."

My fractured soul is bleeding from the blow, and it's only by some miracle that I'm able to hold it together at all. I turn and start to run back down the tunnel, the need to get away so strong that I almost trip over my gown but catch myself at the last second.

"Fate! Don't go!" Cole shouts from behind me.

I run faster. Just before he reaches me, I transition back to my ghostly form and head for the only person left who won't lie to me. The one person that will help me figure out how this all went so wrong.

As the memory begins to fade, the movie in my mind turns into brief snippets, rapidly flickering from one scene to the next. A knife, the feeling of cool night air on my skin, boots kicking my already battered body, blackness, then dirt filling my lungs, before it's all stuffed back inside the locked box in my mind.

My mind is reeling, and my hands have a death grip on the arm of whichever guy is unlucky enough to be holding me at the moment. But I can't trust these guys, right? I abruptly throw the offending arm off, shuffling back a few steps. Then a couple more. It's a struggle to breathe. To think. Tears flood my eyes before I can even stop them.

Looking up from the floor, I scan the room, fat drops rolling down my cheeks. As they land on each guy, it's like some weird connection is made, and their eyes change from concerned to 'what the fuck' in a split second. Their growing horror is nothing compared to the tumultuous level of crazy inside my brain. Do they remember too?

Before I realize it, I've backed myself up against a desk. With nowhere else to go, panic sets in full force. I can't tell the difference between my emotions and Fate's from a hundred years ago. They're all raging through me, twining around each other and creating one hell of a powerful concoction inside me.

My safe haven has been ripped away, and my soul that

was finally whole and happy is keening from the loss all over again. As a combination of two lifetimes of grief converge into one, it seems worse now than all those years ago. I'm all alone, again, questioning who I can trust.

What the fuck did I do to deserve any of this? Did the guys know all along? Have they been praying I wouldn't remember?

"Fate?" Macklin asks gently.

I ignore him. I need to get out of here. I need to go...somewhere. Anywhere. But where?

"Fate," Cole whispers urgently, "you promised."

My eyes dart to his, finding some level of calm. Which doesn't make sense, right? He was the one almost swapping spit with my sister after all. But something in his gaze centers me. Grounds me. Helps clear the fog that is consuming my brain. It slowly erases the residual feeling from the memory and brings me back to myself. To who I am now.

Hastily running the backs of my hands over my damp cheeks, my gaze locks on my sister. Her long, straight hair is pure white, with braids that pull the hair back from her face, meeting at the back of her head in an intricately beautiful knot. I've envied that damn knot for hundreds of years since my own hair can't seem to be tamed. She's dressed in a flowing white gown that is damn near the same color as her super pale skin. She's beautiful, her face radiating pure innocence.

How the fuck does she pull that shit off? I'd probably just look constipated.

That small niggle in the back of my mind has become a large battering ram against my subconscious. Looking back at the vision through what are basically a fresh set of eyes, I remember the odd shimmer in the air, the veil of power just outside the cavern, and something else. Something else that's not quite right.

Walking up to Destiny on unsteady legs, I stand with only inches between us, our eyes locking onto one another. Hers are a pale blue and seem incredibly relieved to have found me yet concerned at my current state. The pounding in my head grows the longer I stare into her eyes. Her eyes. What is it about her eyes?

And then it hits me. Her eyes. The pale blue eyes I'm staring into aren't the same bright green eyes that smirked back at me in the cavern.

"It wasn't you," I whisper.

And with that last revelation, the pounding in my head gives one last beat before my eyes roll back into my head, and I pass out. Again.

Fucking ghost girl problems.

TO BE CONTINUED...

ACKNOWLEDGMENTS

I've got to admit, this is a bit surreal. I wrote a book. But don't think I did this all by myself. No way, no how. This book was made possible by an incredible support team that cheered me on, answered questions, listened to my craziness, and lifted me up when I was down. This is going to be a little long, so grab a coffee, or glass of wine, or whatever tickles your pickle. No judgment here!

First of all, huge thanks to my husband and kids, and the rest of my family, for supporting me and putting up with my crazy writing stories, afternoon Zoom calls, and overall new author mood swings. You've helped me realize my dream. I love you all so damn much!

This book wouldn't be what it is today without help from my AMAZING alpha reader Mel. Girl - you took a chance on me and I'm grateful every day you did. I might never have gotten to this point if you weren't with me every step of the way. I can never thank you enough. You are the Amy to my Tina. Can't wait to see what that friend of yours, Author Genie Martin, does in the future!

To my badass beta babes: Aly, Richelle, Miranda, Louise,

Angela & Sarah. You ladies really rocked it. Thanks for taking a chance on me. I appreciate you all! And I have to give a special shout out to my beta Louise for jumping in with your PA services when I needed them most and creating many of the awesome graphics and forms and posts that were used for promos. Here's to many future shenanigans that will live on in infamy, even if only in our own heads. Grey Sweatpants Challenge, anyone? Oh...and crocheted dicks. They're soft and squishy...friendly little dicks. Ha!

To my awesome editor, Michelle. Thank you for agreeing to work with me and for being a friendly, patient source of support and encouragement. Some hyphens may have snuck into this acknowledgment without your watchful eye to catch them. Sorry, not sorry! #NoMoreAuras #HAA #TowardNoS

To all of my author friends who offered help and advice - with special shout outs to Amanda Cashure, J. Grace, and A.J. Macey - THANK YOU! I want to be like all of you when I grow up.

And a million thanks to Emma Rider with Moonstruck Cover Design & Photography for the FABULOUSLY awesome cover. You worked your magic and brought my vision to life.

Last, but certainly not least, a ginormous thank you to YOU, darling readers, for picking up this new author's book and reading it - you brave, brave souls. Your support means more than you'll ever know.

May life bring you: quiet time for reading, a good glass of wine, donuts, and a crocheted dick - because, why not? ;)

Sin <3

A PERSONAL NOTE FROM SINCLAIR:

Thank you for giving this newbie author a chance. If you enjoyed this book, it would mean the world to me if you'd consider leaving a review on Amazon and/or Goodreads. Us indie authors love nothing more than to know our readers appreciate our work so much that they're willing to take a couple minutes out of their busy day to leave a few nice words about our book babies. Your support will ensure new readers will get to enjoy the world you just stepped out of.

I'm always happy to answer questions...or maybe you just feel like chatting? Email me directly at sinclairkellyauthor@gmail.com.

You can also stalk me for all the latest news on releases, teasers, giveaways, and more:

Facebook Reader Group - House of Sin: A Sinclair Kelly Readers Group
https://www.facebook.com/groups/225146905378562/

Spotify Playlists
https://open.spotify.com/user/n32tc3qcvzbdlese0zjtexzc3?
si=NQhJw9obQp-beHMRU3sirQ

facebook.com/sinclair.kelly.967

instagram.com/sinclairkellyauthor

goodreads.com/sinclairkellyauthor

pinterest.com/sinclairkellyauthor

ABOUT THE AUTHOR

Sinclair Kelly is a paranormal & contemporary romance author who writes to give all of the feral characters in her head a voice. She's fluent in sarcasm and dry humor. She lives in sunny Arizona with her loving husband, three adorably exhausting kids, and a cranky old chihuahua named Sam. She loves reading, writing, coffee, vodka, tattoos, wine, donuts, broody asshole book boyfriends, badass FMCs, wine, all of the friendships she's made since she began beta reading for some totally incredible authors, and can't forget wine!

Keep reading for a sneak peak from Sin's next release: If The Broom Fits

IF THE BROOM FITS - CHAPTER 1

The Witch

"*A*n ogre, a troll, and a witch walk into a bar...sounds like the start of a really bad joke," chuckles the bartender as he wipes off the mahogany bar top in front of us.

We take the three empty stools in front of him and sit wearily.

"Wish I could say you were wrong there, pal, but you're not. Someone, somewhere is cackle-coughing over their hilarity but we're over here confused as fuck." I shake my head in defeat, resting my elbows on the bar. When I attempt to drop my head into my waiting hands, the edge of my new head adornment hits my fingertips. With its wide brim and tall cone, it's the iconic black witches hat. It falls to the floor, but before it can touch the dingy tile, it magically reappears on my head.

Oh, and my broom? It's floating beside me. That's right. I said *broom.*

Fucking hell.

Looking over at Max - the ogre in this tragedy - I can tell he's just as tired as I am. Even the permanent scowl he's been sporting since the first time I laid eyes on him has drooped a little.

His large greenish frame barely fits on the stool, his shoulders slightly slumped as if his whole body is too tired to worry about good posture. I'm not sure how big the guy is in real life, but he's gigantic - and grumpy - now. His forearms - that are easily the size of my thighs - rest on the gleaming wood. His fisted hands are roughly the size of small melons. I'm surprised the dark tartan leggings he's wearing don't burst down the seams - though, note to self, he does not appreciate the term leggings. His oversized linen tunic somehow manages to cover his large chest and belly. Barely. His sword is leaning up against his chair, easily accessible.

"Can you tell us where we are?" he asks, his voice rough and gritty from lack of use. Strange that I can recognize that when I literally just met the man less than twenty-four hours ago.

Between the three of us, he's taken this the hardest. I mean, none of us are thrilled with the situation, but where I've tried to be practical and positive, Max has been surly and cynical. I get it. I do. It's not every day you wake up in a creepy field, the land shrouded in fog and muted colors, with two strangers by your side. And not just any strangers either. I'm talking characters straight out of the movies...and not the lovable children's ones either.

We share only one connection - the strange book that mysteriously appeared on our doorsteps. We had all been reading it when we apparently fell into some kind of magical sleep.

It's a testament to my exhaustion that I can even think that last thought and keep a straight face.

The bartender's voice pulls me from my spiraling mind, "You're in Legends, my boy."

He says it with such casualness, like we should know exactly what he's talking about.

"Where the fuck is Legends?" Max growls. His already thin patience at its limit.

"Hmm...I'd say about two hundred and fifty miles west of Fairytale City and about two hundred miles south of The Realm of Nightmares. We're roughly four hundred miles southeast of the Reality Gateway. "

Max looks at me, his big brown eyes begging me to explain what the hell this guy is talking about. I may be the rational one in our merry little band of misfits, but this is simply outside my level of expertise.

A deep, husky voice pipes in from my other side, "In other words...we're not in Kansas anymore, Toto."

Max just growls at Liam's amused troll face.

I'd be remiss if I didn't mention that even amused, his small trollish features are creepy as shit. With a prominent nose and squinty green eyes, his smile just gives off all sorts of eerie vibes. Where Max tops off at well over seven feet tall, Liam barely brushes three and a half. His short, squat body is on the hefty side, his belly round and protruding over the top of his ratted brown pants. In lieu of a shirt, he's in a green vest that does little to cover the hair that seems to be...everywhere. His arms, chest, and of course - the mass of unruly greyish, black hair on his head that has only one style - sticking straight out in all directions.

But - if there's one thing about the little troll that I can appreciate - it's his constant sense of humor. Without him to lighten the mood during our long, tedious walk here, I may have murdered the grumpy ogre myself.

Double, double, toil and trouble...and all that.

"I take it you three didn't wind up here intentionally?" the bartender questions. A serious look suddenly taking over his face.

"Um...no!" I snort. "Do people normally *choose* to come here?"

"Actually...yes. Adventurers of all types wind up on those stools in front of me. Telling me stories of their travels through our lands with a helluva lot more excitement than the three of you appear to have."

"Listen, man," Max snarls. "Can you just tell us how we get out of here? We just want to go home."

"Of course. You just have to make it to the Reality Gateway and it will take you home."

For the first time in over twelve hours, Max looks at me with a little bit of hope firing up in his eyes. It softens his features and for the first time I get a small glimpse at the man underneath the monster.

Something about the bartender's words rattles around my tired brain for a moment before I ask cautiously, "You said we 'just have to make it to the Reality Gateway'. Feels like there's something you're not telling us. It sounds a little fucking ominous to be honest."

The bartender puts his rag down and places his hands on the counter in front of him. He looks thoughtful for a moment, considering our tired faces.

"Look. I can see you kids have no idea what you're up against here so I'm going to give you a little advice. In the hundreds of years that I've stood behind this counter, I've never once had customers that weren't here willingly. You need to know that someone brought you here for a reason.

What that reason is, I can't say. Just know that your travel to the Gateway isn't going to be easy. You're going to encounter beings you've never seen before. Things you've only ever heard of in books and movies. Don't let any of it fool you. Don't trust anyone or anything. You can only trust each other."

I don't even flinch at the fact the guy is hundreds of years old. Somehow, my brain has accepted the fact that we've landed in a nightmare where anything and everything is possible. The only way to wake ourselves up is to get to this Gateway, and I make a promise to these guys here and now that I'll get us all there if it's the last thing I do.

The Ogre

I can see the gleam in Brenna's eyes. The fierceness that I didn't expect from someone so small. Of course, I'm fucking huge right now, so everyone seems tiny. But something about her slender frame and elegant poise makes her seem fragile. Breakable. That couldn't be further from the truth.

In less than a day, she's proven to be smart, resilient and trustworthy. She led us here. The first place we've found since we landed in that god forsaken field. Part of me is even starting to like the witchy woman.

And when I say witchy, I mean that in the most literal sense. From the black witches hat, down to the tight black dress and the broom that seems to just float beside her. With the classic green skin, and nose that seems impossibly long - wart included - she's the stereotypical picture of the fabled character. Even with the less than attractive image, there's something beneath the surface that keeps calling to me on some level I can't explain. Maybe that's another reason I've been so damn angry. I don't *want* to want the witch. But I do.

What the fuck is wrong with me?

Her voice draws me back to the current conversation, "Do you have a map of the route we need to take?"

The burly bartender eyes her for a second, his head tipped as if he's trying to figure her out. Funny that. The troll does the same thing. What is it about tipping their head sideways that makes them think their brain will work better? I don't fucking get it.

"You should have an inherent knowledge of the land - like an internal compass. You don't have that either?" he ponders that for a moment. Before any of us can answer in the negative, he continues, "Well, this just gets more strange by the second."

"Define strange," I insist. "This whole damn thing is *strange*."

"Those adventurers I mentioned - they all come here with everything they need. The knowledge tucked away just waiting for use. They understand their other forms and have full control over them."

"Other forms?" the little troll demands - even he realizes this is serious and that's saying something since the guy couldn't be serious if his life depended on it.

"Seriously?" the bartender sputters. "You don't even know about your other forms?"

I glance at Brenna and notice she's paled slightly, her green skin looking even closer to that tint normal people get right before they toss their cookies.

"Explain!" I command - trying to get a grip on my increasing ire, but struggling.

Something about my ogre makes me quick to lose my temper. The littlest things set me off. I may not be the most patient of men in my real life, but I definitely wasn't this bad.

"Everyone who owns the book knows about their other form. The other side of themselves. The book is what allows them the opportunity to let that other side have the freedom it could never have in the surface world. They were born knowing and - from an early age - learn how to control it, use it, and protect it."

"You mean...my other form is this...this...witch?" Brenna whispers, horrified.

"A witch, yes. That particular witch, probably not. Since you don't know how to control it, your mind conjures the image that you associate with the form. In this case, because you're in the land of Legends, it's manipulated your form into the quintessential witch. In reality, it's probably a lot closer to your human form."

"That is so not helpful," Brenna mutters.

"But look at the bright side, Babe. Witches have powers. Those will come in handy right?" Liam soothes, his disfigured hand coming to rest on her bright green one.

She eyes him like he's a marble short of a full bag.

"Powers would be great, if I knew how the fuck to use them. I'm more likely to turn you into a toad than I am to give you a bigger dick."

"Hey now," his hands fly down to where his dick would be if his belly wasn't in the way. "There's nothing wrong with my dick. A solid nine inches is more than enough to please a woman."

It's my turn to snort.

"You got something to say, Ogre?" Liam gripes.

"If you're packing nine inches in those trousers, then just call me the Jolly Green Giant."

"To be honest, I haven't actually checked the situation down there since we started this lovely little journey. It kind of freaks me out to even think about what I might find if I actually take a peek when I pull down my pants to take a leak. Hell...can I even see the damn thing with this fucking belly in the way?" he shivers, clearly disgusted with the thought. "I may never get to see my impressive cock again."

Brenna just chuckles. The sound doing strange things inside my chest.

I see Liam's smirk before he hides it. Damn him. He purposely changed the subject to take her mind off the current crazy we're facing. Something tells me he's catching feelings for my girl too and I'm just not sure how I feel about that. Or the fact that I just referred to her as my girl. Fuck!

The Troll

The smile on Brenna's face makes my stomach feel funny. Or that could be all the fat that jiggles when I move. Hard to tell. But there's no denying that something about her calls to something inside of me. And that thought doesn't terrify me nearly as much as everything else about the situation we've found ourselves in.

If someone had told me that I would have another form - troll would not have been my first guess. Mage, maybe...or something equally as badass. If what this guy says is true, though, this isn't the best representation of my other half. Maybe in truth he's taller, leaner, with abs and muscles upon muscles. I don't actually mind the hair. It's growing on me. Literally.

"So, let's summarize this shall we?" I start. "We have these other sides of ourselves, that in this...place...we can let free. Obviously we're behind the curve a bit here, but our best bet would be to learn how to control them, practice our powers and then head for this Gateway you mentioned so we can get the fuck out of here."

"It's not going to be that easy, jackass," the grumpy ogre mutters.

"I never said it would be easy," I retort, tired of his constant negativity. "Just that it's our best bet if we want to go home."

"I'd have to agree with the little man," the bartender nods.

I don't take offense. "Brenna? What do you think?" I ask hesitantly.

Her thin lips pucker and her rather substantial nose scrunches up while she thinks. It really should not be cute - at all - but damned if it doesn't light a little fire in my belly.

"I think you're right, Liam. But that could take days. Where will we stay? We have no money and no spare clothes."

Before I can formulate a response, the bartender replies, "I've gotta admit, I'm feeling pretty bad for you kids. Normally I try to stay out of the outsider's business, but in this case, maybe I can help. There's a room above the bar you can use for the next week - or until you can gain a little control over your other forms. Maybe you can help out around here, cleaning or cooking or bartending, and in return I'll make sure you have food and spare clothes."

Max eyes the man, clearly trying to determine if we can trust him. Can't say I blame the big guy. We've both become pretty protective over our little witch, even though he does his best to hide it. Having made a decision, he turns to Brenna, surprising me.

"It's your call," he answers gruffly.

Brenna bites her bottom lip while she thinks it over and I'll be damned if my whatever-size troll dick doesn't surge a little at the sight. Guess I might have to take a gander down there after all.

"I think it's our only option if we want to make it home safely," she pauses for a moment, turning to look at each of us, the fierce expression locked back into place. "And I promise you both that we *will* get home."

And I believe her. Everything inside me trusts this woman that I barely know and I will do everything in my power to help her keep her promise.

"Let's do this!" I agree.

"Um...but one thing," she says and I can hear the laughter in her voice.

"What's that, Babe?"

"I call the bed."

Only then do I realize what the bartender said. One room. One bed. Three of us. This could get really interesting and I'd be lying if I said I wasn't looking forward to it.

Made in the USA
Middletown, DE
28 August 2023

37469832R00172